PATRICIA WEN
HUE AND CRY

PATRICIA WENTWORTH was born Dora Amy Elles in India in 1877 (not 1878 as has sometimes been stated). She was first educated privately in India, and later at Blackheath School for Girls. Her first husband was George Dillon, with whom she had her only child, a daughter. She also had two stepsons from her first marriage, one of whom died in the Somme during World War I.

Her first novel was published in 1910, but it wasn't until the 1920's that she embarked on her long career as a writer of mysteries. Her most famous creation was Miss Maud Silver, who appeared in 32 novels, though there were a further 33 full-length mysteries not featuring Miss Silver—the entire run of these is now reissued by Dean Street Press.

Patricia Wentworth died in 1961. She is recognized today as one of the pre-eminent exponents of the classic British golden age mystery novel.

By Patricia Wentworth

PATRICIA WENTWORTH

HUE AND CRY

With an introduction by
Curtis Evans

DEAN STREET PRESS

Introduction

BRITISH AUTHOR Patricia Wentworth published her first novel, a gripping tale of desperate love during the French Revolution entitled *A Marriage under the Terror*, a little over a century ago, in 1910. The book won first prize in the Melrose Novel Competition and was a popular success in both the United States and the United Kingdom. Over the next five years Wentworth published five additional novels, the majority of them historical fiction, the best-known of which today is *The Devil's Wind* (1912), another sweeping period romance, this one set during the Sepoy Mutiny (1857-58) in India, a region with which the author, as we shall see, had extensive familiarity. Like *A Marriage under the Terror*, *The Devil's Wind* received much praise from reviewers for its sheer storytelling élan. One notice, for example, pronounced the novel "an achievement of some magnitude" on account of "the extraordinary vividness...the reality of the atmosphere...the scenes that shift and move with the swiftness of a moving picture...." (*The Bookman*, August 1912) With her knack for spinning a yarn, it perhaps should come as no surprise that Patricia Wentworth during the early years of the Golden Age of mystery fiction (roughly from 1920 into the 1940s) launched upon her own mystery-writing career, a course charted most successfully for nearly four decades by the prolific author, right up to the year of her death in 1961.

Considering that Patricia Wentworth belongs to the select company of Golden Age mystery writers with books which have remained in print in every decade for nearly a century now (the centenary of Agatha Christie's first mystery, *The Mysterious Affair at Styles*, is in 2020; the centenary of Wentworth's first mystery, *The Astonishing Adventure of Jane Smith*, follows merely three years later, in 2023), relatively little is known about the author herself. It appears, for example, that even the widely given year of Wentworth's birth, 1878, is incorrect. Yet it is sufficiently clear that Wentworth lived a varied and intriguing life that provided her ample inspiration for a writing career devoted to imaginative fiction.

It is usually stated that Patricia Wentworth was born Dora Amy Elles on 10 November 1878 in Mussoorie, India, during the heyday of the British Raj; however, her Indian birth and baptismal record states that she in fact was born on 15 October 1877 and was baptized on 26 November of that same year in Gwalior. Whatever doubts surround her actual birth year, however, unquestionably the future author came from a prominent Anglo-Indian military family. Her father, Edmond Roche Elles, a son of Malcolm Jamieson Elles, a Porto, Portugal wine merchant originally from Ardrossan, Scotland, entered the British Royal Artillery in 1867, a decade before Wentworth's birth, and first saw service in India during the Lushai Expedition of 1871-72. The next year Elles in India wed Clara Gertrude Rothney, daughter of Brigadier-General Octavius Edward Rothney, commander of the Gwalior District, and Maria (Dempster) Rothney, daughter of a surgeon in the Bengal Medical Service. Four children were born of the union of Edmond and Clara Elles, Wentworth being the only daughter.

Before his retirement from the army in 1908, Edmond Elles rose to the rank of lieutenant-general and was awarded the KCB (Knight Commander of the Order of Bath), as was the case with his elder brother, Wentworth's uncle, Lieutenant-General Sir William Kidston Elles, of the Bengal Command. Edmond Elles also served as Military Member to the Council of the Governor-General of India from 1901 to 1905. Two of Wentworth's brothers, Malcolm Rothney Elles and Edmond Claude Elles, served in the Indian Army as well, though both of them died young (Malcolm in 1906 drowned in the Ganges Canal while attempting to rescue his orderly, who had fallen into the water), while her youngest brother, Hugh Jamieson Elles, achieved great distinction in the British Army. During the First World War he catapulted, at the relatively youthful age of 37, to the rank of brigadier-general and the command of the British Tank Corps, at the Battle of Cambrai personally leading the advance of more than 350 tanks against the German line. Years later Hugh Elles also played a major role in British civil defense during the Second World War. In the event of a German invasion of Great Britain, something which seemed all too possible in 1940, he was tasked with leading the defense of southwestern England. Like Sir Edmond and Sir William, Hugh Elles attained the rank of lieutenant-general and was awarded the KCB.

Although she was born in India, Patricia Wentworth spent much of her childhood in England. In 1881 she with her mother and two younger brothers was at Tunbridge Wells, Kent, on what appears to have been a rather extended visit in her ancestral country; while a decade later the same family group resided at Blackheath, London at Lennox House, domicile of Wentworth's widowed maternal grandmother, Maria Rothney. (Her eldest brother, Malcolm, was in Bristol attending Clifton College.) During her years at Lennox House, Wentworth attended Blackheath High School for Girls, then only recently founded as "one of the first schools in the country to give girls a proper education" (*The London Encyclopaedia*, 3rd ed., p. 74). Lennox House was an ample Victorian villa with a great glassed-in conservatory running all along the back and a substantial garden--most happily, one presumes, for Wentworth, who resided there not only with her grandmother, mother and two brothers, but also five aunts (Maria Rothney's unmarried daughters, aged 26 to 42), one adult first cousin once removed and nine first cousins, adolescents like Wentworth herself, from no less than three different families (one Barrow, three Masons and five Dempsters); their parents, like Wentworth's father, presumably were living many miles away in various far-flung British dominions. Three servants--a cook, parlourmaid and housemaid--were tasked with serving this full score of individuals.

Sometime after graduating from Blackheath High School in the mid-1890s, Wentworth returned to India, where in a local British newspaper she is said to have published her first fiction. In 1901 the 23-year-old Wentworth married widower George Fredrick Horace Dillon, a 41-year-old lieutenant-colonel in the Indian Army with three sons from his prior marriage. Two years later Wentworth gave birth to her only child, a daughter named Clare Roche Dillon. (In some sources it is erroneously stated that Clare was the offspring of Wentworth's second marriage.) However in 1906, after just five years of marriage, George Dillon died suddenly on a sea voyage, leaving Wentworth with sole responsibly for her three teenaged stepsons and baby daughter. A very short span of years, 1904 to 1907, saw the deaths of Wentworth's husband, mother, grandmother and brothers Malcolm and Edmond, removing much of her support network. In 1908, however, her father, who was now sixty years old, retired from the army and returned to England, settling at Guildford, Surrey with an older unmarried sister named Dora (for whom his daughter presumably had been named). Wentworth joined this household as well, along with her daughter and her youngest stepson. Here in Surrey Wentworth, presumably with the goal of making herself financially independent for the first time in her life (she was now in her early thirties), wrote the novel that changed the course of her life, *A Marriage under the Terror*, for the first time we know of utilizing her famous *nom de plume*.

The burst of creative energy that resulted in Wentworth's publication of six novels in six years suddenly halted after the appearance of *Queen Anne Is Dead* in 1915. It seems not unlikely that the Great War impinged in various ways on her writing. One tragic episode was the death on the western front of one of her stepsons, George Charles Tracey Dillon. Mining in Colorado when war was declared, young Dillon worked his passage from Galveston, Texas to Bristol, England as a shipboard muleteer (mule-tender) and joined the Gloucestershire Regiment. In 1916 he died at the Somme at the age of 29 (about the age of Wentworth's two brothers when they had passed away in India).

A couple of years after the conflict's cessation in 1918, a happy event occurred in Wentworth's life when at Frimley, Surrey she wed George Oliver Turnbull, up to this time a lifelong bachelor who like the author's first husband was a lieutenant-colonel in the Indian Army. Like his bride now forty-two years old, George Turnbull as a younger man had distinguished himself for his athletic prowess, playing forward for eight years for the Scottish rugby team and while a student at the Royal Military Academy winning the medal awarded the best athlete of his term. It seems not unlikely that Turnbull played a role in his wife's turn toward writing mystery fiction, for he is said to have strongly supported Wentworth's career, even assisting her in preparing manuscripts for publication. In 1936 the couple in Camberley, Surrey built Heatherglade House, a large two-story structure on substantial grounds, where they resided until Wentworth's death a quarter of a century later. (George Turnbull survived his wife by nearly a decade, passing away in 1970 at the age of 92.) This highly successful middle-aged companionate marriage contrasts sharply with the more youthful yet rocky union of Agatha and Archie Christie, which was three years away from sundering when Wentworth published *The Astonishing Adventure of Jane Smith* (1923), the first of her sixty-five mystery novels.

Although Patricia Wentworth became best-known for her cozy tales of the criminal investigations of consulting detective Miss Maud Silver, one of the mystery genre's most prominent spinster sleuths, in truth the Miss Silver tales account for just under half of Wentworth's 65 mystery novels. Miss Silver did not make her debut until 1928 and she did not come to predominate in Wentworth's fictional criminous output until the 1940s. Between 1923 and 1945 Wentworth published 33 mystery novels without Miss Silver, a handsome and substantial legacy in and of itself to vintage crime fiction fans. Many of these books are standalone tales of mystery, but nine of them have series characters. Debuting in the novel *Fool Errant* in 1929, a year after Miss Silver first appeared in print, was the enigmatic, nautically-named *eminence grise* Benbow Collingwood Horatio Smith, owner of a most expressively opinionated parrot named Ananias (and quite a colorful character in his own right). Benbow Smith went on to appear in three additional Wentworth mysteries: *Danger Calling* (1931), *Walk with Care* (1933) and *Down Under* (1937). Working in tandem with Smith in the investigation of sinister affairs threatening the security of Great Britain in *Danger*

Calling and *Walk with Care* is Frank Garrett, Head of Intelligence for the Foreign Office, who also appears solo in *Dead or Alive* (1936) and *Rolling Stone* (1940) and collaborates with additional series characters, Scotland Yard's Inspector Ernest Lamb and Sergeant Frank Abbott, in *Pursuit of a Parcel* (1942). Inspector Lamb and Sergeant Abbott headlined a further pair of mysteries, *The Blind Side* (1939) and *Who Pays the Piper?* (1940), before they became absorbed, beginning with *Miss Silver Deals with Death* (1943), into the burgeoning Miss Silver canon. Lamb would make his farewell appearance in 1955 in *The Listening Eye*, while Abbott would take his final bow in mystery fiction with Wentworth's last published novel, *The Girl in the Cellar* (1961), which went into print the year of the author's death at the age of 83.

The remaining two dozen Wentworth mysteries, from the fantastical *The Astonishing Adventure of Jane Smith* in 1923 to the intense legal drama *Silence in Court* in 1945, are, like the author's series novels, highly imaginative and entertaining tales of mystery and adventure, told by a writer gifted with a consummate flair for storytelling. As one confirmed Patricia Wentworth mystery fiction addict, American Golden Age mystery writer Todd Downing, admiringly declared in the 1930s, "There's something about Miss Wentworth's yarns that is contagious." This attractive new series of Patricia Wentworth reissues by Dean Street Press provides modern fans of vintage mystery a splendid opportunity to catch the Wentworth fever.

Curtis Evans

Chapter One

MALLY LEE stamped her foot and drew back from Roger Mooring's encircling arm.

"For goodness *gracious* sake, Roger, do try to remember that you're supposed to be in love with me!" she exclaimed.

The ballroom at Curston wore an air of depression. Emptiness and the falling dusk brooded over the rows and rows of chairs which had been marshalled for to-night's performance. Only the little stage, on which the dress rehearsal was in progress, was brightly lighted.

Miss Mally Lee and Mr. Roger Mooring held the stage.

"If you're in love with me, *make* love to me!"

Elaine Maudsley giggled. She had volunteered to prompt, but she divided her time at rehearsals between giggling and dropping the prompt-book. She dropped it now, grabbed at it, and heard the injured Roger say:

"How can I act when you keep interrupting?"

"You weren't acting—that's just what I'm complaining about. We're supposed to be in the middle of a most frantically impassioned love scene, and you hold me as if I were a wet umbrella."

"How do you want me to hold you?" said Roger crossly.

"Jimmy'll show you. Come along, Jimmy, and put your arm round my waist."

"No, I'm hanged if he does!"

Jimmy Lake came out of the wings and hovered. Elaine tittered again. Roger, red with annoyance, put his own arm about the slim waist of his betrothed, and said, in his character of dashing Cavalier, "I love you. I adore you. Let us fly together."

Mally was merciless.

"You get worse instead of better," she declared. "And I won't fly with any one who looks at me as if I were cold underdone mutton. Come along, Jimmy, and show him how to do it."

"Not much!" said Jimmy. "Roger'll break my head if I do, and then where'll you be for a villain to-night?"

"Don't talk about to-night, or I shall scream. We want at least a dozen more rehearsals. Roger gets worse—and worse—and worse."

"Look here, Mally—"

"But you do, Roger—you really do. You make love worse than any one I've ever come across. Now don't you think you could make a really terrific effort and look as if you did like me a little?"

Roger's handsome features remained impassive; the set of his mouth betrayed temper.

"Miss Lee—" This was Colonel Fairbanks speaking from the other side of the footlights with a certain deliberate weariness— "Miss Lee, are you stage-managing this piece, or am I? I don't mind, you know; I only ask, because—"

"You are—and you do it too beautifully," said Mally. "I'm frightfully sorry. I won't do it again."

She turned back to Roger with a swish of her full Stuart skirt, tossed her ringlets, and dropped him a curtsey. Voice and manner changed suddenly and became sweetness itself.

"Ah, my dear love," she breathed, taking up her cue and wickedly pleased to observe that this sudden address brought the embarrassed blood to Mr. Mooring's manly cheek.

The love scene proceeded on its unequal way. Roger could look handsome and hold himself well, but there his capacity as an actor ended. He was further handicapped by the fact of his engagement to Miss Mally Lee. In the circumstances, he hardly knew which was worse—to make stage love to her himself, or to allow Jimmy Lake to do so. In either case Elaine would giggle and the county be amused. He cursed all private theatricals, and continued to walk steadily through his part and to hold Mally, in rose brocade, as if she were a wet umbrella.

"I'm glad I'm not engaged to you," said Jimmy Lake as they stood together in the wings, waiting for the abduction scene.

"So am I," said Mally Lee very heartily.

"Love all! You *are* a little devil, you know. Why do you do it?"

"Dunno. You might as well ask why I breathe, or sleep."

"You'll go too far one of these days—honest, you will, Mally."

Mally dropped to the floor in a curtsey, and made a beautiful recover. She was a slim slip of an insignificant creature, with a provoking something in her greenish-hazel eyes.

"Thank you, Jimmy dear. But you'd better be careful too. You're the villain of the piece, and don't you forget it and start preaching, or—Gracious! There's my cue!"

An hour later an exhausted company trooped in to tea. Lady Mooring, plump and comfortable, detached herself from her novel with an effort and inquired vaguely:

"Well, my dears, and how did it go this time?"

Six people speaking at once said, "Awful!" Colonel Fairbanks made a silent gesture of despair, and Jimmy groaned.

"Well, the worse it goes now, the better it will go to-night. That's always the way, isn't it? At least I'm sure I've been told so, or else I read it somewhere—I really don't know which. Elaine, my dear, will you pour tea? Jimmy, don't you think another log on the fire—? Yes—thank you. And now let's be comfortable and think that it's all going to be a splendid success."

Lady Mooring was invariably described as "such a kind woman." Her reputation for extreme good-nature was really founded upon the fact that she found it too much trouble to disagree with any one. As long as she could eat four meals a day and read innumerable novels, she asked no more of life. She addressed most of her acquaintances as "my dear"; but if some cataclysm had suddenly removed them all, she would, to be sure, have murmured, "How sad!" But her enjoyment of the entrée and the after-dinner novel would have been unimpaired. Roger alone had the power to penetrate this comfortable indifference; and where Roger was concerned, she could be as jealous and exacting as any other mother of an idolized only son. Roger was of course the handsomest, cleverest, and altogether most desirable young man in England. If she did not go beyond England, it was because England was to her the universe, and Curston was her world.

"Where's Roger? Jimmy, where's Roger?"

"Roger? I don't know." Jimmy's mouth was full of cake.

"But he was with you, surely. Marion, my dear—"

Miss Mally Lee disclaimed all knowledge of Roger's whereabouts.

"If he's as hungry as I am, he'll be here in no time. Jimmy, cut me some cake—there's a love. Rehearsing gives me the most frightful appetite, especially when Roger and I have been quarrelling all the time."

Lady Mooring, who disliked Mally, as she would certainly have disliked any girl who aspired to Roger's hand, began to dislike her a little more and to wonder vaguely but resentfully what Roger or any one else could possibly see in her. Just now, of course, dressed up and rouged, with those absurd ringlets, she was looking her very best; but as a rule, with her short hair and her short skirts, she was more like a little schoolgirl than the future mistress of Curston—not pretty, and not smart; and goodness alone knew who her people were. Not a penny, and working for her living, too. Under Lady Mooring's placid exterior such thoughts as these took shape.

Roger came into the room with an air so gloomy and abstracted as to give some food for thought. He plumped into a chair as far as possible from Mally, and took a cup of tea after the manner of a man who commits some desperate act. When he refused cake, Lady Mooring's spirits rose. After all, an engagement was not a marriage.

A little later Mally herself had the same thought. She and Roger were for the moment alone in the big ballroom, now brightly lighted from end to end. Under the lights Roger's air of gloom seemed suddenly oppressive. She slipped a hand inside his arm, only to have it shaken off again.

"As bad as all that?" she said, and blew him a kiss. "Poor old Roger!"

"I don't know what you mean."

"Don't you?" She looked at him wickedly out of the corners of her eyes and assumed a cooing voice: "Was'ums, did'ums then?"

Roger glared at her.

"That's right. Go on. Laugh at me. You're always laughing at me."

"It's so frightfully good for you to be laughed at."

"Well, look here, Mally, I'll tell you one thing—I won't be laughed at in public. You'll go a little too far one of these days."

Mally made a graceful pirouette.

"I do love the way these long skirts swish. There's no satisfaction in twirling round in a skirt that only comes down to your knee—is there? What did you say, Roger?"

"I said you'd go too far one day." His voice was low and furious.

Mally stuck her chin in the air.

"And what would happen then? How fearfully exciting!"

"You'll be sorry—that's all."

"I wonder." She twirled again. "Roger, you don't know what you miss in not having a skirt. It does feel lovely."

"Look here, Mally—" He paused. His face was full of angry color.

"I'm looking," said Miss Lee in a small, cool voice. "You're awfully red, Roger. Are you feeling hot? That sort of cloth is a bit stuffy—isn't it?"

"Look here, Mally—"

"I am looking. What is it?"

"I want to know why you got engaged to me, if I'm such a laughing-stock."

"Of course I'd never seen you *act*." This was in a very small, whispering voice. Then quickly:" Oh, Roger, don't be so awfully cross. I haven't the slightest idea why I got engaged to you—I haven't really—and I don't suppose I ever shall have. Cheer up, and think what a splendid bit of luck it was for you." As Roger showed no signs of cheering up, she added, "Of course, when you say engaged—well, what do you mean by engaged?"

"What everybody else means. You said you'd marry me."

Mally gave a little shriek.

"Never! Good gracious, Roger, what a horrible fib!"

"What did you say then?"

Mally came up close, took hold with either hand of the lace ruffles which were one of the uncomfortable features of Mr. Mooring's present attire, tweaked them, and said with emphasis,

"I said"—tweak—"I'd be engaged"—tweak—"and see how I liked it"—tweak—"if you were very, very, very good. And if you call it being good to groan and glare and glump and gloom like you've been doing all this afternoon, I don't. So there!"

Her laughing, teasing face was very near. Roger might have kissed it; but he chose to stand on his dignity. He was at this moment very much aware of what a good match Mally would be making if she married him—Mally, who hadn't a penny and was neither pretty nor—nor anything special at all. There were other girls in the world besides Miss Marion Lee.

He drew back a step and examined his ruffles with an air of concern. Mally burst out laughing.

"Roger, you do look so cross! Jimmy—"

"Now look here, Mally, you've gone far enough. There's too much Jimmy altogether. As my mother says—"

Mally stopped laughing.

"What does Lady Mooring say?"

Roger blanched a little.

"I don't suppose you mean any harm. But considering that you only came down here a week ago, I must say—" He paused; something in Mally's face made him pause.

She repeated his last words:

"You must say—What must you say? Go on—say it—*say* it!"

"Oh, nothing."

"No, Roger, that's not *fair*. Go on."

"Well, it's nothing really."

Mally caught him by the arm and shook him.

"Considering I'd only been here a week—What?"

Roger looked at her with frowning dignity.

"Well, you're pretty well at home with every one, aren't you? Christian names all round, and all that sort of thing."

The color went away from Mally's face, leaving the rouge in two brilliant, unnatural patches. Somewhere inside her the real Mally quivered like a child who has been struck. She had loved it all so. It had been so delightful. She was enjoying herself so much. She had never in all her life had such a lovely, lovely time before. And now Roger, *Roger* had spoiled it all.

She felt her hands taken and held.

"Mally, don't look like that. You didn't mean any harm—I said you didn't mean any harm. I—"

"Let me go, please!"

Roger tried to draw her nearer.

"Mally!"

"No, let me go!"

"Mally, be reasonable!"

Mally flashed a look at his flushed, handsome face. The sulky look was gone. Gone too for the moment was Roger's sense of being King Cophetua to a beggar maid. To placate Mally, to prevent her from breaking their engagement, was all that mattered. He put her hands to his lips.

"Mally, I was jealous—you made me jealous."

She relented a little. After all, she had teased him unmercifully.

"Did I? You get jealous very easily."

Chapter Two

"MALLY, ALICE TOLLINGTON can't come."

Roger made the announcement blankly, and the whole assembled cast exclaimed: "What?" in varying tones of horror and dismay.

"She can't come—she's just rung up. They can't get the car to start, and it's too late to go and fetch her."

"I said Alice would fail—she always does," said Elaine Maudsley with a giggle.

"Well, we must cut out her songs, that's all, unless—" Colonel Fairbanks turned to Mally. "That interval between the acts is a most awful nuisance. Now if you could sing something. You're not on at the beginning of the next act, you know. Do you think you could come to the rescue?"

"No, of course she can't!" Roger began. And Mally instantly decided that she could; she had just been rather nice to Roger, and felt that the pendulum required a push in the opposite direction—Roger got uppish so easily.

"I can manage beautifully. What shall I sing?—that's the only thing. Something old-fashioned because of the dress. I shan't have time to change."

"You better sing *Mally Lee*," said Jimmy Lake with a teasing look.

Mally caught Roger's eye and clasped her hands.

"I'd love to! Dare I? Shall I?"

Roger Mooring rushed upon his fate.

"What rubbish! Of course you can't! Jimmy, what a perfectly crass suggestion! No, sing—'m—ah—oh, there are plenty of songs without dragging in—"

"I shall sing *Mally Lee*, and Jimmy shall play my accompaniment on a ukulele."

Roger took her by the arm.

"Mally, you can't."

"I shall—I will—I'm going to. Tune up the ukulele, Jimmy. You've just got time."

"Mally, I forbid you to."

The worried voice of Colonel Fairbanks arose: "Miss Lee, the curtain is due to go up in three minutes, and you're on."

Mally pulled her arm away from Roger. She blew him a kiss and Colonel Fairbanks another, and ran lightly on to the stage, where three minutes later she was discovered humming a tune and writing a love-letter.

The hall was quite full and the audience an indulgent one, the play no better and no worse than others of its kind. When the curtain fell on the first act there was some very stimulating applause, which was renewed when Miss Mally Lee appeared behind the footlights, dropped a neat curtsey, and began to sing to the accompaniment of a ukulele—off.

She sang:

"As Mally Lee cam doun the street her capuchin did flee—
She cuist a look ahint her back to see her negligee—

She had two lappets at her heid, that flaunted gallantly,
And ribbon knots at back an' breist o'bonny Mally Lee."

She had a pretty, clear voice, and she acted the song, as well as sang it. With a swish of her rose-colored skirts, she walked a few steps, looked over her shoulder, and gave the refrain:

"And we're a' gane east and west, we're a' gane agee,
We're a' gane east, we're a' gane west, coortin' Mally Lee."

She took the second verse with considerable spirit:

"A' doun alang the Cannongate were beaux o' ilk degree,
An' mony a yin turned roond aboot the comely sicht tae see.
At ilka bob her ping-pong gied, ilk lad thocht 'That's tae me';
But fient a yin was in the thocht o' bonny Mally Lee."
She gave the refrain in a laughing, lilting fashion:
"Oh, we're a' gane east and west, we're a' gane agee;
We're a' gane east, we're a' gane west, coortin' Mally Lee."

She ran off, waving her hand, and bumped into Jimmy in the wings.

"I say, that was tophole! But what in the world's a ping-pong?"

Mally gurgled.

"I haven't an idea. Jimmy, I must fly and put on a cloak to be abducted in. Tell them it's no use their clapping like that—I can't give an encore."

The curtain rose on an act full of duels, hairbreadth escapes, and villainous machinations. Mally was very realistically abducted, and much less realistically rescued. When the play ended with Jimmy lying up-stage, decently shrouded in a cloak, and Mally, close to the footlights, locked in Roger's stiffly reluctant arms, the applause was all that could be desired. Lady Mooring was surrounded by people with pretty things to say about Mally's acting and Roger's looks: "What a becoming dress!"; "Oh, Lady Mooring, you ought to make him have his portrait painted in it"; "He's really awfully like the Cavalier picture you've got upstairs—isn't he?"

Lady Mooring thought he was. She beamed placidly upon the speaker, and then turned to beam again at Mrs. Armitage from Upper Linden.

"Lady Mooring, you said I might bring my niece, Dorothy Leonard. And she's so excited because she says she is sure she was at school with Miss Lee—Dorothy, my dear—"

The tall, fair, eager girl beside her bent towards Lady Mooring.

"I recognized her the minute she came on and sang that song. We always used to make her sing it at school. Not at concerts, you know—Miss Martin wouldn't have thought it proper—but at school singsongs. We both left two years ago—and I'd quite lost sight of her. I went straight out to India to my people. And—oh, do you think I might go behind the scenes and find her?"

She was gone almost before the smiling permission had been given. Lady Mooring composed herself to listen once more to praise of Mally.

Miss Leonard found the space behind the scenes crowded with laughing, chattering people, all telling one another how well the play had gone. Mally appeared to be the centre of the group, and the only person who was not laughing and talking was Roger Mooring, who was wrapped in gloom. Not only had Mally defied him, but she had made herself ridiculous by singing a ridiculous song. In making herself ridiculous she had made him ridiculous; he felt convinced that people would laugh. He therefore gloomed furiously and stood apart.

Mally felt herself touched on the arm, and turned to see and recognize Dorothy Leonard.

"Dorothy!"

"Mally!"

"How on earth—"

"Mally, where have you been?"

"Nowhere—absolutely nowhere. Look here, I've got to get some of this grease paint off. They're going to clear away the chairs for us to dance. Come along with me, and we can talk whilst I tidy. I shan't change—this dress is much too becoming."

Upstairs in Mally's room Dorothy looked at her admiringly.

"Mally, you're engaged, aren't you, to that frightfully good-looking Mr. Mooring? I'm simply dying to hear all about it. Do tell me!"

Mally pinned up her ringlets out of the way and began to wipe the grease paint off her face.

"Beastly stuff! I hate it!" she murmured.

"Mally, tell me all about it. Where did you go when you left?"

"I went into the depths of Dorset to my Aunt Deborah, and it was deadly dull. Dorothy, you've no idea how dull it was—how dull everything's been until now. Mercifully, Aunt Deborah's great friend, Mrs. Marsden, had two grandchildren home from India, and she asked if I'd come and teach them in the mornings, just to break them in for school. They were little fiends, but they weren't dead and buried like Aunt Deborah and old Mrs. Marsden."

"Poor Mally! Then what happened? Do go on!"

"Aunt Deborah died. And she'd been living on an annuity, so I hadn't a penny. The fiends were going to school, and I was just wondering what was going to happen to me, when Mrs. Marsden said her niece, Lady Emson, wanted a nursery governess, and would I go if she recommended me?"

Mally turned round, towel in hand, her face pale and shiny.

"And you went?" Dorothy appeared to be breathlessly interested.

"Went? Of course I went. I hadn't anywhere else to go. But it was fairly grim."

"Mally!"

Mally, having removed the grease paint, was applying powder to her little nose. She waved the puff at Dorothy.

"My child, it was. The che-ild was the limit—mother's joy, and 'She's so sensitive, Miss Lee—you mustn't cross her.' Cross her?" said Mally viciously. "If ever there was a child that wanted crossing morning, noon and night, it was darling Enid. Yes, it was grim—it really was. I'd have wheeled her into line all right if I'd been let—but I wasn't. And Lady Emson is one of those people who look upon a governess as a sort of educational implement, not a human being.

Oh, how I hated it!" She began to put on a little rouge very delicately. "What made it worse was that Blanche, the grown-up Emson girl, was just my age and having a frightfully good time."

"Oh, poor Mally! But do tell me about Mr. Mooring. How did you meet him?"

Mally laughed.

"Oh, he came to stay. He's a cousin of the Emsons. And he and I fished darling Enid out of a muddy pond together. Frightfully romantic, wasn't it? And then next day he came up to the schoolroom to ask how she was. And the day after we met by accident in a wood."

"Accident! Oh, Mally!"

"Of course he made the accident," said Mally composedly. She was darkening her eyebrows. "And then there were some more accidents. And then he said, would I be engaged? And I said I'd try and see if I liked it. And *then*"—she paused and sparkled—"*then* there was a most hair-raising row, and I had to go and stay with my cousin Maria, who hasn't a baked bean in the world, whilst Roger broke me gently to his mother."

"Mally, how thrilling!"

"Some of it," said Mally, "was almost too thrilling."

"And is Lady Mooring all right to you?"

"Oh, she's frightfully kind. Every one is. I'm having the time of my life. Jimmy Lake, you know, the villain—there's something awfully comic about Jimmy being the villain—, he's a cousin of the Moorings, and he's like the very jolliest sort of brother. And Colonel Fairbanks—he's a perfect old dear. And—"

"And *Roger*?"

Mally's enthusiasm became rather less marked.

"Well," she said frankly, "just at this moment Roger and I are in the middle of a quarrel. We generally have about seven a day—quite amusing, you know, and *fearfully* good for Roger."

Dorothy flushed.

"Oh, Mally, you shouldn't quarrel! Do go and make it up!"

"'M—presently. I think that's just about the right amount of rouge, isn't it?"

"You usen't to rouge at all."

"I don't now, except in fancy dress. Is this right?"

Dorothy nodded.

"Mally, *do* make it up! It'll spoil the evening if you don't."

Mally turned from the looking-glass, laughing.

"My child, leave it to me. You don't know Roger. Quite between ourselves, he's got to be reformed. At present he's rather like darling Enid—he mustn't be crossed. So I make a *point* of crossing him a million times a day. At intervals it boils up into a quarrel. You've no idea what a lot of moral uplift Roger gets out of a quarrel with me."

"Oh, Mally!"

"Oh, Dorothy!"

"But when are you going to be married?"

Mally made a face.

"Not for ages and ages and ages. So if you hear of any one who wants to give a nice large salary to a perfectly untrained person, just be an angel and think of me."

"Oh, but Mally—"

"Well? Come along, we must go down, or Roger'll think I've eloped—he's in that sort of mood."

"No, but Mally, they wouldn't like you to go out again—the Moorings, I mean. You don't really want a job, do you?"

"Yes, I do." Mally turned serious. "I *do* really. I won't marry Roger yet. I—I'm not sure enough. I won't stay here, and I can't go anywhere else, so I must, must, *must* have a job."

They were at the head of the stairs as she finished. Quite suddenly she laughed, called over her shoulder, "Race you down, Dorothy," and took the stairs at a break-neck rush.

Chapter Three

"MALLY, I WANT to introduce Sir George Peterson."

Mally looked up and saw a big man with marked features, not exactly handsome, but rather impressive. Silver-grey hair emphasized a florid complexion.

Dorothy Leonard performed the introduction and rejoined her partner, and Mally found herself dancing with Sir George. He danced well in an old-fashioned way, and talked in a very agreeable manner about the play, the weather, and Mally herself. Presently, when they were sitting out, he said, with a change of manner:

"Your friend, Miss Leonard, has just told me that you are looking for something to do."

Mally nodded.

"I'm looking for a job. I want one terribly."

Sir George smiled.

"Do you know, that's rather curious, because in the middle of your play I turned round to Mrs. Armitage—I came over with them, you know—and I said, 'Now that's the sort of girl I want for Barbara.'"

"For Barbara?" said Mally, rather slowly.

"I've been abrupt. Let me explain. Barbara is my only child. She's eight years old, and I do not wish to send her to school. I want some one to look after her. My sister, Mrs. Craddock, lives with me and manages the house—"

"Sir George, I'm not trained. Did Dorothy tell you that?"

"Yes, she did. That's the whole point. I don't want a governess; I want some one who'll interest Barbara and be interested in her. The fact is the child's crazy about drawing. By the way, can you draw?"

Mally spread out her hands in a little gesture of disappointment.

"No, I can't—not a line. Oh, what a pity!"

Sir George's smile was rather an odd one.

"If you could draw, you wouldn't do," he said. "I just wanted to make quite sure. I hate this craze of Barbara's. She's got to be broken of it. But she's more obstinate than you would think possible."

"Don't you want her to draw?" said Mally in a wondering voice.

Sir George's bushy dark eyebrows drew together; something rather frightening looked out of his eyes for one instant. Mally was not easily frightened, but a little danger-signal went off like a flare somewhere in her own mind.

"No." The word was very harshly spoken, but next moment he was smiling again. "I want some one who'll interest Barbara in other things—some one young, and lively, and attractive. When I saw you to-night you struck me as being exactly what I was looking for. I rather gave up hope when I heard you were engaged to young Mooring. Miss Leonard tells me that you will not be getting married just at present, and that meanwhile—" He paused.

"Meanwhile, I want a job—yes, I do want a job," said Mally in rather a flat voice.

The music had begun again. Sir George got up and offered her his arm.

"Will you think it over, Miss Lee? I don't ask you to take me on trust. Mrs. Armitage is an old friend; she will tell you anything you care to ask. And as regards salary—well, I'm prepared to give a hundred and fifty to the right person."

Mally was speechless. A hundred and fifty a year was wealth. It was the most wonderful thing that had ever happened. It was too wonderful; there was bound to be a catch somewhere.

She broke away from her next partner and caught Dorothy by the arm.

"Quick, Dorothy, quick! Take me to your aunt. I've got twenty million things to ask her."

Mrs. Armitage was a comfortable and ample person; there was as much grey satin in her skirt as would have made several frocks for Mally. She sat on three chairs, or at the very least concealed them. She waved Mally to a fourth, against which the tide of grey satin had been stayed.

"Well, my dear, have you and Dorothy had a nice long talk?"

"Yes—" Mally was rather breathless.

"She was so excited when she saw you. Really, she quite pinched me, and she said, 'Oh, Aunt Laura, I'm sure it's Mally Lee.'"

"Yes—Mrs. Armitage—"

"And you had a good talk about old times. Dear me, how much I should like a talk with some of my old schoolfellows! Philomela Johnson now—I've often wondered what happened to her—yes, really quite often."

Mally, having no interest in Miss Johnson, broke in. She had a feeling that if she didn't break in, Mrs. Armitage would begin to tell her all about everybody she had ever known since she first went to school.

"Oh, Mrs. Armitage, *who* is Sir George Peterson?" It sounded dreadfully abrupt. She made haste to add, "He told me to ask you. He wants me to go and look after his little girl, and he said you could tell me all about him—and—and please *will* you?"

Mrs. Armitage looked a trifle bewildered. She had a great deal of grey hair, which she wore arranged over a cushion after the fashion of twenty-five years before. She put up her hand to her hair and patted it.

"My dear, to be sure. But I don't quite follow."

Mally restrained her desire to ask twenty million things at once. Her eyes danced, but she said, speaking slowly and demurely:

"I'm so sorry. I'm in a dreadful hurry, I know—and of course I haven't explained a bit. Sir George wants some one to look after his little girl—and he thinks I would do—and he said you would tell me all about him."

"But, my dear, I thought you were going to be married!" Mrs. Armitage's kind blue eyes expressed astonishment.

Mally summoned all her discretion.

"Not for *at least* six months," she murmured. "And please, will you tell me about Sir George?"

Mrs. Armitage looked a little happier.

"Well, I've known him a long time. At least I've known Lena Craddock a long time. We were at school together, and she and I and Philomela Johnson—"

"Dear Mrs. Armitage, *who* is Lena Craddock?"

"Well," said Mrs. Armitage meditatively, "we were at school together. But do you know, I've never been quite sure whether we were friends or not. Now her husband was a most *charming* man—so clever, so amusing—"

"Sir George spoke of a sister who kept house for him. Is Mrs. Craddock the sister?"

"Yes, but they are not at all alike—not at all. I know some people admired her, but—no, they are not at all alike. Now Sir George, to my mind, is a very good-looking man—don't you think so?"

"Yes. Mrs. Craddock lives with him?"

"Lena—yes, she lives with him. As I was telling you, I was at school with her—she's a widow now—and I remember Philomela Johnson liked her better than I did. And of course that's how I got to know Sir George, who was then quite a young man and just Mr. Peterson."

"Yes? That was what I wanted to ask you—what is his profession, I mean. You see I don't really know a single thing about him."

Mrs. Armitage seemed surprised.

"He's quite well known. He's head of a shipping firm. They had terrible losses in the war, and every one thought he was ruined. Something to do with his buying up Spanish ships and their being sunk. I remember Lena was dreadfully upset about it. But somehow or other it all came right, and now he's much richer than he was before. Lena says little Barbara will be a great heiress. She's an odd child—mad about drawing. And of course Sir George doesn't like that."

Mrs. Armitage had a comfortable, billowy voice; it was rather rich and deep, and whatever words she used acquired a certain soothing quality.

Mally broke in with a little vigorous gesture.

"But why? Why doesn't he want her to draw?"

"Oh, my *dear!*" Mrs. Armitage sounded quite shocked. "After that sad affair of the mother, can you be surprised?"

"But I don't know of any sad affair. Please tell me."

"My dear, really it was very shocking. Of course you may say that a man of Sir George's age is foolish to marry a young girl. But it does not excuse her—no, no, no, it really cannot be held to excuse her."

Mally felt as if the kind, rich voice were smothering her. She had a dreadfully wicked desire to run a pin into one of the grey satin contours.

"What did she do that couldn't be excused?"

"He was, to be sure, her cousin," said Mrs. Armitage, "and it would, of course, have been far better if she had run away with him before she married Sir George instead of afterwards."

"Much better. Why didn't she?"

"He hadn't any money. Artists never seem to have any money somehow, until quite suddenly when they are knighted, or die, or something like that. And of course Sir George had so much."

"She ran away with an artist, and that's why Sir George won't let Barbara draw?"

"My dear, you can't be surprised. Nella never had a pencil out of her hand. She never had time for him, or the child, or anything. And when she eloped, it was the last straw. So you can't wonder at Sir George's feelings on the subject—can you?"

"N-no."

There was a little pause. A most curious sensation came over Mally. For the first time since her engagement she wanted to marry Roger and be looked after. She didn't want to go to London. She didn't want to find a job. She didn't, didn't, *didn't* want to look after Barbara Peterson.

"Philomela Johnson," said Mrs. Armitage in the tone of one who settles down comfortably to reminiscence, "Philomela Johnson used to say—"

Mally roused herself, and caught Roger's eye fixed gloomily on her. Her own implored a rescue.

She said "Thank you so very much" to Mrs. Armitage and was presently borne away by a young man whose every look and gesture expressed silent reproach. Still under the influence of that curious wave of feeling, Mally looked at him with softened eyes. She wanted him to be nice to her. She wanted him to make her feel that he cared, and that he would stand between her and the world. She said "Roger" with an unusual inflection of timidity.

Roger continued to dance correctly and silently.

A sparkle replaced the softness in Mally's eyes. She said "Roger" again, and then added *"darling"* and shot a wicked upward glance.

There was no response.

She gave a sudden, vicious pinch to the arm she was holding.

"You needn't listen if you don't want to. I thought you *might* have been interested to hear that I'd been offered a job in London. But if you're not, you're not. Don't say afterwards I didn't tell you—that's all."

Roger frowned, and the music stopped. When they had found a sitting-out place on the deserted stage, Mally said coaxingly:

"Oh, Roger, I'm so tired of being quarrelled with! Do be nice, just for a change."

"What were you talking about just now? What's all this nonsense? You're going to marry me, aren't you? What do you want with a job?"

"Of course I *should* have my work cut out if I married you—shouldn't I? I just thought perhaps I'd take a holiday first."

Roger's gaze became ferociously intense.

"What are you talking about?"

"About my job, *darling*. Sir George Peterson wants me to go and look after his little girl."

"I suppose you'd like me to think you're serious?"

"Of course I'm serious. And so is he—fearfully, frightfully, furiously serious. Why, my good Roger, he's going to give me a hundred and fifty lovely paper pounds for doing it."

"Look here, Mally, that's about enough. I won't hear of your doing any such thing."

Mally's little face became suddenly grave and set.

"Won't you, Roger?"

"No, of course I won't! The whole thing's ridiculous. Who on earth is this Peterson?"

"My employer," said Mally. "He wasn't going to be, but now he is."

She stood up, ran down the steps that led from the stage to the ballroom, and turned to say over her shoulder:

"Thank you for making up my mind for me. I'm going to tell him that I'll start work as soon as he likes."

Chapter Four

MALLY ARRIVED at Sir George Peterson's London house in the dusk of a January evening. The house was very large and imposing. The square in which it stood was very dim, discreet, and austere. Beyond lay a busy thoroughfare where the common, roaring tide of commercial activity ebbed and flowed; but the square itself was silent.

Mally came into a marble hall that looked chilly and felt warm. A number of uncomfortably posed statues, in the extraordinarily small amount of clothing affected by mythological persons, stood around the walls. She followed a footman up a marble stair with shallow steps and a massive balustrade.

At the turn of the stair a black column supported a bust of Sir George Peterson. Mally met it rather suddenly, and in vivid vernacular admitted to herself that it gave her the pip. Sir George in the flesh was really quite handsome, with his eyebrows, black and rather tufty, his bright dark eyes, red color, and silver hair. But Sir George in white Carrara marble! Mally took two steps at a time to get away from him, and would have taken three if it hadn't been for the footman, who was used to the bust and not disposed to hurry.

Mally never quite recovered the impression which made her want to run away. She never got nearer to it than the bald statement that the thing gave her the pip. It wasn't the whiteness, or the coldness, or the immobility, or anything she could put into words; but she wanted to run a hundred miles and never come back. Instead, she followed the footman along a corridor, and was ushered in upon a strictly domestic scene.

In a room of reassuringly moderate size blue curtains were drawn, a fire burned pleasantly, and a middle-aged lady sat knitting, whilst close to her, hunched up in a large armchair, a slim little girl pored over a book, with a hand on either cheek and untidy hair tumbled all about her face. In the very middle of the hearth an orange Persian cat and a pale, malevolent pug sat side by side.

"Miss Lee," said the footman, and departed.

The pug, the little girl, and the cat remained unmoved by the announcement; but the middle-aged lady said, "Oh, dear!" dropped a stitch, said, "Oh, dear!" again, got up, and becoming mysteriously entangled in her wool, let her knitting fall to the ground, and stood still, looking at it helplessly.

By the time Mally had picked it up, unwound the tangle, and been thanked, she began to feel herself again.

Mrs. Craddock would not have daunted the most timid person on earth, being herself in a perpetual state of apologizing for something she had done or explaining why she had done it. She wore a lugubrious grey dress braided with black, and was further adorned with a necklet and ear-rings of bog oak. Her fuzzy, faded hair was curled in a formal fringe and held tightly to her head by a hair-net and a great many hairpins.

"I'm so grateful, Miss Lee. And you've picked up the stitch, too! Now I call that really kind. And did you have a pleasant journey?"

"Yes, thank you."

"Barbara—Barbara my dear, this is Miss Lee, your new governess. Won't you come and shake hands with her?" She used the tone which people employ when they make a request which they are pretty sure will be refused.

Barbara continued to pore over her book.

"She's so spoiled," said Mrs. Craddock in a whisper calculated to arrest any child's attention. "So dreadfully spoiled! Sir George refuses her nothing."

"Then why doesn't he let me draw?" said Barbara without looking up.

"My dear—Barbara my dear—I think—I really do think you should come and say how d'you to Miss Lee."

"Don't bother her," said Mally sweetly. "I expect she's frightened, poor little thing."

The tumbled hair was thrown back with a toss, two very bright dark eyes looked out of a round pale face, and an indignant voice said:

"I'm *not*."

Mally gave her a little nod.

"Aren't you?"

"No, I'm *not*."

Barbara scrambled down from her chair. There was a challenging gleam in Mally's eye.

"I'm not frightened of any one. I just don't like governesses. Bimbo doesn't either—he'll probably bite you in a minute. He bit three people last week—they all screamed."

The pale pug produced a slight rumbling growl at the sound of his name; his eyes slid round swivel-wise and looked coldly at Mally's ankles; his black lip lifted and showed a line of milk-white teeth.

"I have a frightfully loud scream," said Mally. Her eyes danced at Barbara.

Barbara bit her lip, screwed up her face, stamped quite viciously, and then broke into sudden, uncontrollable laughter.

"She's so dreadfully spoiled," wailed Mrs. Craddock in the background. "Barbara my *dear*! Bimbo! No—*no*—not biting! Good little dog!"

Bimbo snuffled.

Mally went and sat down beside Barbara in the big chair.

"Show me your book," she said in a laughing voice. "And do let's be friends. It'll be more amusing really, because I know about three hundred stories; and if we're all biting and screaming, I can't possibly tell you any of them—can I?"

Sir George came in half an hour later, to find Barbara on Mally's lap, and a story just arrived at the happy ever after stage. He greeted Mally gravely and kindly, refused tea, and seemed to be hurried and preoccupied. After ten minutes or so he got up to go.

"I'm dining out, Lena. What have you arranged with Miss Lee?"

Mrs. Craddock dropped a stitch.

"Well, George, really I don't know. I don't think I've arranged anything. I really didn't know—I'd no idea—I'm sure I'm very sorry if you meant me to."

Sir George turned to Mally with a slight frown.

"My sister was going to ask you what you would like to do about your evening meal. We should be delighted if you would dine with us—or with my sister when I am out. But if you would prefer to have supper with Barbara and feel that the evening is your own to do just as you like with, well—" He completed the sentence with a smile.

Mally felt her arm pinched; it was clear enough what Barbara wished her to say. She said it obediently, and saw at once that she had pleased Sir George. She had an impression that the pleasure went deep.

Barbara fairly bounced on her lap.

"She'll tell me stories all the time," she announced.

When Sir George had gone out, Mrs. Craddock gazed mournfully at Mally and heaved a sort of sniffing sigh.

"I'm afraid my brother thinks I was remiss. But really there was so little time, and—now, what do you think? Would you have said that he was vexed?"

"No. Why should he be?"

"Well, my dear Miss Lee, I don't know. Gentlemen are very often vexed without much reason—don't you think so? Now, my brother—he is of course very busy, very occupied; but he never forgets anything, and it puts him out quite terribly if other people don't remember things."

Here her knitting slipped to the ground and Mally picked it up with a dexterous swoop. Barbara clutched her, shrieking with delight. Bimbo growled, and Mrs. Craddock continued without an appreciable pause:

"Thank you—oh, thank you. I mean my memory has always been very bad; and if you've got a bad memory, why, you've got a bad memory. But there, it always vexes him just the same, though I'm sure if I've told him once, I've told him a hundred times that I haven't got his head."

Barbara took Mally upstairs presently and showed her their domain—a pink bedroom which was Barbara's; a blue bedroom which was Mally's; and a sitting-room with white walls and chintzes covered with parrots and birds of paradise. There was a connecting door between the pink bedroom and the blue bedroom. "So as I can come in in the morning and get into your bed, and you can tell me a new story *every* day."

Mally laughed.

"Suppose there isn't a story in my story box?"

"Do you keep them in a box?"

"In a *secret* box. Sometimes when I open it there's nothing there—I never know. You'll have to take your chance."

Barbara flung herself upon her in a sudden hug.

"I *do* like you!"

They hugged each other. After a moment Barbara let go, stepped back, and said in a tone of ferocious intensity:

"But I shan't if you're going to like Pinko."

"Who on earth's Pinko?"

"He's my father's secretary, and I hate him worse than I hate snails, and worms, and slugs, and spiders with hairs down their legs."

"Why do you hate him? It's frightfully silly to hate people."

"Pinko isn't people; he's Aunt Lena's nephew and his outside name is Paul Inglesby Craddock. And I call him Pinko because he hates it, and because his face is pink, and because he told my father about my pictures and they took them away. Yes, they did."

Barbara turned very white over the last words; her voice dropped to a low unchildlike tone. Then suddenly she flung herself on Mally again.

"Promise me, promise me, promise me that you'll hate him, too!"

Chapter Five

SIR GEORGE'S DINNER engagement was one which quite a number of people would have envied him. He was a member of the small dinner club which called itself *The Wolves*.

No one talked politics at *The Wolves*' dinners, and no one talked business; yet it was said that the complexion of more than one political problem had been changed, and the financial status of more than one undertaking determined as the result of these informal gatherings.

The chief guest this evening was neither politician nor man of business, but Sir Julian Le Mesurier, head of the Criminal Investigation Department. The romantic name sat oddly enough upon a man who was universally known as Piggy. The aptness of the nickname stared one in the face; Sir Julian bore the strongest possible resemblance to a very large, clean, healthy and intelligent pig. The fact that he was married to one of the most charming women in the world, and that she adored him, is a proof that women are not always swayed by outward appearance.

A good many years ago he and Sir George had been at school together. There had survived one of those odd intimacies which is not a friendship, though it uses the outward forms of friendship.

When dinner was over, Sir George found himself beside his guest. He clapped him on the arm with a ribald "Well, Piggy, and how's crime?"

Piggy crinkled up the corners of his eyes.

"We shan't get into mischief from having idle hands."

"Busy—eh?"

"Fair to middling."

"That was a pretty good coup you made over the forged French notes last year. Mopped up the whole gang, didn't you?"

"Oh, that?" Piggy waved a large white hand. "My dear man, you might just as well talk about the Cardinal's Necklace or the Gunpowder plot. Mr. Bronson and the late Guy Fawkes are both upon the shelf. In fact, it's a case of 'Each day brings its petty crimes, our busy hands to fill,'—and I owe Matthew Arnold an apology for that." Sir Julian was very comfortable in a large armchair. He spoke in a lazy, drawling voice.

Sir George laughed. He had an extremely pleasant laugh.

"If you've nothing but petty crimes, you're in clover, I suppose. You don't burn the midnight oil over erring haberdasher's assistants or defaulting clerks, I imagine."

"No," said Sir Julian. "No. By the way—" He paused, his small eyes almost closed, his voice vague and dreamy. "Er—what was I saying?"

"Well, first you said 'No,' and then you said 'By the way.'"

"Er—yes—uncommon good dinner you gave us—" He paused again. "Now what the deuce was I going to say? Must have been going to say something. Yes, dates—it was something to do with dessert. Pineapple—no, not pineapple, though I congratulate you on it. You know, as a rule, Peterson, I hold to the heretical opinion that the pineapple out of a one-and-fourpenny tin is immensely superior to the inordinately expensive variety which one encounters at banquets. Now your pineapple, Peterson, was *fully* the equal of the chap in the tin. But it wasn't pineapple—I'm digressing—not pineapple, nor peaches, nor pomegranates, nor peppermints. Ginger—yes, that's better—ginger and cumquats—in fact China. All the world to a China orange—yes, that was undoubtedly it. I mean I was going to ask you whether you'd ever been to China."

Sir George gazed at him indulgently.

"Once," he said.

Piggy's voice sank to a dreamy whisper. "Interesting country, China. You know, I always think that line of Kipling's about the dawn—lemme see, how does it go?" He began to beat on the arm of his chair and to hum in a perfectly toneless, tuneless voice. "That's it—I've got it! Funny how the tune'll bring the words back, isn't it? Ever noticed it yourself?" He beat out the rhythm strongly and declaimed with enthusiasm: "'The dawn comes up like thunder out of China crost the Bay.' That's it! Finest line he ever wrote by a long chalk. Talking of China always brings it back. Varney, now—did you know Varney in China?"

Sir George said "No" in his quiet, casual voice, and then, "I don't know—I met a lot of people I've forgotten. I was out there just after the war, you know."

"Yes, I know. Ah, music! Who are we going to have? You always give us something pretty good."

"It's the Hedroff Quartet. Wonderful artists, I think."

Sir Julian composed himself to listen, with half-shut eyes and big idle hands. The wild Russian air fell strangely on the ears of comfortable men in peaceful after-dinner mood. It was as if the rare and icy air of the steppes had rushed into the warm, well-lighted room—a savage song, exquisitely sung and ending on a sudden tragic note as sharp as a dagger thrust.

Piggy nodded slowly as the sharp note died.

"Yes, wonderful artists. Wonder what it was all about. I should say they were out to get some one, and that they most undoubtedly got him."

"How professional!" said Sir George. "And talking about getting people, Piggy, why don't you gather in the cat burglar, or burglars?"

"That," said Piggy, "is mere plagiarism from the *Evening Scream*. They ask that question six times a week."

The Hedroff Quartet began to sing again, a soft and melancholy lullaby.

When Sir George reached home, he turned into his study and found his secretary still working. After standing for a moment or two looking over his shoulder, Sir George moved to the fire and stood there frowning.

Mr. Paul Craddock finished a letter, put it in an envelope, addressed it, and got up.

"You're late," said Sir George.

"I'm just through, sir. Do you want me for anything?"

"No."

There was a pause. Paul Craddock picked up a sheaf of letters and moved towards the door; but before he had gone a yard, Sir George's voice arrested him:

"Le Mesurier dined with us to-night."

Paul Craddock's eyebrows rose. He turned with the letters in his hand.

"I hope you had a pleasant evening."

Sir George was still frowning. He put his hand to his chin and said, "He asked me if I knew Varney."

Chapter Six

MALLY MADE Mr. Craddock's acquaintance at breakfast next morning. Having been implored to hate him, she was naturally a good deal predisposed in his favour. He was taller than most men, and broad-shouldered, but he had a long, thin neck, and a small, rather pear-shaped head upon which the hair was already wearing rather thin. He shaved very clean indeed, and had the brilliantly pink and white complexion which had provided Barbara with a nickname for him. To any one who had once heard it, Pinko he was, and Pinko would remain to the end of the chapter.

"He's such a comfort to my brother," said Mrs. Craddock when Paul had gone out. "Such a comfort in every way—and so much nicer than having a stranger in the house, which is always a great trial. Oh, my dear Miss Lee, I do beg your pardon—I do indeed. A most unpardonable thing to say. But I always do say the wrong thing without meaning it. It used to vex my poor husband most dreadfully—he was such a tactful man himself. And it vexes George quite terribly, too. I remember my husband saying to him once— No, I've forgotten what he said. I've a shocking memory, and it doesn't really matter. But you will forgive me, won't you?"

Mally felt quite breathless. She said, "Oh yes, yes," and fled with Barbara to the chintzy schoolroom, where they did highly amusing and unconventional lessons until it was time to go for a walk. The walk was amusing too, and no real governess would have approved of a single minute of it.

Instead of walking in the Park and combining fresh air and exercise with a lesson in deportment, they strayed down Bond Street, looking at the shops and playing the entrancing game of buying in make-believe all the things they liked best. By the time they had furnished a castle in the air with everything from Crown jewels to chocolates, they were both very hungry.

Barbara, rushing joyously upstairs, bumped into Sir George, coming down.

"Hallo!" he said, and then became aware of Mally just behind. He looked from Barbara to Mally, and back again to Barbara—a Barbara with pink cheeks and eager eyes. "You're in a great hurry."

"We're so hungry." Barbara was hopping on one leg.

"Well, that's new. What have you been doing to her, Miss Lee?"

Mally only laughed, but Barbara poured out a torrent of excited words.

"We've had lovely lessons and a lovely, lovely walk. And we're going to do it all over again tomorrow, or else something nicer. And she told me a story in bed. And she says she will every day if I'm good. And she isn't a bit like a governess. And oh, *please* may we go and have our lunch, because we're so *frightfully* hungry."

The days went on very pleasantly. It is agreeable to be adored—and Barbara made no secret of her adoration. It is also agreeable to feel that one is pleasing one's employer and one's employer's sister. Mally told herself that she was in luck, and became daily in less of a hurry to marry Roger and settle down at Curston. She was like a child in her enjoyment of London. She and Barbara explored together, and ranged enthusiastically from Museums to the Zoo.

She had been installed for about a week, when Roger Mooring rang up. Mally, arriving breathless from the top of the house, was surprised to find a little glow of pleasure warming her. She said, "Roger!" and then, "How near you sound!"

"I *am* near—I'm in town."

"For the day? What energy!"

"No, I'm up for some weeks settling up Aunt Catherine's affairs. I'm at her flat, which is just as she left it. You'd better take the address and the telephone number."

"How do you know I want them?"

Roger took no notice of this impertinence. He said, quite eagerly for him, "I want you to come out and dine with me to-night. We'll go somewhere where we can dance."

"Do governesses dance?" said Mally with a little gurgle. "I'm a governess now, you must remember—and my employer mightn't like it."

Roger said something cross under his breath.

"What did you say?"

"I said, 'Ask him.'"

"No, you didn't. But I will. You'd better hold on."

She ran down to the study and stood for a moment by the door, wondering whether Sir George would be alone. Then as she turned the handle she heard him say in a harsh voice, "I've not the slightest idea whether he meant anything or not," and with that she came into the room and felt a sudden chill, a sudden constraint. The chill was in Sir George's voice, and the constraint in his manner as he asked:

"What is it, Miss Lee? Do you want anything?"

He was sitting at his table, and Mr. Craddock was standing beside him. Mally came to a standstill a yard from the door.

"I'm sorry—you're busy. I'll come some other time."

"No, no. Let's have it now. What is it?"

She felt the strongest possible desire to get out of the room.

"It's only—Roger. He rang up. He wanted to know if I could dine with him to-night."

Sir George laughed a little; but it seemed to Mally that the chill was still there—in the laugh, in Mr. Craddock's pose, in the way Sir George looked at her when he said, "Of course, of course—arrange it with my sister."

"Thank you," said Mally, and was gone. It was nice to have the door between her and the study. As she ran upstairs again, she remembered that Paul Craddock had never once raised his eyes or looked in her direction.

The telephone lived in its own telephone room, very nobly installed, with directories, reference books and tablets in profusion. Mally left the door open, and caught up the receiver.

"It's all right—he says I can. What time?"

"Eight o'clock at The Luxe."

"Where's that?"

Roger restrained himself. He—he, Roger Mooring—was engaged to some one who had never heard of The Luxe! He said patiently:

"I'll come and call for you at a quarter to eight."

Mally hung up the receiver and went to find Mrs. Craddock. When Roger was patient with her he roused all her worst passions. She thought of several things which she would have liked to say, and felt inordinately virtuous because she had not said them. She opened the door to Mrs. Craddock's sitting-room upon a sight so odd that she forgot Roger and his misdeeds.

Mrs. Craddock, on her hands and knees, seemed to be slowly prowling across the carpet, patting it as she went. Her knitting lay half under a chair, and three balls of fleecy wool trailed with her as she went, and became more inextricably entangled at every moment. She looked up vaguely at Mally and said:

"Oh, Miss Lee, have you—I mean—I suppose you haven't seen it anywhere—but it really must be somewhere, mustn't it?"

"What is it? Your knitting? It's under the chair."

"Oh no, not my knitting. It's really very careless of me, indeed, because I certainly knew the pin was loose. But it must be somewhere."

"Your wool?"

Mrs. Craddock sat back on her heels. She looked very flushed and unhappy.

"Oh *no*, not my *wool*. I thought I'd explained."

"No, you didn't. Do let me help you up—you look so frightfully uncomfortable. What have you dropped? I'll look for it."

Mrs. Craddock allowed herself to be assisted to a chair. When her knitting and her fluffy balls of wool had also been picked up, she said, "I thought I'd told you all about it. I must have dropped it last night, because I know I was wearing it on the front of my dress. But the catch must have come undone. And my brother is dreadfully vexed—quite, quite *angry*, in fact."

"You haven't told me now what it is that you've lost," said Mally.

"My *dear* Miss Lee! My grandfather's diamond of course. That is to say, the pendant was really my grandmother's. She was a Miss Warrender, and he met her in Grand Canary. But my grandfather had the diamond put in the centre instead of the ruby that was there before. He brought it—I mean the diamond—from the East Indies.

And I believe it belonged to a great Mogul or some one else with one of those names that one really can't be expected to remember, though George *does* get annoyed with me about it."

"Oh," said Mally, as the poor lady stopped to take breath. "And is it the diamond you've dropped, or the whole pendant?"

"Well, it isn't exactly a pendant now, because my mother had it made into a brooch. And the pin has never really been very secure. And what with the diamond being so valuable, and my brother so put out—But then I keep on saying to myself it must be *somewhere*. Oh, my dear Miss Lee, it really must, mustn't it?"

"You dropped the whole thing?"

"Oh, yes, the whole thing."

"And when did you miss it?"

"About half an hour ago. At least I didn't miss it, but my maid did. And she asked me if I'd taken it to be mended. And of course I *ought* to have. And if I *had*, it would have been safe—wouldn't it? Only I *keep* saying to myself that it *must* be somewhere."

"Of course it must," said Mally cheerfully.

But the hours passed, and still a most rigorous search failed to discover that somewhere.

Chapter Seven

ROGER MOORING was quite surprised to find how eagerly he was counting the minutes until Mally came. It was a matter of minutes now, because he was waiting amongst Sir George's cold statuary, with a taxi ticking by the curb outside.

When he was with Mally, he quarrelled with her most of the time, or rather she quarrelled with him; but when he was away from her, other people seemed dull and life went stodgily.

He stood amongst the statues and watched the staircase with quite an ardent gaze, yet his first glimpse of Mally brought a faint line of disapproval to his brow. He had made a pleasant picture of a Mally chastened by absence coming sedately down the shallow steps, with the modest light of welcome in her eyes, and perhaps—

so far had fancy led this misguided young man—perhaps a slight, delightful blush upon her cheeks.

Actually, Mally whisked round the corner by Sir George's bust and took the remaining steps three at a time with a laughing, "Am I late? Have you been waiting? I don't want to lose a single instant. *Do* let's come along quick! We *are* going to dance, aren't we?"

The pleasant vision of Mally fled. Roger looked at the actual Mally, and for a moment wished that he had not suggested The Luxe. Mally's one evening dress, known familiarly as Old Black Joe, was certainly not up to Luxe standards; and Mally herself, with her short dark hair, cut by a country hairdresser, and her little pale face, had neither the beauty nor the distinction that can carry off an old frock.

The thought was hardly there before it was gone again. Mally's odd greenish, dancing eyes, with the eager something that was half laugh, half sparkle, met his; Mally's little nose wrinkled at him; and Roger ceased to be aware of anything but that she was Mally and that he had not seen her for a week.

Mally came home between one and two in the morning in a sort of delightful golden dream. She had never enjoyed herself so much in all her life before—never. The Luxe was like a fairy palace, and she herself exactly like Cinderella at the King's ball, except that the whole delightful dream went on in spite of the clock striking twelve. Such an amusing dinner. Such thrilling things to eat. And Roger to tell her that the fat, bald man at the corner table was the terrifically rich Mr. Marcus Aurelian, and that the lady in pearl ropes and a very little silver tissue was Mlle. Tanga Miranda, the world's most sinuous dancer. Then the dancing floor—you *couldn't* really have a floor like that except in a dream. And whatever Roger was or was not, he certainly could dance. Yes, the whole evening was like a dream. And wonderful beyond all other wonders, she and Roger had not quarrelled even once.

Mally passed the statues, all coldly awake and staring, and went up the stairs, leaving a sleepy-eyed young footman to the congenial task of putting out the lights. As she turned by Sir George's bust, she saw them vanish one by one, leaving her in semi-darkness, with all the light there was coming from above.

At the top of the stairs she stood for a moment looking along a rather dim corridor. The door of the telephone room was ajar. Light streamed out of it, and just as she was wondering who could be telephoning at this hour, Mr. Paul Craddock opened the door wide and stood there looking at her.

Mally was friends with all the world to-night. She beamed at Paul and said:

"How late you are! I'm so glad some one else is late besides me. I've had such a *frightfully* lovely time."

He switched off the light and opened the door of the next room.

"Come in and have a sandwich and tell me about it. There ought to be coffee and sandwiches here."

Mally hesitated. She knew very well that she ought to go to bed. If you are a governess you don't eat sandwiches with strange secretaries at two in the morning.

She sniffed the coffee and was lost. There was a lovely fire too, and the room had crimson curtains and looked so warm after the marble staircase. Before she could make a good resolution she was eating a sandwich and telling Paul Craddock about Tanga Miranda and her pearls.

Paul Craddock listened with an amusement which began to pass into interest. He had had a very dull evening, and he found Mally stimulating. He had asked her to share his sandwiches on an impulse born partly of boredom, and partly of something else.

"I must go," said Mally, finishing her coffee. "I don't want to, but I must. I hate going to bed after a party—don't you? I would have liked this evening to go on, and on, and on, and on, and on."

Paul Craddock smiled. He put down his cup and got up, all rather slowly and lazily.

"Well," he said, "why not let it go on a bit longer?"

Mally got up too.

"No, it's got to stop. I'm really Cinderella, you know, and it's hours past twelve."

"Only two hours. There's no hurry. Since you're so fond of dancing, when will you come and dance with me? Or"—he smiled a little more—"does Mooring not allow it?"

Mally stuck her nose in the air. She knew very well that she ought not to stay. But she stayed—to put Mr. Paul Craddock in his place.

"How sudden of you!" she said. "Really, Mr. Craddock, I think you're the suddenest person I ever met. This afternoon, when I came into the study, you wouldn't even see me, and now—*l'invitation à la valse*." She made him a little bob curtsy. "*Sir*, your most *obliged*."

"What does that mean?" He was leaning over the back of the chair from which he had risen.

"It's a *very* polite way of saying 'No.'"

"And why 'No'?"

"Because—Oh, has Mrs. Craddock found her diamond?"

"No, she hasn't. Why won't you dance with me?"

"Because I won't, Mr. Craddock. Good-night."

Paul stepped back and leaned against the door this time.

"Then Mooring does want all the dances? Selfish fellow!"

"Mr. Craddock, I want to go upstairs."

"All in good time. What are you afraid of? That he'll break my head—or the engagement?"

"Will you let me pass, Mr. Craddock?"

Paul Craddock laughed.

"I think you'll have to pay toll, Mally."

Mally walked straight up to him with her eyes like green fire.

"Let me pass at once! I'll scream if you don't."

"Then I must stop your mouth," said Mr. Craddock, still laughing; and as he laughed, he caught her by the shoulders and bent to kiss her.

Mally ducked. Mr. Craddock exclaimed. The kiss grazed the top of her head, which she instantly jerked upward, causing him to bite his tongue. He swore, felt a vicious pinch on the inside of his raised arm, and, recoiling from it, received a very hard, stinging slap in the face. The next instant the door had opened and banged again. Mally was gone.

When she had reached her own room and locked the door, she told herself with some truth that she was a perfect little fool, and that it was all her own fault. Then she reflected with a good deal of pleasure upon the hardness of the slap which she had administered. Mr. Craddock had a good sort of face to slap—the sort that feels soft.

"Ouf!" said Mally. "Slug! Pink slug!" She spread out her fingers and looked at them. Then she went to the washstand and washed them very carefully.

Downstairs Mr. Craddock had passed from incoherent soliloquy into a dangerous silence. He stood for some time with his elbow on the mantelpiece, looking down into the fire. From time to time he thrust savagely at the embers with his foot and stirred them into a blaze.

When about half an hour had gone by, he slipped his left hand into his waistcoat pocket and took out something which he laid in the palm of his other hand. The light dazzled on a heart-shaped wreath of diamond leaves from which hung pendant-wise a very large and brilliant diamond.

Mr. Craddock stared at the diamond. Then he said, "I wonder," and slipped it back into the pocket from which he had taken it.

Chapter Eight

MALLY OVERSLEPT herself next morning, and Barbara got no story. This cast a gloom over the breakfast table, where Barbara behaved very badly indeed, becoming ruder and less tractable with each of Mrs. Craddock's rather plaintive reproofs.

After breakfast Barbara disappeared. Mally searched the house for her in vain, and arrived reluctantly at the conclusion that the naughty little thing had taken refuge in the study. To the study she therefore went, knocked, and, receiving no answer, opened the door.

Sir George was not there, but Paul Craddock was standing by Sir George's table, holding the table telephone in one hand and the receiver in the other. His own writing-table, littered with papers, was behind him. The safe beside it stood open.

Mally had begun to draw back, when something moved by the window. Barbara's head looked round the corner of the curtain, Barbara's eyes glowered at her, and Barbara's tongue shot out defiantly. Instead of running away, Mally ran into the room and pulled the curtain back.

Paul Craddock scowled at her entrance and then rather ostentatiously turned his back.

"Ah yes, Jenkinson," he was saying. "Well, Sir George would like a reply. Yes, that's the message he left with me—he would like a reply by the end of the week without fail. No, I don't think it would be any use your ringing up again. No, he's not in the house—I can't say when he'll be back. He left a very definite message, and nothing would be gained by your calling up again."

"Barbara!" said Mally while this was going on. "How could you? Come quick, before he stops telephoning." She had her lips against Barbara's ear, and spoke in an almost soundless whisper.

Barbara twisted away, put out her tongue again, freed herself with a jerk from the folds of the curtain, and ran across the room and out at the door. Her feet made no sound on the thick carpet. Paul Craddock had not seen or heard her go.

Mally straightened the curtain and followed Barbara out of the room. By the time she reached the foot of the stair, Barbara was already out of sight. As Mally took the marble steps three at a time, she thought of quite a number of pungent things to say to the little wretch later on.

She was running along the corridor, when the door of Mrs. Craddock's sitting-room was opened and Mrs. Craddock's worried face looked out.

"Have you found her? Where was she?"

"Yes. She's run upstairs. She was in the study."

Mrs. Craddock came out of the door and caught her by the arm.

"Oh, don't talk so loud! Oh, my dear Miss Lee! Oh, *please* come in here."

"But Barbara—"

"Hush. Oh, please hush. Come in here and I'll explain."

Mally followed Mrs. Craddock into the sitting-room.

"What is it? What's the matter?"

"Oh, my dear Miss Lee! Oh, please shut the door. Are you sure it's shut? Did you say she was in the study?"

"Yes—hiding behind a curtain. And now she's run upstairs. I really ought to go to her, Mrs. Craddock."

"In the study?" Mrs. Craddock actually wrung her hands. "Was any one there? Did any one see her?"

"Why? Does it matter?"

"Yes, yes, it matters. Tell me, did any one see her?"

Mally had been considering.

"Mr. Craddock was in the room, but I don't believe he knew she was there."

Mrs. Craddock looked terrified.

"If Paul saw her—"

"I don't think he did. She was behind the curtain, and when I opened the door, she looked out at me and made a face. But he had his back to her, telephoning."

"And then?"

"I went across and pulled the curtain back. He didn't look round, and—no, he couldn't have heard anything either. She pulled away from me and ran out of the room. And he was very busy, talking all the time and giving a message from Sir George; and I don't believe he knew anything about Barbara being there. But—but why does it matter? Mrs. Craddock, I *really* ought to go."

Mrs. Craddock clutched her arm. Mally saw with surprise that she was trembling.

"No, wait—I must tell you. My brother mustn't know about Barbara being in the study." She dropped her voice so much as to be scarcely audible. "If Paul knows, he'll tell him. But you won't—will you?"

"But why?"

"Because—Oh, my dear Miss Lee, you don't know my brother. He spoils Barbara in most things; but he has a terribly violent temper, and he has forbidden her to go into the study. She took some paper once to draw on, and he—he caned her for it. It seems too dreadful, but he did. He won't have her draw, you know. And—and—he mustn't know, he really mustn't know." Mrs. Craddock dropped her voice still further and shook quite dreadfully. "Miss Lee, she *screamed*. It was—oh, terrible! I couldn't bear it again. He mustn't know."

"Well, I shan't tell him," said Mally briskly. "Dear Mrs. Craddock, do sit down and compose yourself. You'll see it'll be quite all right. And now I really must go and find that little demon and scold her."

Mally found her little demon miraculously transformed into the Angel Child of romance. With neatly brushed hair and an expression of seraphic calm, Miss Barbara Peterson sat bolt upright at the schoolroom table doing sums.

Mally's lecture slid smoothly from a shield of impenetrable virtue. When told how bad she had been, Barbara sighed, glanced at the cornice, and observed:

"Yes, Mally darling, but I *do* want to get on with this sum, and you're interrupting me dreadfully."

Downstairs in the study Sir George Peterson sat with his chair pushed back from the writing-table, staring incredulously at his secretary.

"Craddock! Craddock, what are you saying?"

The bright pink color in Paul Craddock's cheeks had changed and hardened till it looked like clumsy daubs of paint.

"It's gone," he said. "It's gone!"

"What are you saying? Pull yourself together."

"It's gone," said Paul Craddock in an odd, breathless voice that sounded as if he had been running very fast uphill. He stood on the farther side of the table, his two hands holding the edge of it, his big shoulders stooped forward. His whole frame shook a little as things seem to shake in a heat haze.

"How? And when?" Sir George spoke sharply.

"Just now. She must have taken it."

"Who?"

"That girl, Miss Lee—she came in. It's gone."

Sir George fixed him with an icy look.

"May I suggest, for the second time, that you should pull yourself together and tell me quickly and exactly what you suppose to have happened. Whine about it afterwards in prison, which is where you'll certainly find yourself if you lose your nerve. *Now!* Drop your hysterics and tell me what happened."

Paul Craddock drew a deep breath, put his hand to his long throat, and swallowed once or twice.

"I beg your pardon, sir. It was so sudden—I got rattled. I'm all right now."

Sir George nodded.

"Tell me exactly what happened. So far you've merely been incoherent."

"It knocked me over. You know, sir, I always thought I ought to lock the door when I was decoding anything. But you said 'No.'"

"Of course I said 'No.' You might just as well advertise a criminal conspiracy, and have done with it. Get on and tell me what happened?"

"I took Varney's last code message out of the safe and sat down to decode it. It was the one that came last night—I told you. When I'd nearly done, Jenkinson rang up. I went over to your table and gave him the message you left. He kept me on the line whilst he went and saw Magnay. And when he came back, he went on about wanting to talk to you personally. Whilst I was in the thick of it, the door opened and Miss Lee looked in. I thought she was going away again, but she didn't. She went across the room to the window first. Then she went out. When I went back to my table, Varney's message was gone. She must have taken it."

Sir George got up.

"Come round to the telephone and show me how you were standing. Like that? Sure?" He went over to the door. "And Miss Lee came in here? And went across to the window?" He began to walk in the direction indicated. "Stop me where you lost sight of her."

Paul Craddock stopped him midway between door and window. "And then?"

"I don't know. Jenkinson was being very pressing—I was attending to him—I didn't look round."

"Ah! You left a decoded message from Varney lying on your table, and you didn't look round. How long was Miss Lee in the room?"

"Not more than a minute. I can't say for certain. I think she walked to the window and back again—but I was talking—I didn't notice."

"You didn't hear the rustle of paper?"

"I should have looked round quick enough if I had. I just saw her come in, and then—I didn't really see her go out because I'd turned a little more this way. But I heard the door shut. Jenkinson kept me another five minutes gassing about nothing, and I'd just got back to my table when you came in. She must have taken it."

"How long had you been here before she came to the door?"

"I don't know—quarter of an hour, twenty minutes perhaps."

"And you haven't left the room since?"

"No. Why?"

Sir George walked to the nearest window without replying. Heavy curtains of maroon velvet hung from ceiling to floor, looped back with tasselled cords as thick as a man's wrist. He looked behind each curtain, passed to the other window, and lifted the curtain that had screened Barbara. It would not have hidden a grown-up person, but the child, kneeling on the floor, had been able to pull the ample folds about her below the looping. Paul Craddock's writing-table, making an angle with the window-frame, had helped to screen her.

Sir George crossed to the last curtain, lifted it, and let it fall again. Then, turning, he surveyed the room. It afforded no other possible hiding-place.

"Yes," he said grimly, "it looks as if she had taken it. But why? *Why?*"

Craddock threw him a glance full of fear. He moistened his lips and said:

"No one would have taken it unless they had known what they were taking. She hadn't a minute to think. If she hadn't come here as a spy—"

Sir George interrupted him.

"You think that?" He spoke curiously.

"What else is there to think? If she didn't come here as a spy, what possible motive could have made her snatch that paper from my table? It's not the first time she has done that sort of thing either. Only a practised hand, and a cool one, would have risked it and brought it off without making a sound."

Sir George had come back to his chair. He sat with an elbow on the table, looking down, his face frowningly intent.

"Yes," he said at last; and then, "What was on the paper? Just what had you decoded? Can you remember? Go over there and sit down and write it out."

Paul Craddock hesitated, then turned about and flung himself into the chair before his own table. For a few moments his pen moved rapidly. Then he got up and laid the scribbled paper in front of his chief.

There was a moment's silence. Sir George stared at the paper and set his jaw. Then he reached for the matches, lit a taper, and watched Mr. Craddock's oddly written half-sheet of note-paper blacken and fall into ash.

He had put out his hand to the table bell, when Paul Craddock asked sharply and nervously:

"What are you going to do, sir?"

"Send for Miss Lee—have her searched if necessary. She's probably got the paper on her."

"No, sir, wait! That won't do."

Sir George looked at him icily, his hand still on the bell.

"Wait? Till she gets away with it? Are you by any chance turning an honest penny over this yourself?"

Craddock ignored the insult. His sense of his own peril rendered him impervious to anything else.

"No—*sir*—think! It won't do. Say she's got the paper—say we get it from her. She goes straight to Scotland Yard and tells them what's happened. You can't have her down and search her as if she'd taken a brooch or a ring."

"Or my sister's diamond. Yes. There's something in it."

A curious look passed like a flash over Paul Craddock's face. He came a little nearer and dropped his voice.

"Aunt Lena's diamond. Yes, it would have been quite easy if she'd only taken that. *Why shouldn't she have taken it?*"

"What do you mean, Craddock?" said Sir George very deliberately.

Paul stooped forward and laid his closed hand on the table in front of Sir George.

"What's this?"

The hand opened slowly. On the palm of it lay the Mogul's diamond in its circle of little brilliant leaves.

Chapter Nine

MALLY AND BARBARA were still doing sums, when the door opened and Sir George came in.

"Lessons?" he said; and then, "Do you know, I'd rather like to stay and plumb the depths of Barbara's ignorance. Don't let me disturb you. Carry on just as if I were not here." He strolled over to the sofa as he spoke, sat down in the corner of it, and took up a book.

The lessons proceeded, Mally hoping that her consternation was not apparent, and Barbara continuing to be unnaturally seraphic. Sir George made no comment. He appeared to be reading; yet Mally was aware that his attention was focused upon her—upon her, not Barbara. He did not look at her, but she was conscious of a most disturbing attention. Never in all her life had she been so glad to hear the lunch bell ring.

Mr. Craddock was at lunch, and conversation fluttered about the loss of Mrs. Craddock's diamond ornament. The poor lady herself made feeble endeavours to change the subject, but even the most devious paths led back again to diamonds, or thefts, or mysterious losses that were never cleared up. It was a most uncomfortable meal, for Barbara, discarding the rôle of Angel Child, was inclined to be pert, whilst Mrs. Craddock hovered nervously on the verge of tears and Sir George was by turns sarcastic and silent.

When the coffee came in, Mally got up and excused herself; Barbara was supposed to rest after lunch and there were still the lesson-books to put away. A good deal to her surprise, Sir George emerged from a prolonged fit of silence to say:

"Oh, don't go without your coffee, Miss Lee."

"I really don't want any."

Sir George frowned.

"Nonsense! Sit down and drink it. What difference does it make whether you put Barbara to bed at half-past two or five-and-twenty to three?"

Paul Craddock had taken his coffee and was dropping candied sugar into it slowly and thoughtfully. He took three spoonfuls and stirred his cup with a curious smile that made Mally feel like a volcano. What business had he to smile like that?

Mrs. Craddock looked at her imploringly, and Mally took a cup from the tray and drank the coffee with one quick gulp.

"Now, Barbara," she said, and they went upstairs together.

"Do you like coffee? I don't," said Barbara, hopping on one leg round the table.

Mally made a face.

"I didn't like *that*," she said. "It had a perfectly horrid taste. Don't hop, Barbara. Make haste."

"Must hop," said Barbara calmly.

"Not when I say 'No.'"

"Must. You see, I've simply promised my left leg not to walk on it till I go to bed." Barbara's tone was mournful and earnest.

Mally made a dive at her, picked her up, shook her, and ran laughing and panting into the bedroom, where she deposited her with a bump in the middle of the bed. After a rather riotous five minutes decorum was restored. Barbara and a golliwog were tucked up under an eiderdown, and Mally went back into the schoolroom.

She sat down on the sofa, yawned, and took up the book Sir George had been reading. She felt suddenly so sleepy that she would have liked to be Barbara under the eiderdown. She yawned again, opened the book, and found herself reading the same sentence over and over, with no idea what it meant. She stared at the page and saw the lines running one into the other. She closed her eyes so as not to see them, and slipped down into the sofa corner, with her head against the arm and a sound like rushing water in her ears.

She did not know how long she slept, or how deeply; but she woke suddenly, with a start that shook her from head to foot and a little choking cry. The start and the cry had come with her out of a dream in which she was running, running, and running down a steep and stony road. Something was running after her. There was no sound of following feet, yet something followed. She started, cried out, and was awake.

She was sitting up, facing the door into the corridor, and the door was closing. Mally did not know why this frightened her so; but the slow, slow movement of that closing door turned her cold with terror.

The door ceased to move; the handle turned a little; the latch clicked—and that was all. There was no sound of a withdrawing foot. There was no sound at all. Mally sat in a dead silence, and was cold with fear. She could not take her eyes from the door, and the drowsiness, which she had only half shaken off, flowed and ebbed, and flowed and ebbed again.

It was the thought of Barbara that roused her and brought her trembling to her feet. If there was anything wrong, she must go to Barbara. Then, as she began to move, the fear and the drowsiness were gone together, leaving her wondering at herself.

Really, at her age, to drop asleep and wake up scared to death because she had had a dream! "Idiot!" she said to herself. All the same it was time for Barbara to get up.

She went to the door that led into the bedroom, and turned the handle. The door was fast. She shook it, but it held. She was calling "Barbara—Barbara!" when a sound behind her made her swing round with a little cry. Sir George Peterson was coming into the room, with Mr. Craddock behind him.

Paul Craddock shut the door, and Sir George said in a low, grave voice:

"Barbara is not in her room."

Mally cried out:

"What has happened?"

His eyebrows rose.

"To Barbara? Nothing. She was removed by my orders. You will not see her again."

"Sir George!"

"Does that surprise you?"

Mally's chin went up. She stood leaning against the locked door, wondering if this was still a dream.

"It *does*—very much. Will you explain?"

"Does it need explanation?"

Mr. Craddock had not come very far into the room. He stood leaning over the back of a chair, staring maliciously at Mally, whilst Sir George stood grave and erect by the table, with a hand resting lightly upon one of Barbara's copy-books.

"Sir George—what is the matter? What do you *mean*?"

"Don't you know? My dear Miss Lee, this is a delightful but quite unconvincing display of innocence. You really have a great deal of histrionic ability. But just at the moment, I'm afraid, it's wasted. Will you kindly give me back the paper which you took off Mr. Craddock's table this morning?"

Mally put her hand behind her and gripped the handle of the door. It was a quite instinctive movement, but it had the effect of a denial.

Sir George came a step forward.

"Come, hand it over!" he said very harshly.

"I don't know what you mean."

He seemed to control himself with an effort.

"Miss Lee, I don't want to be hard on you. It was my sister's loss that opened our eyes. It was an act of the most criminal stupidity to take so marked a jewel as the Mogul's Diamond. But we are not anxious for a scandal. Give back the pendant and the paper that you were foolish enough to take this morning, and we shall not prosecute."

Mally listened to these unbelievable words without making the slightest sign that she had heard them. In a sense it may be said that she did not hear. The sound of them fell upon her ears, but her mind made nothing of them. She said in a quiet, puzzled voice:

"I don't understand—I don't know what you are saying."

And just at that moment Paul Craddock laughed.

It was something in his laugh that brought Mally sharply to herself. She saw Sir George turn a look of frowning anger upon his secretary and then face her again with a grave and judicial air.

"Miss Lee, what is the use of taking up this attitude? You came into this house in a position of trust. You have abused that trust. I feel that I am in part to blame—I made too few inquiries. But Mrs. Armitage is an old friend—" He broke off, made a gesture as if waving something away, and then went on, using a harder tone: "Well, I was precipitate, and I'm paying for it. Now, I don't want a scandal, for Barbara's sake, for my own sake, and for my sister's sake—she will in any case be most terribly upset. Give back the jewel and the paper, and I won't prosecute."

Mally was still gripping the handle of the door behind her. Her fingers seemed to have grown to it; she could not move; they were cold and stiff. Her mind had begun to take in the words of Sir George's accusation; but they were just words.

"I haven't got any paper."

The instinct that made her take hold of the words last heard was one that did her more harm than she could guess, for it confirmed both the men in their conviction that she not only had the paper, but knew its value.

Sir George's self-control gave way. With an oath he took a great stride forward and dropped his hand upon her shoulder.

"You damned little liar! Give it up—give it up, I say!"

Mally had courage enough and to spare. Sir George's violence steadied her. She tilted her head back and said hotly:

"How dare you touch me? Let me go at once—at *once*. Are you mad? I don't know anything at all about any paper."

Craddock said, "Sir George!" in a low, warning voice, and Sir George let go of her and fell back a pace.

"Now look here—" there was a threat in every word—"stop all this nonsense and hand it over. You can't bluff me, and you can't get away with it. I'll give you five minutes. And if you don't hand it over, I'll have you searched, and you'll go to prison as a common thief. Come, is it worth it? I don't know what put it into your head to take the paper, or who paid you to do it. But just consider whether it's worth while. If I have you searched, the Mogul Diamond will be found on you. I should think you'd get a year's imprisonment, and you'll come out ruined for life. Is it worth it?"

Mally did not speak. She set her mouth in a straight, pale line and groped amongst Sir George's words for something that she could understand. She saw him, once more controlled, return to the table and lay his watch upon Barbara's copy-book. It was a bright-blue copy-book with a white label pasted on it. Mally knew what was written on the label—"Barbara Peterson. Sums." The words were enclosed in a thin black line with twirls at the corners.

Sir George had laid his watch just under the label. The copy-book had round corners, and the pages were edged with red. Mally took particular notice of these things.

"Three minutes," said Sir George.

Mally went on looking at the copy-book. The blue was rather a nice, dark blue with a watered line in it like *moire*. Lady Mooring had a black *moire* dress. It didn't suit her; it was much too stiff. She wore a Honiton lace collar with it, and a diamond brooch.

A whole sentence of Sir George's sprang up suddenly in Mally's mind and blotted out the picture of Lady Mooring in black *moire*: *"If I have you searched, the Mogul Diamond will be found on you."* The words seemed to hang in the air. They were like one of those sky-signs which she had seen last night when she and Roger were crossing Piccadilly Circus. They sprang out of the darkness and blazed with a horrid glaring light: *"If I have you searched, the Mogul Diamond will be found on you."*

Mally remembered the queer taste in the coffee which Sir George had pressed upon her. She remembered her sleep, her terrified awakening, and the silent closing door. She remembered that Paul Craddock had laughed.

"Your five minutes are up, Miss Lee. Are you going to be sensible?"

She did not know that she was going to speak; but she heard herself speaking, saying what she had said before:

"I don't know what you mean."

It was true. She didn't know. She only knew one thing—that some dreadful unseen net was closing down upon her. They would search her. And they would find the Mogul Diamond. And she would go to prison. Why these things were happening she could make no guess; she only knew that they were happening and that she could not possibly escape from them.

"Come, come, Miss Lee, be rational. I'm asking you not to ruin yourself. Give me the paper, and you go scot-free. Come!"

Mally did not speak. There was nothing to say. No, nothing that she said would make any difference. If they meant to ruin her, they would ruin her. There was nothing she could do.

Sir George turned and went out. The door fell to behind him with a heavy, jarring slam that shook the room.

"What a fool you are!" said Paul Craddock. "He'd have struck you if he'd stayed. But it would have been better for you if he had. He's going to have you searched, all most properly and respectably. And when the diamond's been found on you, you'll wish you hadn't been quite such a fool, Mally, my dear—you really will. Look here, suppose we do a deal. That paper's of value to Sir George, and I happen to know that he'd give a very considerable sum for its recovery. Hand it over, and you shall go away with a couple of hundred pounds in your pocket, and no harm done. You'll give back the diamond, of course, but—" He laughed maliciously—"We won't be too particular about asking how you came by it."

Mally did not say a single word. She put back her head against the wooden panel of the door and fixed her eyes upon Paul Craddock's face. She went on looking at him quite silently and steadily. Paul had expected anger, fear, perhaps—most pleasing thought of all—a terrified plea for help. Instead, Mally's greenish-hazel eyes just rested on him in a look that passed from surprise into bleak, withering contempt; and under their gaze Paul Craddock felt a discomfort that surprised himself. He looked away, and then looked back again.

Mally's face was quite pale and expressionless, but her eyes judged him.

Chapter Ten

THE DOOR OPENED, and there came in, Mrs. Craddock, who was trembling very much, and Mrs. Craddock's maid, a tall and most stiffly respectable person of the name of Jones. Sir George followed them a little way into the room and beckoned to Paul Craddock.

"We shall wait outside. Now, Jones, you quite understand? You will search Miss Lee thoroughly in Mrs. Craddock's presence. If she makes any difficulty, just let me know and I will send for the police. Take any letters or papers which you find, and let me see them. If you don't find the diamond ornament on her, her room must be searched."

"Oh!" said Mrs. Craddock. She sank limply into a chair beside the table and dabbed at the tears which were rolling down her cheeks.

"Oh, Miss Lee, how dreadful! Oh, George, I can't believe it."

"My dear Lena, I don't ask you to believe anything; I merely request that you will remain in this room whilst Jones carries out my instructions." He passed into the corridor as he spoke, and shut the door.

Mally had not moved. She stood with her head thrown back against the panel of the bedroom door, her fingers clenched upon the handle. She heard Mrs. Craddock sniff and sob.

Jones touched her on the arm.

"Now, miss, come along."

It was Jones's touch that roused her effectually. She sprang away from it, stamped her foot, and said:

"What does it all mean? I think you're mad—I think you're all quite mad! Mrs. Craddock!"

"Now look here, miss—"

"Mrs. Craddock!"

Jones stepped between Mally and the weeping lady.

"What's the sense of upsetting her more than she's upset already? What's the sense of any of it? If you're innocent, you're innocent, and no harm done. And if you've forgot yourself and taken things that don't belong to you—well, isn't it better for me to find 'em than to be taken off by the police and searched at the station? Which is what'll happen if you're foolish. You take and be sensible, and don't go upsetting Mrs. Craddock, that wouldn't hurt a fly."

Mally looked at the large, impassive woman, and her anger died. What was the good of being angry? The thought of the police station chilled her. Jones noted the change. She became the maid, brisk and business-like.

"Let me have your jumper and skirt to start with. It won't take long if you're sensible. Come along."

Mally slipped off her dark-blue jumper and stepped out of the short skirt that matched it. It was cold without them. Jones felt the jumper all over and hung it over a chair. Then she ran her hands down the skirt, turning it this way and that, whilst Mrs. Craddock cried continually and Mally stood watching her.

"Oh!" said Jones suddenly. It was a very sharp exclamation. She dropped a fold of the skirt, then picked it up again and stared accusingly. "A pin ran right into my finger!"

Mally stood with her bare arms crossed. She held a cold elbow in either hand and saw Jones turn back her blue serge skirt at the hem and feel it gingerly. Just by the seam the stitching had come undone.

"Oh!" said Jones again. She pinched the hem and slipped a finger and thumb into the hole.

Mrs. Craddock's handkerchief dropped from her eyes. She looked, Jones looked, and Mally looked at what the finger and thumb brought out—a bright something that flashed, a wreath of diamond leaves woven heart-wise about a central, gleaming drop, which caught the light of the dull wintry afternoon. Mrs. Craddock's mouth fell slowly open; she looked as if she were screaming, but she did not make any sound. Mally heard herself say "No!" in a sort of piercing whisper. Jones dropped the skirt in a heap.

"Well, I never!" She spoke slowly, almost abstractedly; and when she had spoken, she went over to the table and laid the Mogul Diamond down on Barbara's blue copy-book.

Standing there, with her back to Mally, she said roughly, "Put on your clothes. I'll have to call Sir George."

Mally bent and picked up her skirt. How did a thing like this happen? It didn't. It couldn't. It was simply bound to be a dream. She fastened the hooks at her waist and slipped the jumper over her head. And then Sir George was back in the room, and she heard him talking to Jones, and Jones answering:

"No, sir—only this, sir."

"You searched thoroughly? There are important papers missing."

Mally's mind took hold of the word papers. It puzzled her; she looked at the word and didn't know what to do with it.

Sir George went out of the room again and shut the door. Jones came back to her.

"What's all this about papers? What's the sense of taking other folks' papers? You hand 'em over. Hand 'em over, and you save yourself and me a heap of trouble."

"I haven't got them," said Mally.

She looked into Jones's plain, respectable face with some faint hope that the woman might believe her, might even help her. It was a very faint hope, because Mally did not really see how any one could help her. The Mogul's Diamond had been found hidden in the hem of her dress, and what could any one do or say that would blot out this damning fact?

The second search was a good deal more thorough than the first. When Mally had dressed herself again, Jones went to the door and stood just outside it. Mally could hear her voice, but not what she was saying. After a moment she returned and touched Mrs. Craddock on the arm.

"Now, now, ma'am." Her voice was suddenly soft. "Don't you take on so. You come along with me and have a bit of a lay-down, and don't upset yourself any more. Sir George don't want us now, so you just come along."

"Oh, it's so dreadful!" Mrs. Craddock had a fresh access of sobbing. "So dreadful! So very dreadful!"

She held on to Jones and stood up, shaking and weeping. But before she had been piloted more than half-way to the door she stopped, turned back, and lifted her streaming eyes to Mally's face.

"Miss Lee, how could you, *could* you do it?"

"I didn't." Mally's answer came with a ring and vigour which surprised herself. She didn't know what was going to happen to her; but her shocked apathy had passed, and whatever came, she meant to meet it fighting.

Sir George, coming in, was aware of a change, and put it down to the fact that the paper had not been found. He stood over her with a flushed face and threatening manner.

"What have you done with the paper? Where is it?"

"I don't know what you mean."

"Oh, don't you? You'd better think, Miss Mally Lee, or you'll find yourself in Queer Street. Why, you little fool, what's going to save you from going to prison? Nothing, if you persist in being obstinate."

Mally stood her ground, looked straight up into the furious face, and said in a small, cool voice, "How did Mrs. Craddock's pendant get into the hem of my skirt?"

"I think a jury would say that you had hid it there."

"I wonder."

"Are you going to give me the paper?"

"I don't know anything at all about any paper."

"You took a paper off Mr. Craddock's table this morning. I want it. If you give it up, I won't prosecute."

A little spurt of anger warmed Mally and loosened her tongue.

"That's frightfully kind of you. Do I say 'Thank you very much'?"

Sir George set his jaw.

"You give me the paper, or you go to jail."

Mally stepped back from him with a little laugh. Now that she was angry, she could laugh.

"How can I give you what I haven't got?"

"Where is it? What have you done with it?"

"How do I know?" She laughed again. "I think you know more about the diamond than I do, and about this stupid paper which seems to upset you so much."

As soon as she had said the words, she felt a stab of fear. Sir George's face changed; there was a black, bleak silence. After a moment he turned stiffly and went to the window. It was about four o'clock in the afternoon, and there was a touch of dusk upon the January air. The fire had gone out because no one had thought to make it up.

After the silence had lasted an interminable time, Sir George came away from the window and switched on the light. Then he called in a loud, harsh voice to Paul Craddock.

Chapter Eleven

MALLY SAT on a hard chair in a small bedroom high up on the fourth floor of the big hostile house. A single unshaded electric light showed a neat hard bed, the square of Turkey carpet, and furniture painted white.

She had just decided to her own satisfaction that the carpet must belong to Mrs. Craddock and had graced her dining-room; it was so exactly the sort of carpet that Mrs. Craddock would have in a dining-room. The furniture was probably Mrs. Craddock's, too—the furniture of a servant's bedroom, not considered good enough for Jones's use. That nobody used this room was plain enough; it had the neat, cold, unlived-in feeling which clings about empty houses. It was an hour since the door had been locked on Mally, and two hours since Sir George had called to Paul Craddock. Mally had never heard of the third degree, but she had been put through it with merciless efficiency. The fact that she had no knowledge of the missing paper helped her to weather the long, battering cross-examination to which she had been subjected. In the end it was Sir George who lost his self-control, suddenly, terribly, shockingly, and Paul Craddock who had stood between her and actual physical violence. It was Paul who had marched her upstairs, told her to take the night to think it over, and locked her in.

Mally got up from her chair, went to the window, and pulled up the blind. She looked out over the square, with its soft central darkness of trees to the rows of lighted windows that marked the houses square, with its soft central darkness of trees, to the left of the hall door. The light made an odd, shiny circle on the wet road and damp pavement. The far edge of the circle touched the iron railings which shut in the garden, where the trees and shrubs lived like prisoners behind bars.

Mally looked at the railings and began to wonder what being in prison was like. She would soon know, because she did not see how there could be any way out of her going to prison.

She was able to think quite clearly now. She had gone over every minute of the day since breakfast. She was quite sure in her own mind that some one had drugged her coffee, and that Paul Craddock had put the diamond pendant inside the hem of her skirt. It would have been easy, because she had been very deeply asleep; he had only to open an inch of the hem with those very neat fingers of his, and to push the diamond in. It was quite easy. But she could never, never prove that he had done it, any more than she could prove that she had not hidden the diamond there herself.

She was quite sure that it was Paul Craddock who had put the Mogul's Diamond into the hem of her skirt. But why had he done it? She had slapped his face of course; but it didn't really seem an adequate reason. If you kissed a girl, or tried to kiss a girl who didn't want you to kiss her—well, you deserved all you got. "And if he hadn't ever been slapped before, I expect he often will be again. And anyhow he asked for it—*absolutely*," was Mally's conclusion. No, that there was something more in it than Paul Craddock's slapped face and Paul Craddock's injured feelings, Mally was sure. But further than that she could not get. This talk about a missing paper—was it a blind? Or had they really lost something which they needed at all costs to recover?

Mally stared thoughtfully out of the window. She was up against something that she did not understand. She felt as if she were trying to walk in a dark, slippery place, where a step in any direction might be dreadfully dangerous. Slippery—yes, that was the word; wherever she turned, she had a sense of the ground sliding from under her feet.

She pressed closer to the window. The night, the trees, and the wet roadway were more friendly than this house. If she could only get out and get away. She watched a cat stroll across the wet road. It came out of the shadows like a shadow, stood for a moment in the lighted circle cast by the street lamp, and then slipped like a black streak into the shadows again.

Yes, if she could only get away—if she could only get out. There was something more than strange about the whole thing. If she could get to Roger, he would help her.

She had a most comforting vision of Roger and herself leaving London far behind them, slipping through the night in Roger's car and coming safe to Curston. She had a feeling that at Curston she would be safe—if the Moorings stood by her she would be safe. She did not reason about this feeling; but it was all the stronger because it was purely-instinctive. Roger would take her to Curston, and at Curston she would be safe. *But how was she to get to Roger?*

On the instant Mally became severely practical. She opened the window and leaned out. The room in which she had been locked was on the fourth floor. On the next floor was a window immediately below her own; and this window had a little stone balustrade.

Mally looked at the balustrade. It enclosed a ledge not more than a foot wide, which might have held three flower-pots. Mally looked earnestly at the ledge. It was ten or twelve feet below her. You can't hang from a window-sill and drop ten or twelve feet on to a ledge three flower-pots wide unless you are a cat, burglar or an acrobat.

Mally wasn't any of these. She had done a certain amount of gymnasium work at school, and she had a good head; but even with prison as an alternative, she did not see herself hanging from a fourth-story sill and dropping gracefully on to a third-story ledge— not without something to hold on to anyhow. She could have done it at a pinch with a rope.

She turned back into the room and looked about it. The small, narrow bed was covered with one of those loosely woven honeycombed counterpanes which have a little knotted fringe all round and are so extraordinarily heavy to sleep under. Mally whisked the counterpane off the bed and measured it along her arm. It was of the size described in catalogues as two by three.

She went to the open window and let the counterpane hang down, holding it by one corner so as to get the length diagonally. The fringe dangled just above the balustrade. She drew it up again quickly. What could she fasten it to? There ought, of course, to have been nice easy window bars; but as there weren't any window bars, she would have to find something else.

She went to the bed, moved it, and felt a horrible conviction that it would tip up the minute any weight came on it. Flimsy, cheap, and light, it might be a last resort, but it would certainly be a horribly dangerous one. She went back to the window, pulled down both sashes, and, wrapping the counterpane about her arm and hand, she very deliberately broke a hole through the glass immediately under the transverse bars of wood, taking care that no splinters should fall down outside.

Now, supposing any one were to come, what would she do? Mally went to the door and stood there listening, holding her breath. From far away downstairs, a dull booming sound reached her. That meant either the dressing gong or the dinner gong. In either case she was safe for at least an hour. She rather thought that she was meant to go supperless—Paul Craddock had, in fact, said as much. But, anyhow, no one would come near her until dinner was over.

She pushed the corner of the counterpane through the holes she had made in the two sheets of glass, and looked in dismay at the immense thickness which would have to be knotted. Even if she could run the knots tight, they would take up so much of the stuff that what was left would not reach nearly far enough. If she could slit the corner and get two ends which she could tie, it would be ever so much better.

She stooped down to look for a piece of glass with a sharp cutting edge, and as her knee touched the floor, she heard a footstep far away down the passage—a man's step, quick and impatient.

Mally did not stop to think. She was not at all conscious of thinking. She heard the footsteps, and found herself at the other side of the room with her fingers on the switch of the electric light. Darkness rushed down upon her; the walls, the window, the bed, the Turkey carpet, were all one soft blackness. She stood there and heard the handle rattle. If any one came in, it was all up. The handle rattled again, and Paul Craddock's voice said:

"Hallo! Have you thought any better of it yet?"

Mally did not speak, but she went very softly into the middle of the room and waited.

"Sulky, are you? You'd better think it over, you know. You really won't like being in prison."

"When am I going to have something to eat?" said Mally. It cheered her a good deal to find that her voice was cool and steady, though her heart would beat in an unmanageable way.

"I really don't know. I shouldn't be surprised if you didn't get anything. Fasting's good for the conscience." He laughed. "See you in the morning. So long."

The footsteps went away again. Mally turned on the light, found her piece of glass, and made shift, between cutting and tearing, to slit the corner of the counterpane diagonally for about a couple of feet. She knotted the ends over the cross-bar of the window, switched off the light, and climbed out over the sash on to the window-sill.

The light was all below her now—yellow, unsteady light from the street lamp. The balustrade which she must reach looked small and black against it. She held the sash and let the counterpane fall to its full length; and it was when the limp, heavy folds slid down the wall that Mally's courage went cold in her and she would have given nearly everything in the world to have been able to turn back.

She was kneeling on the window ledge, with its rough granite gritting into her knees through her thin stockings; her feet hung out over the four-story drop to the wet pavement and the spiky railings; her hands clung to the sash as if they would never let go. And from across the square all the lighted windows watched her.

Mally felt herself rocking. The house seemed to sway with her, slowly, monotonously, rhythmically, like the pendulum of a clock. And then all at once she was talking to herself in a hard, angry whisper:

"*Rabbit!* Do you want to go to *prison*? Do you want to fall down *squash* on the pavement? Do you want *Paul Craddock* to find you here and laugh at you? Yes, idiot—*laugh* at you. Stop being an invertebrate jellyfish this instant!"

The house stopped rocking.

"Now!" said Mally. "*Now*, rabbit! Take your hand off the sash and catch hold of the counterpane. Now your left. Get your weight on it. Now shift your knees."

Mally did just as she was told. If she had waited a second, she could not have done it. But she did not wait. The most frightful moment was when her knee slipped off the edge of the sill and she hung on the loosely woven stuff and felt it stretch, and give, and stretch again. The window ledge pushed her body out from the wall, so that she was not hanging clear. She shifted her grasp a little at a time until her hands touched the sill. Then she had to hang by one hand whilst she felt for a grip on the counterpane lower down. It was so frightfully thick; she could not grasp it all or nearly all. But she got past the sill somehow and came down inch by inch.

When the counterpane became easier to hold she knew she must be coming near the end. And then, before she expected it, her dangling feet just touched the balustrade. She looked down for the first time since she had begun the descent; and instantly she was giddy—so giddy that even when she had dropped into the little space between balustrade and window, she could only crouch there, shaking from head to foot.

Two men passed down the road below. She heard their voices; one of them laughed. Mally roused herself. Any one might look up at any moment and see that dangling counterpane. Fear of discovery drove out all other fear. She slipped off a shoe, broke the window in front of her, and almost before the splinters had stopped falling, pushed through the broken pane into the room behind. The curtains had been drawn, and the glass falling against them made very little sound.

Mally stopped just beyond the curtains; her left hand clutched them together behind her. They were of smooth glazed chintz, very cold to the touch. The room in front of her was pitch-dark. It was one of the spare bedrooms, and she thought that the door was immediately opposite the window by which she had entered. She let go of the curtains and began to feel her way towards it. When her groping right hand touched the panel, she stood still and felt for the handle; and as she did so, the thought came with a rush, "What if the door is locked on the outside?" Careful housemaids did lock the doors of unused rooms on the outside. Suppose she were locked in here, to be tracked and most ignominiously found by Paul Craddock.

In a panting hurry she twisted the handle and pulled. The door opened, and the long, empty corridor lay before her, lit from end to end by softly shaded lights. She stood on the threshold, listening acutely. She was on her own floor now; her room and Barbara's were at the end of the passage. Still breathing fast, she stepped out of the room, shut the door behind her, and ran lightly and quickly down the corridor.

In the darkness of her own room she began to think. She must get away. She must get to Roger. A hat—that was the first thing—a hat and coat. She felt for them and put them on. Her purse was in a hand-bag, and the hand-bag in a drawer with her gloves. The nuisance was that the drawer creaked. She would just have to chance the creak. She must have the money. It was little enough; but she must be able to take a taxi.

She pulled gingerly at the drawer, got it open an inch, and pulled again. Of course the wretched thing must needs creak, and creak loudly. Mally bit her lip, fished out her bag, and was just cramming the gloves into it, when she heard a sound. Some one was opening a door—not the door into the passage, but the one from Barbara's room. With a click the light went on, and there, quite close to her, was Barbara in her nightgown, her face chalk-white, her dark eyes round and staring.

She said "Mally!" in a sort of sobbing whisper, and then ran forward and caught at Mally's arm.

"You're going away!"

"Oh, Barby darling, hush!"

"You're going!"

"I must."

They were both whispering. Suddenly, above their own voices, there came to them the sound of another voice. It was Jones, outside in the corridor, and she was speaking to some one. They heard her say, "She'll be quite all right." And then, quick as lightning, Barbara had switched off the light and was pulling Mally with her. They had reached the bed and were standing beside it, when the door into the passage was opened a little way and they could see Jones, the half of a black shadow against the light behind her.

She stood there and listened for a little, whilst Barbara clutched Mally and Mally clutched Barbara. Then she said in a low, cautious voice, "Are you asleep, miss?" and listened again. She said this two or three times, then turned and spoke over her shoulder: "She's fast as fast, ma'am. You come along back to your bed and let me get down to my supper." She shut the door on Mrs. Craddock's murmured answer.

"Mally," said Barbara in the darkness, "*are* you going away?"

Mally picked her up, put her into bed, and covered her. It was a cold night and the child was shivering.

"I must."

Barbara threw off the clothes and sat bolt upright.

"They said I shouldn't *never* see you again." Mally was silent. Barbara's little hard, cold hands held her wrist. "Why must you?"

"Barby darling, I must. Let me go."

"Is it because of Pinko? Is it?"

"Yes, it is. He'll hurt me if I don't go quick. Barby, let me go!"

"I knew it was because of Pinko. Wait—I want to give you something—wait just where you are."

She wriggled out of bed, and Mally heard her bare feet padding on the carpet. She was back again in a moment with something that rustled, something that, pushed into Mally's hands, resolved itself into a packet of papers.

"What is it?"

Barbara jigged up and down on the bed. Her whisper was tinged with triumph.

"It's my drawings, what I hid, so that beastly Pinko couldn't tell about them and get them burnt like he did the others."

"Did he?"

Barbara stopped jigging.

"It was *murdering* of him. They were mine—I made them my own self. And he told, and they were all torn up and burnt. And I hid these so as even you didn't know. And I want you to take them right away out of the house and keep them safe, and when I'm grown up you can give them to me again. Now go quick, because I'm going to cry."

Mally caught the little shaking figure in a tight hug; a hot tear ran against her cheek. And then Barbara pushed her away.

"Go quick, quick, quick!" And Mally went.

It seemed like madness to come out into the lighted passage and down the stairs, and yet there was no other way of it. The thought of the back stairs she dismissed at once; they would be far more dangerous. Sir George and Paul Craddock would still be at dinner, and there was a chance that she might be able to pass through the hall and get away without being seen.

She stood by Sir George's bust and looked down at the marble statues and the cold tessellated pavement. The study lay on the left and the dining-room on the right. The hall was empty. Mally ran down the shallow steps and through the swing doors into the vestibule. The front door was before her. She took hold of it to open it, heard the door behind her swing again, and whisked round to face Herbert, the second footman, a tall and personable youth with a fresh complexion and eyes that were inclined to stare. They stared at Mally now, and she gave a little imperious nod.

"Open it!" she said, and waved to the door.

Herbert stood stock-still and considered. He had no wish to lose his place. It was a good place, and as the first footman was thinking of leaving, Herbert had hopes of promotion. He was not quite sure what Mally was supposed to have done, but he knew that she had been locked up, and that Mr. Craddock had given particular instructions with regard to her.

"Open it!" said Mally, a little more imperiously than before.

Herbert came slowly forward. He liked Mally, but that would not have moved him from the path of duty. Mr. Craddock had been most particular. Herbert did not like Mr. Craddock. Mr. Craddock had tried to kiss Alice, the second housemaid, not a week ago; and Alice had boxed his ears and told Herbert, with whom she was walking out.

"Open it!" said Mally for the third time. She stamped her foot a little.

Her hair was the same color as Alice's hair.

Herbert stepped to the front door and opened it in a beautifully silent manner. As it swung towards her and the cold night air rushed in, Mally's heart beat hard and fast. She had not really thought that he would let her go.

She put her hand to her throat and turned shining eyes on Herbert. Then, with a decorous "Thank you, Herbert," she slipped into the dark street and was gone.

Chapter Twelve

THE LATE Lady Catherine Cray's collection of china and Bristol glass is quite well known to connoisseurs. Mr. Roger Mooring, her nephew by marriage, was engaged in cataloguing it. Himself something of a collector, he naturally found this a sufficiently absorbing occupation, and having dined in the drawing-room of the flat, he had drifted back into the dining-room, where the collection occupied every available inch of space.

The light, glitteringly enshrined in a magnificent cut-glass chandelier, flashed down upon a medley of goblets, bottles, dishes, and epergnes. The lustrous apple-green Bristol, the turquoise blue, the translucent white, and the very rare pink gave color to the display. Roger's eye dwelt upon it lovingly. He picked up a large azure jug flecked with silver and held it to the light. Only two had ever been made, and Lady Catherine had always hoped to secure the pair. The light came softly through the blue. Roger was just going to set it down, when the door was opened with a rush and shut again with a bang.

Mally Lee stood with her back to it and said "Roger!" in an odd, breathless voice; and Roger very nearly dropped the precious jug on the top of an even more precious cup and saucer, where a pheasant flaunted among peonies on a ground of silver lustre.

He frowned at Mally reproachfully, put the jug in a safe place, and said, "What is it?"

Mally looked at him without speaking. There was something odd about her appearance, he thought; she had a bright color, and she looked rather untidy—hair ruffled, hat crooked, and coat unbuttoned. Untidiness did not appeal to him.

"Roger!"

"My dear Mally, what on earth's the matter? You oughtn't to come here, you know. You really—" He stopped because Mally gave a queer little dry sob.

"If I can't come here, I can't come anywhere. I've—I've run away."

Roger stared.

"My dear girl, what on earth do you mean?"

Mally came forward. When she reached the end of the table, she stopped.

"I've run away. I want you to take me to Curston."

"To Curston?"

"Roger, I shall scream if you go on repeating what I say. If I say Curston, I mean Curston. And I mean *now*."

Roger instantly offended again.

"Now?" he said, and stared with all his eyes.

Mally picked up a turquoise bottle with a filigree gilt top and banged on the table with it.

"Yes, now, *now*, NOW! And when I say now, I mean now! You've got to get that old car of yours and drive me down to Curston—*now, at once*, or you'll have the police bursting in and arresting me—and you won't like that a bit."

Every time that Mally said, "Now," she rapped the table hard with the little bright blue bottle. Its peril distracted Roger. Catching her hand in an impassioned clasp, he said hoarsely:

"You'll break it!"

"I don't care if I do. Roger, you're not attending. I said the *police* would burst in and arrest me."

"Why on earth—? Oh, I say, do be careful of that bottle—you *will* break it!"

Mally lost her temper.

"I shall want to break it if you go on being so maddening. I want you to help me, and you talk about a miserable bit of blue glass. Roger, I'm in a hole. I've run away. And I should think the police would be here any moment. But if you'll get me down to Curston, I don't believe they'll do anything. No, *I don't*, for I'm sure there's something behind it all—something horrid and wicked and disgraceful. They think I'm nobody, and they think they can try it on me. But you, and Lady Mooring, and the whole country solid behind you—no, they won't risk it. I'm sure they won't risk it. I'm *sure* they won't."

She pulled her hand away and put the bottle down with a push that set the pendant lustres swinging and tinkling on an apple-green candlestick. Then she caught at Roger's arm and pinched it hard.

"Oh, Roger, *say* something, *do* something. There isn't any time to lose—there isn't, really."

"I don't understand—I say, don't pinch like that!"

He stepped back. Mally stamped her foot, and the telephone bell went off beside them with the suddenness of an alarm clock.

"Bother!" said Mally. "Say you're out—say you've gone to Brighton—say you've eloped."

"S'sh!" This was to Mally. To the telephone Mr. Mooring remarked courteously, "Hallo!"

Mally darted to his side, covered the mouthpiece with her hand, and whispered fiercely.

"You haven't seen me—you don't know where I am! Do you hear?"

Roger glared.

"You're tickling. And I don't know what you're talking about."

Mally still clutched the mouthpiece.

"You haven't seen me since last night!"

The whisper tickled again. Then she let go of the telephone and clutched Roger's arm instead. Faintly she heard what he was hearing—faintly but quite distinctly.

"Is Mr. Mooring—"

"Speaking." Roger's voice still sounded annoyed.

"Oh, Mooring, it's Sir George Peterson. We—we are concerned about Miss Lee. Do you happen to have seen her?"

Mally's fingers sank into Roger's arm in one of the hardest pinches he had ever felt. He threw her a raging glance and said stiffly:

"She dined with me last night."

Again the thread of sound that was yet so unmistakably Sir George's voice, suavely pleasant:

"My dear Mooring, it's a very delicate matter. We're all deeply concerned. Er—have you seen Miss Lee to-day?"

Roger jerked the arm that Mally was pinching.

"Why do you ask?"

"Well"—hesitation—"Well, Mooring—"

"What is it?" Roger was becoming exasperated.

"Well, the fact is that something very unpleasant has happened. Miss Lee is a very charming girl, and we all took a great fancy to her—my sister especially. And now, I'm sorry to say, we have all received a shock, a very severe shock."

Mally's little nose wrinkled. Her lips formed the word "Beast," but it remained unspoken.

"What has happened?" It seemed to Roger that it was about time that some one told him. He put the question with a good deal of force.

"Er"—hesitation again—"Really, Mooring, it's extremely painful to me to have to tell you."

"*What has happened?*"

"I will ask you to believe that I'm very hard hit about it all. I could have sworn—but there, one doesn't know what the temptation may have been."

"I don't know what you're driving at."

"Well, the fact is I haven't liked coming to the point. But I've got to. Here it is, Mooring. My sister yesterday missed a very valuable ornament containing a jewel known as the Mogul" Diamond. Naturally, no one would have dreamed of connecting Miss Lee with its disappearance, but—" The voice stopped.

"What do you mean by 'but'?" said Roger Mooring slowly. Mally's fingers still gripped his arm; he thought they shook as he asked the question.

The voice took up its thread of speech again:

"No one would have suspected Miss Lee if a valuable paper had not disappeared this morning in circumstances which made it impossible that any one else could have taken it. She was searched by my sister's maid in my sister's presence, and I regret to say that the Mogul Diamond was found in her possession."

"What?"

"The diamond was found in Miss Lee's possession. Believe me, I would rather it had never been found at all."

There was a silence. Roger lifted his head and looked at Mally, and Mally let go his arm and went a step backwards. If Roger could look at her like that, he could say what he liked. He could—

Faint, very faint, Sir George's voice:

"Have you seen Miss Lee? We thought she might go to you. Have you seen her?"

"No!" Roger said the word sharply; and as he said it, he thrust the receiver violently back upon its hook.

Mally put her hand out as if she were pushing something away. She said "Roger!" in an angry, shaking voice. Then she stamped her foot and burst into tears.

Roger went on looking at her in a dazed, horrified way. He did not say anything, because for the life of him he could not think of anything to say; besides, Mally was speaking, and sobbing, and blowing her nose, all at the same time and with the utmost vigour.

"Aren't you going to *do* anything? Aren't you going to take me away? Aren't you going to get your car? The police may be here at any minute. We ought to have gone ages ago—simply ages. Any one—*any* one would have known I was here from the way you spoke to the *wretch. Roger!*"

Still Roger did not speak.

Small causes sometimes produce quite big results. Shakespeare, Bacon, or Another has remarked on this. It is nevertheless true. If a tuft of Mally's hair had not hung down over her left eye; if her hat had been poised at its usual becoming angle; and if she had been less drastic in her treatment of a blue Bristol bottle with a gilt filigree top, Roger Mooring would have been less disposed to believe her guilty in the matter of the Mogul Diamond.

"*Roger!*" said Mally again. There was command, not appeal, in her voice. Perhaps if she had appealed—but she was much too angry to appeal.

She rolled her wet handkerchief into a tight ball, thrust it deep into her coat pocket, winked the last hot tear away, and read Roger's distrust in Roger's face.

Up to this moment she had merely thought him maddeningly, idiotically slow; now she saw quite plainly that this slowness was deliberate. He didn't go and get the car, because he didn't mean to go and get the car. He didn't want to take her to Curston. He didn't want to do anything. He believed Sir George. It had simply never occurred to Mally that Roger would believe Sir George. *Roger*— he ought to be stamping up and down, using up his very best vocabulary on the entire Peterson household. Alternatively, he ought to be sprinting, simply sprinting, for his car. He wasn't doing either of these things; he was standing there looking at her with gloomy suspicion.

The room waved up and down under Mally's feet for a moment. It felt odd, just like being on a ship; all that glitter and sheen of glass ran, and dazzled, and rocked soundlessly. She turned very white, and took three little, careful steps sideways until she came to the table and could catch hold of it. She held the table-edge with one hand and the other, groping, came down on a tall white translucent lustre. The pendants jangled. Mally's hand closed hard on one of them, and the sharp edge of it cut her palm. The room stopped waving up and down. She faced Roger Mooring and said in a whisper:

"How dare you? Oh, how dare you?"

"Mally!"

"Don't speak to me! You believe him—I saw you believing him!"

"Mally, why did you do it?"

At this point it becomes impossible to excuse Mally's actions. She said "Oh!" with a little furious gasp; a wild and whirling rage descended on her like a cyclone. She pulled off her engagement ring and threw it with a remarkably good aim straight at Roger's face. It hit him on the left cheek-bone, and the diamond drew blood. He swore, and Mally picked up the tall white lustre that had cut her hand.

Roger plunged forward with a shout:

"Look out! Look *out*! You'll break something!"

"I'm going to," said Mally, and flung the lustre with a crash into the midst of the crowded table.

There was an awful shattering sound, the ring and tinkle of falling glass, and hard upon it the slamming bang of the door.

Roger Mooring wiped the blood from his cheek and surveyed the ruins of Lady Catherine Cray's collection.

Chapter Thirteen

SIR GEORGE PETERSON turned from the telephone and said briskly:

"She's there. He lied about it, of course—but damned badly. She's certainly there."

"What next? The police?"

"My good Paul! No, get on to Makins and Poole. Tell 'em it's a confidential matter. Tell 'em about the diamond, and say we don't want to prosecute in deference to my sister's feelings, but we've reason to believe she's gone off with important private papers, and we *must* have 'em back. Offer a reward that will ginger 'em up without making 'em suspicious. Tell 'em to put a real good man on to the job. And, above all, no publicity."

Mally Lee ran all the way down the stairs from Lady Catherine's flat, and when she came out into the dark, wet street, she ran as far as the corner, where she hailed a bus and got the last inside seat. It was only half a seat really, because a very large lady, with a string bag and a beaded mantle trimmed with aged rabbit fur, billowed voluminously over two-thirds of the bench.

Mally sat on the edge and got back her breath. She paid her fare to the conductor, took her ticket, and put it inside her purse. It had for company a half-crown, a shilling, three pence and a bent farthing. Mally shut the purse. She had three and nine-pence farthing in the world.

What can you do with three and ninepence farthing, when the police are after you and you have simply *got* to get away and hide? How far can you get with three and ninepence farthing?

Mally bit her lip, because the answer was certainly, "Not nearly far enough."

When her pennyworth was up, she got out of the bus, and watched it go rumbling and clattering away, with something of the same feeling with which a marooned sailor watches his departing ship. She was at the junction of two streets—one dark and quiet, the other more brightly lighted and full of the roar of traffic. She did not know the names of either of these streets, and she had no idea where she was.

She began to walk down the darker street because it occurred to her that if she stood still, people would notice her and wonder what she was doing. She walked as far as the next crossing, and then turned back again because the road ahead had a deserted look and instinct turned her towards the lights. She walked slowly and tried to think. It was raining, with the sort of icy rain which might turn to snow at any moment; it was very cold.

Mally reached the lighted corner, turned it, and walked on down the street. It was about seven hours since she had had anything to eat. Every time she began to think about her plans, irrelevant visions of hot soup, and penny buns, and muffins, and buttered eggs, and mince pies, kept bobbing up and down and interrupting her train of thought.

It was because of this confusion in her mind that she did not at first perceive that she was being followed. She was waiting on the curb to let the incoming traffic from a side road go by, when some one whispered in her ear. The whisper was sound, not words, to Mally. She said involuntarily, "I beg your pardon," and turned her head.

A man was standing quite close to her, smiling; and at the sight of his smile Mally ran in front of a taxi, dodged round a bus, collided violently with a stout old gentleman, and narrowly missing a private car, arrived breathlessly on the opposite pavement and fled along it without looking back. She was angry, but she was also frightened. No one had ever looked at her like that before, and it filled her with a shuddering rage.

When she had run about twenty yards, she took a pull on herself and slowed to a walk. "You little fool—little *idiot*! You're not to run. You'll make every one look at you. Stop at once and walk properly."

She stopped, and began to walk properly. It wasn't very easy, because she was feeling creepy-crawly all down her back with the thought of what might be coming up behind her. "You're not to look round—it's the worst thing you can do—you mustn't do it." And at once she did look round. The man with the smile was about a dozen yards behind. Mally's heart gave a loud, hard thump, and she began to run again.

This part of the street was rather empty. There were houses on either side, which showed no lights; the shops were all shut; and there did not seem to be a policeman anywhere. Mally was fleet of foot, and the man behind her not desirous of making himself conspicuous by running. His idea was to wait until she was out of breath and then come up with her comfortably. It was quite a good idea, but Mally spoiled it by taking cover just as her breath really did begin to fail. She saw, on her right, three steps leading up to an open doorway from which a light was shining. A light meant people, and people meant safety. That, at least, was the way in which it looked to Mally.

She ran up the steps and into a paved and empty hall from which a stone stair wound upwards. There was no one there, and there was no sign of a lift. But it was at least a place where she might take breath. Perhaps the creature who was following would think she lived there and go away.

The thought had hardly come and gone before he was peering round the door. Without an instant's hesitation Mally ran up the stairs. Once started, she was quite unable to stop. The stair went up and round, and round and up, and up and round again. There were doors with names on them, but Mally never paused to see what the names might be. She ran with all the desperate energy of panic until she had reached the very topmost floor, and there—oh, joy!—was a door that stood ajar.

Mally leaned against the jamb and panted. Her legs felt like the dangling legs of a marionette; they shook and threatened to give way beneath her. She held on to the jamb, and from inside the room she heard a murmuring voice repeating strange words in a sort of fervent whisper. It was a man's voice, and the words sounded, as Mally said afterwards, "utterly barmy."

"Spatial," said the voice in earnest tones. "Spatial; glacial; racial; facial; palatial." A deep groan followed.

Mally pushed the door a little wider and beheld an attic room, a littered table, and a young man in his shirt-sleeves sitting before a pile of smudgy manuscript. The right-hand cuff of the young man's shirt was in an extremely disintegrated condition, and would certainly have fallen off if it had not been secured to the sleeve by no fewer than three black safety pins.

The oddness of seeing three black safety pins together had an extremely calming and reassuring effect upon Mally. She stepped into the room, closed the door behind her, and said "Please."

The young man lifted his head. He bore an astonishing resemblance to a half-grown sandy cat, and it was out of eyes of a milky blue that he looked vaguely at Mally and repeated tentatively:

"Peaks glacial; æther spatial; torrents facial."

There was a slight tinge of defiance about the last word; the pale-blue eyes held a hint of obstinacy.

"Torrents *what*?" said Mally. She was now feeling completely reassured. This was an authentic poet in an authentic garret, and poet and garret were both as harmless as could be.

"Facial," said the young man. "I *said* facial."

"I know you said it. But what on earth does it mean?"

"It means torrents that run down the face of rocks."

Mally sat down on a very rickety chair and began to laugh.

"Torrents do run down the face of rocks," protested the injured poet.

Mally groped in her coat pocket for her handkerchief. It was still soaking wet with the tears of rage which she had shed in the flat. She made it a little wetter still with tears of pure laughter. Then she shook her head.

"Ah," said the poet moodily. "It's always the same. Anything original, anything distinctive, and the disintegrating tooth of destructive criticism battens on it—positively battens."

"Don't!" said Mally. *"Don't!"* She clutched her side. It was better to laugh than to cry. But she didn't really want to do either; she wanted something to eat.

The young man took up his pile of manuscript and cast it passionately on the floor.

"All right—have it your own way—*have* it your own way! Why do I write? Why does any one write? What's the good of it? Why didn't I go into an office?"

"I don't know," said Mally politely.

With startling suddenness the injured poet became a humanly inquisitive young man. He looked at Mally as though seeing her for the first time, said "Hallo!" in a puzzled tone, and inquired:

"I say, do you want anything?"

"Yes," said Mally, "I want something to eat."

"Something to eat?"

Mally repeated her remark in tones of most creditable firmness:

"Something to *eat*—E—A—T, *eat*."

The poet's mouth dropped open on one side. It was ten o'clock at night; Castleby was out, and wouldn't be back this side of midnight; he, Wilfrid, was alone, absolutely alone and unprotected; and here was a strange girl blowing in from nowhere at all and wanting something to eat. It was a most extraordinary situation. It was so extraordinary that the glacial peaks, the spatial æther, and all the rest of it faded away and were not.

For one insane moment Wilfrid Witherby actually wished that his Aunt Judith were present. His nerve failed him and, reverting to the stammer so severely checked by Aunt Judith in his childhood, he said:

"What s-s-s-sort of thing t-to eat?"

A hopeful gleam brightened in Mally's eye.

"*Anything*. I'm *starving*."

"St-t-tarving!"

"*Yes. I am.* Have you any soup—or coffee—or sardines—or—or bully beef—or buns? Because I could eat them all."

"B-b—buns?"

"*Anything,*" said Mally desperately. She began to have a low opinion of his intelligence.

"We haven't got any b-b-buns."

Mally sprang up and beat her hands together.

"Don't keep on saying buns, or I shall scream. *Have* you got anything to eat, or haven't you?"

"C-c-castleby has some b-b-biscuits."

Mally uttered a cry of joy.

"Where are they?"

As in a trance, Mr. Witherby rummaged in a corner of the room and produced a tin box without a lid. He set it on the table.

"They're g-g-gingernuts. Castleby likes gingernuts. Personally I think they're foul."

Mally drew the rickety chair up to the littered table and began to eat gingernuts. They were not good gingernuts, being soft and no longer in their first youth; but there were plenty of them. Mally ate about a pound and a half, and then demanded something to drink.

"There isn't anything to drink."

Wilfrid had recovered his speech, but was still conscious of feeling rather dazed. Whilst Mally ate biscuits, he watched her with a fixed stare and the feeling that the whole thing was probably part of one of his odder dreams, and that at any moment Mally might melt into thin air or dissolve into somebody else.

"There isn't anything to drink," he said.

"Nonsense!" said Mally. "There must be."

"There isn't."

"Don't you *wash*?"

"Oh, *water*."

It was quite obvious that Wilfrid did not regard water as something to drink. Mally looked at him reprovingly; she even reminded him for a moment of his Aunt Judith.

"Get me some water—please."

The water, when it came, was not very nice; it had a vague, far-off taste of shaving soap about it. Thirsty as she was, Mally did not drink it all. When she had set down the cracked tumbler, she heaved a sigh and smiled a sudden, dazzling smile.

"Thank Mr. Castleby for his biscuits—won't you?" Then, quite shamelessly, she put half a dozen in her pocket. "Will he mind?" she asked, and smiled again.

Wilfrid decided that this was an agreeable dream and that he would like it to go on.

"He'll be d-d-delighted. He's an awfully good f-fellow—he really is. He's not a bit like what you'd expect a detective to be like."

A nasty little cold shiver ran all up one side of Mally and all down the other. She picked up another gingernut and looked at it fixedly.

"Is Mr. Castleby a detective?"

"I should think he was. I should hate it myself, but he seems to like it. He's dashed off to-night on a v-very special job looking for this girl who's gone off."

Mally, staring at the gingernut, saw it as a very large brown disc with a wavering edge. This was only for a moment. Then it was its natural size again; but her fingers had closed on it so hard that they had bent it out of shape. She put it thoughtfully into her pocket with the others, sucked a sticky finger, and smiled for the last time upon Wilfrid Witherby.

"Thank you so much for my kind supper," she said, and was gone.

Chapter Fourteen

IT MAY BE SAID at once that Mr. Castleby's errand had nothing whatever to do with Mally Lee. If Mally had seen an evening paper, she would have discovered that the world of yellow journalism was concerning itself with the simultaneous disappearance of a certain Miss Ellen Marshman and the contents of her employer's till. Her own affair, nevertheless, was receiving the expert attention of Mr. Alfred Dawson, one of the brighter minions of Messrs. Makins and Poole.

Messrs. Makins and Poole were not a firm who suffered the grass to grow beneath their feet. On receiving Mr. Paul Craddock's telephoned instructions, they acted with commendable promptitude. Expense being no object, their Mr. Alfred Dawson departed for Lady Catherine Cray's flat in a taxi. It was not his fault that he arrived too late to see Mally get into her bus; but he certainly had a stroke of luck in encountering an injured lady who would have liked the seat which Mally took. She was a stout and voluble lady, and when she had a grievance, she wished the whole world to share it.

"Little bit of a chit of a thing, and me the mother of fifteen! Smacking—that's what girls want nowadays. And all mine had it and lived to be grateful for it when they'd got 'usbands of their own. Don't you take no lip from nobody, man or woman, not without you give back as good as you get. That's what I says to them all—'I never took no lip from any of you, and well you knows it.' And—where was I, mister?"

Mr. Alfred Dawson, waiting for the next bus on the curb beside the voluminous lady, responded with professional politeness:

"You were telling me about the young lady who took your seat."

The stout woman snorted.

"Lady indeed! *Lady!*" she snorted again. "I 'ope I'm a lady myself. And I 'ope I knows a lady when I sees one. Lady indeed!" She paused, and then went on with extreme rapidity and bitterness. "And as for that there conductor, if you want to know what I think of 'im—a squit of a fellow, the very moral of a rabbit, that oughter 'ave been drowned when 'e was born, instead of being dragged up by the scruff of 'is neck to insult respectable women at my time o' life, with 'is 'Houtside—plenty of room houtside!' And I says to 'im—and I only 'opes as 'e 'eard me—'*Houtside* yourself,' I says, 'you and all such whipper-snappers.' And 'make room,' I says, 'for ladies that weighs double what you ever did or will do and isn't a-going to risk their necks a-climbing your back stairs.'"

"Ah," said Mr. Alfred Dawson. "And what did you say the young person was like that took your seat?"

Mr. Dawson displayed a good deal of energy and resource in tracking Mally's bus. Having tracked it, he interviewed the whipper-snapper of a conductor and induced him to remember where Mally had got down. He himself reached this spot at precisely the moment when Mally had put six gingerbread biscuits into her pocket and was staring at the seventh.

He looked up the road and down the road, tossed for which way he should take, and began to walk in the direction which Mally had taken. The odds against his coming across anything that would be of the least use to him were considerable; but he was a conscientious young man and meant to do his best.

Mally ran down the six flights of stone stairs even more quickly than she had run up them. She knew now what criminals felt like; at every turn of the stair she expected to meet Mr. Castleby with a warrant for her arrest. The fact that she had just eaten a pound and a half of his ginger biscuits added poignancy to the situation.

In the little hall she stood for a moment, then slipped cautiously to the doorway, peeped round the corner, and emerged breathless upon the wet and empty pavement. Thank goodness, the slimy horror who had followed her was gone.

Mally's spirits rose, though with little enough reason. The rain had turned to sleet, and would certainly be snow before morning. She had nowhere to go. She did not know a soul in London except Roger and the Petersons. She had only three and ninepence farthing. She had no umbrella. On the other hand, she had just had something to eat, she had dodged Mr. Castleby, and she had broken off her engagement to Roger Mooring.

Mally had just reached this point, when she and Mr. Dawson met and passed each other. Once more Mr. Dawson's luck was in. A street lamp shone full on Mally as he passed her. He saw a girl in a dark-blue coat and a black felt hat and ran rapidly over the official description with which he had been furnished: "Five foot four; very slight; small features inclined to be pale; eyes greenish hazel with black lashes; hair dark; probably wearing navy-blue jumper and skirt, dark navy coat without fur, close black felt hat turned up in front, with a small paste ornament representing basket of flowers."

These faithful details were due to Jones. Every one of them, with the exception, perhaps, of the little basket of flowers, would have applied not only to Mally Lee, but to an indefinite number of other young women. London is full of small, slight girls in navy-blue coats and black felt hats. Most of the coats, it is true, have fur upon them, and very few of the black felt hats would be likely to carry a paste ornament in the shape of a basket of flowers.

Alfred Dawson allowed Mally to reach the corner before he turned and began to follow her. When she passed him, he had only seen the right-hand side of her hat. He had to see the other side. And if it was fastened back by a brooch or pin in the form of a basket of flowers, he would make pretty sure that he had had the inconceivable luck to come up with Miss Mally Lee.

Mally went straight on across the road and up the long, wet street. She wished that she had thought of asking Wilfrid Witherby where she was. She walked on with the intention of stopping the first respectable looking woman she met and asking to be directed to the nearest railway station.

Waterloo—her fancy played fondly about Waterloo. She had an idea that trains would be coming and going all night. She could take a ticket for a quite near station, and then the people at Waterloo would let her stay in a waiting-room. The waiting-room would be warm. She thought it was a lovely plan, and the only difficulty about putting it into instant execution was the fact that she hadn't the remotest idea of how to get to Waterloo.

She tramped on until her shoes began to squelch. It was whilst she was noticing what a horrid noise they made that she noticed Mr. Alfred Dawson's footsteps. She frowned and walked a little more quickly. He might be perfectly harmless, or he might not.

After she had walked at varying paces for nearly half a mile she became quite, quite certain that the footsteps had a purpose, and that that purpose was to follow her. She thought the road would never end. And then, quite suddenly, it ended, coming out into a flaring highway, where buses ran and crowds of people jostled one another. A big cinema just opposite the corner was emptying itself. In a flash Mally saw her chance and slipped into the crowd.

Hopeless to try for a seat in the bus. The crowd was not a very gentle one, and there was some rough pushing going on. Mally turned, twisted, and wriggled her way to the outskirts. Then she asked a girl about her own age the way to Waterloo. The girl stared at her, and Mally asked again.

"Dunno, I'm sure," said the girl.

Mally tried again with an older woman, and received bewilderingly fluent directions, which ran all together in her mind and made confusion there:

"First to the left, second to the right, third to the left, and tike the tube."

That was what it sounded like. But she wasn't at all sure that she hadn't got the number of the turnings mixed. She was just going to ask again, when, creepy-crawly all over her, went the feeling that she was in danger. The man who was following—perhaps it was Mr. Castleby, perhaps—Mally didn't wait to think of any other explanation. She began to run.

Mr. Alfred Dawson was, as a matter of fact, only a dozen yards away. He had seen Mally, and he had seen, perched up on the left-hand brim of her hat, a little basket of sparkling flowers. Triumph flooded his mind. And in the very moment of his triumph came disappointment. He saw Mally look frightened, and he saw her begin to run. Then, as a bus drew up beyond him, he was caught in a surging rush and carried backwards towards it.

It may be said that he did his best. He shoved three stout ladies in succession, and was told with three degrees of rudeness that he was no gentleman. He trod on a messenger boy, and was called a nasty barging brute by another lady. In spite of all his efforts, the stream carried him away, and when its violence abated and the bus had gone, Mally had disappeared.

He ran down the road as a man will run to catch a train; there were three hundred yards of it without a turning. What in the world, or out of it, had happened to the girl? She wasn't in the road, and when he reached a corner, he looked round it into a little empty cul-de-sac. It was a very angry as well as a very puzzled young man who presently gave up the search and went home.

Mally had certainly had a narrow escape. When Mr. Alfred Dawson looked at her, she saw him as one of the crowd. She had actually begun to run before she realized that she was running because this tall young man had looked at her, and that this look was one of triumphant recognition. She left the crowd behind, and found herself with the long stretch of pavement clear before her; not a turning, not an archway, not a bit of cover anywhere; houses, very tall and dark; shuttered shop fronts; more houses; more shops. And then a row of petrol pumps and the front of a large garage flaring scarlet under the arc light overhead. It was so bright that it almost hurt, coming up suddenly out of the wet and the dark—such a wash of scarlet. And as Mally looked at it, a sliding door moved and a lad came out whistling. He stood for a moment looking down the road, and behind him, between him and Mally, there was a foot-wide gap in the scarlet.

Mally slipped through the gap and was inside, in a place that seemed pitch-dark for the moment. She must get away from the door. She couldn't wait for her eyes to get accustomed to the sudden change from dazzle to dusk. She must get away quick before the boy came back. She kept her hand on the inside of the sliding door and moved to the right; and by the time she had taken half a dozen steps she was able to see her way.

The place was full of cars parked in rows—the most splendid hiding-place in the world. She reached the side wall, slipped between a Rolls Royce limousine and a Lanchester landaulette and heard the boy come whistling back and shut the door with a bang.

Mally leaned against the Rolls, quite still, holding her breath. Suppose he came this way. Suppose he *did*. But the boy passed down the middle of the long garage, and the strains of *Tea for Two* faded away.

Mally was filled with thankfulness for her garage. If an enchanted palace had suddenly started up to shelter her, she couldn't have felt more grateful about it. It was dry; and she became aware of how very wet she was. It was warm; and she discovered that she was shaking with cold. Above all, it was beautifully, beautifully safe. The boy had shut the door. The unbroken scarlet wall flared to the street again and told nothing. No one, *no one* would dream of her being here. Shelter, warmth, dryness, and safety—who could possibly ask for more? Yet more was to be had. Any of these cars would provide her with a luxurious bed for the night.

When this brilliant thought flashed into her mind, she almost laughed aloud, and then set about choosing her quarters with a good deal of discretion. Not the Rolls Royce, and not the Lanchester. Limousines and landaulettes were more likely to be London owned than a touring car. Dimly at the back of her thought there lurked the beautiful vision of sliding rhythmically out of London into the darkness of country lanes.

It was the faint echo of the plan she had made about a hundred years ago, when she was still engaged to Roger and she had thought that he would drive her to Curston and keep her against the world. So she looked for a touring car, and found a large four-seater Wolseley, well splashed with mud. The hood was up, and all the side screens closed. She opened the rear door and got in, feeling before her gingerly.

There was a large rug lying in a heap, and she nearly tripped over it. The seat was alluringly comfortable. But Mally was not to be lured from the stricter path of safety. If she sat on the floor with a bit of the rug under her and all the rest of it snuggled up round and over her, no one could possibly guess she was there unless they actually wanted some of the back seat for themselves. In that case, of course, all would be over.

Mally was not inclined to look for trouble. The rug was most beautifully soft and warm. She ate three more of Mr. Castleby's ginger biscuits, and had some idea of embarking on a fourth; but just then drowsiness came down on her like a thick, blank fog, and she went fast asleep instead, very fast asleep, on the floor of a Wolseley touring car with her head against the seat and the warm rug pulled all over her.

Chapter Fifteen

ABOUT THE SAME TIME that the excellent Jones was engaged in searching Mally Lee, Sir Julian Le Mesurier was reading a detailed and confidential report which he had that day received. It was concerned with the affairs of Peterson & Co., the shipping firm of which Sir George Peterson was the only surviving partner.

The report disclosed a state of affairs extremely difficult to reconcile with the style in which Sir George lived and the extremely comfortable balance at his bank. When a man has more money—and a very great deal more money—than his profession can account for, there may very easily be good reason for the Criminal Investigation Department to keep an eye on his affairs.

Piggy finished the report, and sat looking at it. When he was thinking deeply, it was his practice to draw cats. He began to draw them now—two cats with arched backs and bottle-brush tails spitting at one another. He drew neatly and with an excellent attention to detail. Each cat showed three sharp claws unsheathed, and each had four whiskers on one side and three on the other; their eyes bulged with malice.

When he had sketched a garden fence for them to fight on, he pushed the report on one side, took up the receiver of the telephone on his desk, and asked for his cousin Julian Forsham's number. Mr. Forsham's voice, a little bored, said, "Hallo!"

"Hallo, Ju-Ju!"

The boredom vanished.

"That you, Piggy? I was coming to see you to-morrow. Only arrived to-day."

"So *The Times* informed me."

Mr. Julian Forsham, it may be remembered, was of some note both as an explorer and a literary man. He groaned.

"My first twenty-four hours in town is spent at the telephone! It's a beneficent invention."

Piggy laughed.

"All right, I won't keep you. You're up for the Wolves' dinner to Lawrence Marrington, I take it. I'd really almost forgotten you were a Wolf."

Julian groaned again.

"If I hadn't come, every one would have said it was a case of two of a trade. Anyway that's what Amabel said they'd say. So she packed my bag and shoved me into the train. She said I'd enjoy it—which is what I call insult piled on injury."

"You don't know when you're well off. Now, I'd give anything to be in your shoes. Seriously, I'd like to meet the fellow."

"Why on earth?"

"A passion for Aztec pyramids, and sun-worship, and—er—Virgins of the Sun, and things like that." Piggy's voice was perfectly expressionless.

It was Julian Forsham's turn to laugh.

"What a colossal fraud you are! I'm quite positive you've never thought of Peru since you got 'Prescott' as a prize away back in the dark ages. What *do* you want?"

"I want to come to the dinner to-night. Or if that's impossible I'd like to drop in afterwards."

The sound of Mr. Julian Forsham whistling came faithfully along the wire. The tune that he whistled had a ribald intention; it was, in fact, the well-known air from *The Pirates of Penzance*—"With catlike tread upon our prey we steal." Then he broke off to say:

"All right, I invite you. You can dine. And mark you, Piggy my lad, your luck's in. Carstairs was my guest" (Carstairs was a Cabinet Minister) "and he rang up only ten minutes ago to say the Prime Minister had sent for him to go down to Chequers. If he hadn't failed, I don't see what I could have done. Every one in London wants to meet Marrington. He's made some amazing discoveries and brought some marvellous stuff over with him."

"I don't see Peterson," said Sir Julian Le Mesurier, looking up from his soup. The little eyes that saw everything looked down the table and up again.

"Do you want to see Peterson?" inquired Julian Forsham.

Piggy said, "'M," and went on eating soup.

His other neighbour, a small, bright-eyed man with a pointed beard, Manisty, the artist, answered for the absent Sir George.

"Peterson's coming on afterwards. He rang up. Couldn't get away in time to feed. Important business engagement. Board meeting. Always wonder they don't spell it B-O-R-E-D. Bores to the board. Glad I'm not in business. It's all bulls and bears and bores and bankruptcy. Especially bankruptcy. 'Hang on the line and stay solvent,' is my slogan."

Piggy put down his spoon, picked up the menu, produced a pencil from somewhere, and began to draw a frieze of cats rampant.

"Peterson," he said vaguely, "—er—Peterson is, I imagine, rather more than solvent."

Manisty dropped Peterson and began to be amusing about the Official Receiver. Piggy let him go on whilst he drew three more cats, and then brought him back to Sir George again.

Julian Forsham laughed inwardly. "Piggy on the trail!" was his inward comment. "Virgins of the Sun indeed! I wonder how long he could talk to Marrington without being caught out. What an old humbug he is! And why did he want to come here to see the wretched Peterson?"

His eyes and his thoughts strayed to Lawrence Marrington. And then in a minute Manisty was leaning forward with a "Well, what do you make of him? D'you know him at all?"

Julian shook his head.

"Now I do," said Manisty. "That's to say, I did. Came across him two years ago when he was ranging London like a hungry lion seeking for a financier to devour. He'd got this expedition planned, and he hadn't got a bean. I tell you he was raging."

"Well, he brought it off all right."

Manisty nodded.

"Odd how things come off—isn't it? Two years ago nobody'd ever heard of him. Two *months* ago nobody'd ever heard of him. And now"—he made a gesture and a grimace—"*I'm* going to paint his portrait."

"Quite a good subject."

Manisty nodded again.

"I'd like to call it *Breaking up the Type*, but I suppose I can't."

The three men looked at Lawrence Marrington.

"See what I mean?" said Manisty. "He started as the typical aristocrat—long, well-bred, well-featured, rather high in the nose, rather narrow between the eyes. That's the type before it was starved and burned to the bone and scared to breaking point. The type has a calm and ruminative eye; this fellow looks round the corner to see who's coming for him next."

Julian Forsham burst out laughing.

"I hope you'll never want to paint me, Manisty."

Piggy went on drawing cats. Manisty went on talking.

"He's had a good press—hasn't he? Ignorance is the mother of adulation. I know nothing of Peru. You know nothing of Peru." His bright, restless eyes challenged Piggy, challenged Julian. "From the depths of our abysmal ignorance we behold the man who knows an Inca from an Iguana—a Being who can pronounce words like Quetzalcoatl, and the things that end in 'hualtepec. Naturally we fall on our knees before him. We lionize. We adulate. We entertain him. We spare him a column or two from politics and the police court. Ha, Forsham? We were doing it to you last year. Chaldea, wasn't it? If it's possible to know less about anything than I know about Peru, Chaldea has it. Names are easier to spell though—nice and short like Ur. Ha, ha, nose out of joint? What's it feel like? Oh, Lord! Do you know, I've got to make a speech in about a minute. That's why I'm so silent and depressed."

He got up presently and made his speech, looking very much at his ease. The only head that did not turn in his direction was that of Mr. Marrington, who sat well back in his chair in a lounging attitude and looked bored. When he looked bored he reverted completely to his type, and was the handsome indolent aristocrat to the life.

"Thoroughly accustomed as I am to public speaking," began Manisty, "it would be quite easy for me to—er—spoof you all. Spoofing is, in fact, the end and object of public speaking. But I am a candid, honest soul first, and a public speaker last. I will therefore make a clean breast of it and confess that all I know about Peru and—er—Aztecs was snatched from a handy encyclopædia as I dressed for dinner this evening. Mr. Lawrence Marrington"— He passed into well-phrased compliment, said the right things in the right way for the right space of time, bowed to the guest of the evening, and sat down with a groan.

Slowly, almost reluctantly, Lawrence Marrington rose to reply. He was a very tall man, very lean, very brown, with the line of an old scar running like a puckered seam across one cheek. He began to speak in a low, inaudible manner, and for five minutes boredom waited on his halting repetition of platitudes. Then there was a change. He began to tell of actual experiences, hardships, dangers, delays, suspense, achievement. His voice rose and cleared; the long languid back straightened itself. The passion of the enthusiast, the fanatic, mounted in him like a fire. In the end the man was actually eloquent, with the eloquence of pure passion.

Sir Julian Le Mesurier, watching his cousin, saw the dark face as rapt and as intent as Marrington's own. He reflected that it wouldn't be long before old Ju-Ju hit the trail again.

Sir George Peterson came in just as Marrington finished his speech. Manisty beckoned him, and he came down the table and pulled in a chair between Manisty and Chetwynd Case, the K.C.

"Well, you've missed the best of it," said Manisty. "I hope your business was worth it?"

Sir George laughed his genial laugh. He had just seen Sir Julian Le Mesurier.

"Hullo, Piggy! Evening, Forsham!" Then turning to Manisty, he gave a belated answer to his question: "Worth it? Scarcely. As a matter of fact, it wasn't business at all, but a domestic contretemps—a nursery governess with kleptomania, and my sister so upset that I couldn't leave her. Extraordinary thing, kleptomania."

"It seems to have come down in the world," said Manisty dryly. "It used to move in Society with the largest possible S. A duchess might have kleptomania; but a nursery governess—stole. What's the matter with the plain English of it?"

Sir George frowned.

"I don't know. I felt sorry for the girl. We all liked her. One prefers to think she's unhinged. Well, I'm sorry I missed Marrington's speech."

"Have you met him at all?" asked Sir Julian.

"I? No. I don't suppose many of us have. Why?"

"I'd like to meet him. Where's he staying, Manisty?"

"Oh, he's not in town—shies off the reporters. He's staying with the Lennoxes down in Surrey. I believe he's going back again to-night. Oh, Lord, that bore, Crewthorn, is going to speak!"

Chapter Sixteen

WHEN LAWRENCE MARRINGTON left The Wolves, he declined a taxi, a lift, or company.

It was an exceedingly unpleasant night, the pavements wet with rain that was half-way to being ice, and the air full of a stinging sleet which was most undoubtedly turning to snow. Lawrence Marrington drew a good breath of this icy air and appeared to find it enjoyable. He took off his opera hat and strode bare-headed along the black and empty streets.

He walked for a full half-hour, and came to a four-cross-way. A huge new cinema stood at the left-hand corner, its flare of lights all dead, its ugly bulk visible only as a black and formless mass.

Marrington crossed the road. A few hours earlier he would have had to thread his way warily through cross currents of traffic; now he could walk across without so much as a backward look. He followed the pavement a couple of hundred yards, and stopped where an arc light broke the darkness and lit the long scarlet front of a garage.

Mally Lee had gone down into the deepest waters of sleep beyond all reach of sound. Dreams do not visit those depths. She slept without moving. Her head was against the seat, and the rug covered her. If a thunder-storm had roared overhead, it would not have wakened her.

The whirr of the self-starter, the pulsing of the engine, the sound of the horn as Marrington backed out of the garage, simply did not come near her at all; she continued to sleep, breathing gently, slowly, deeply, with one hand under her cheek and her lips parted in a child's smile.

It was perhaps half an hour later that she began to come back from those deep places, to rise again towards the surface of consciousness. She began to dream that she was in an aeroplane, flying high beneath a blazing moon. She was being pursued by Paul Craddock, who was flying after her in a bright green omnibus that made a noise like all the traffic in the world. Mally knew that if she could only reach the Milky Way, she would be quite safe. But the omnibus gained on her terribly, and the noise was so loud that she could neither think, nor scream for help. The bus came roaring up, and just as Paul made a grab at her, she jumped and fell down, down, down with a sickening plunge. And then, all at once, she had wings that bore her up again. They were queer, flabby wings, very hard to fly with, because they were made out of the limp, honeycombed stuff which is used for cheap counterpanes.

Mally began to sink again slowly, slowly, slowly until her feet touched the ground and suddenly the moon went out and it was dark. It was to this sense of darkness that she awoke. The moon had been so bright, and now she couldn't see anything at all. She moved, felt the impeding rug, and was aware of stiffness; the hand under her cheek was cold; her feet were cold. She pushed the rug away, sat up, and felt the movement of the car.

It was running smoothly, rhythmically, swiftly; and as she raised herself a little she could see black hedges slipping by. It was just as she had pictured her flight; only it was to have been she and Roger on their way to Curston and safety. She stared at a head silhouetted against the glow of the headlights. There was no Roger any more— and *thank goodness for that*. She was driving with a stranger to some unknown destination.

An extreme and violent curiosity took possession of Mally. The situation was exhilarating in the extreme. She had got out of London. She had got out of London without parting with a single one of her few and precious coins. It was exhilarating beyond words. But she was simply flooded with curiosity. She could see no more of the man who was driving than the shape of his head with an ear on either side. The ears didn't stick out; they only jutted a little. Mally felt that she would have hated to be rescued by a man whose ears stuck out.

She went on considering the back of his head, but it told her nothing. She wished that she dared get up on to the seat; now that she was awake, the floor felt dreadfully hard. She wondered if she could manage it, but decided that it was too risky. And then, just as she reached this conclusion, the car turned in at a gate and ran between trees for perhaps a quarter of a mile, and so to a paved yard and a garage standing open.

The man got down from the driver's seat, came round to the back of the car, and before Mally guessed what he would be at, he had the door open and a hand on her rug. The hand caught at the rug, began to pull, and stopped.

It took Marrington just a second to stop himself. The rug, which should have been cold, was warm.

"Who's there?" he said without raising his voice at all.

Mally moved away from his hand, sat bolt upright, and said, a shade defiantly.

"I am. If you'll get out of the way, I'll come out."

Marrington did not move; but he laughed.

"I want to get out."

He laughed again.

"You're pretty cool for a stowaway. Of course I'm delighted to be of service to a lady and all that. But may I ask why you chose my car?"

"I didn't. I went to sleep. I didn't choose it. It was just a car, and—and I got into it."

As Marrington turned to feel in one of the front pockets, she flung away the rug and jumped out. Next moment his hand went up with an electric torch in it.

Lawrence Marrington saw a small, crumpled girl in navy blue; she had hazel eyes and brown hair under a black felt hat. Unlike Mally, he had read the evening papers. He laughed once again rather dryly and remarked:

"Miss Ellen Marshman, I imagine?"

"Who on earth is Ellen Marshman?" Mally's tone was tart; she didn't like having torches flashed on to her when she knew she must be looking like nothing on earth.

As she spoke, she stepped back out of the ray.

"Oh, come! I've read the papers, you know. You got a paragraph next to the one announcing my arrival. It was a bit longer than mine. But then, of course, crime has first call—hasn't it?"

A well-known tingling sensation informed Mally that she was going to lose her temper. It is a regrettable fact that, on this occasion at least, she lost it with a good deal of pleasurable anticipation. As a preliminary, she wrinkled her nose haughtily at Lawrence Marrington, who had turned his torch on her again, and said, in what she herself would have described as a snorky tone of voice, "Don't keep doing that! I don't like it. Turn it off!"

Instead of turning it off, he made the ray play up and down her.

"What in the world am I going to do with you?" he said.

Mally's foot tapped the concrete floor.

"I asked you to turn that off. I don't like it."

"I'm afraid you'll have to put up with it."

Mally's temper went. She snatched the torch. The light dazzled on Marrington's face. Who was he? And why did he have paragraphs in the paper?

And then he caught her wrist and had the torch again. She pulled away from him furiously and heard him say in a voice of exaggerated boredom: "Of course, what I ought to do is to hand you over to the police."

The color ran up into Mally's cheeks.

"How dare you?"

"Oh, easily enough, my dear. But it would be a bit of a bore." He yawned. "I believe I'm too sleepy to be bothered with you."

He lowered the torch, took a couple of steps forward, and dropped a sudden hand on Mally's shoulder.

"Like to kiss me good-night?" he said.

An uncontrollable panic took hold of Mally. Afterwards she had a good deal to say to herself on the subject. There were things she might have said to him, and things she might have done; but at the moment all that she wanted was to get away. With a little gasp of rage and fright she wrenched free and ran away into the darkness.

Chapter Seventeen

MALLY RAN BLINDLY into the dark. First there were cobblestones underfoot, then she was out of the yard and on gravel. She ran full tilt into a large bush or shrub that sent out an aromatic smell and scratched her outstretched hands with its sharp twigs and hard foliage. With a little gasping cry she stopped, and then pushed her way in between the branches until she felt the trunk and could hold on to it. She wanted something to hold on to because, now that she had stopped running, she was trembling very much.

She stood there in the dark and called herself names:

"Idiot! What are you afraid of?"

She really had not the slightest idea. The panic fear had come pouring down on her like a douche of ice-cold water. She felt drenched with it to the very marrow; but she did not know why. She heard the garage door shut with a bang. And then, whistling to himself and flashing an idle torch here and there, Lawrence Marrington went by.

The white light danced like a malicious Jack-o'-lanthorn. She saw snow-sprinkled gravel just for a second, and then scarlet holly berries amongst prickly leaves. The light went by. Lawrence Marrington went by. The sound of his footsteps died away. He turned a corner and the last dancing spark went too. Mally felt the black dark close round her with a comforting sense of safety. Her bush smelled strong and sweet. She leaned back against its resilient branches, and stopped shaking.

What on earth was she going to do? It must be somewhere about two o'clock she thought—two, or perhaps three in the morning; and it was really frightfully cold. The sprinkled snow on the gravel had been white and crisp; the earth under her foot was as hard as stone; and all the trees in the garden moved restlessly under a steady wind from the north.

Mally came out of her bush and made her way back to the yard. The garage door was locked of course—that went without saying. But there might be some outhouse, empty loose box, or loft.

Mally was certainly not going to freeze in the open if there was shelter to be had. She began to feel her way about the yard. Now that Marrington was gone, a sense of adventure buoyed her up. After all, she had done pretty well; she had got out of London, and she still had three and ninepence farthing in cash and four ginger biscuits in kind.

She felt a gate with an iron hasp, and narrowly escaped coming down over a staple driven into the ground. Then there was a length of fence which ran down to a corner and met a brick wall. Mally felt along the bricks and collided with a ladder. From the fact that it did not move when she hit it rather hard with her shoulder, she deduced that the upper end of it was fixed. A fixed upper end meant a loft door or hatch. She began to climb hopefully, and found what she had hoped for.

At the top of the ladder was a loft with an open hatch, and—joys of joys—the loft was half full of hay. It was only when the hay closed round her and she felt its warmth that she realized how cold she was. Hay was beautifully warm, if rather tickly. She snuggled down into it and went to sleep.

It was broad daylight when she woke to a clattering, swishing noise. The sound of men's voices came in through the open hatch.

The chauffeur was washing the car, and another man came and went. Mally could not hear what they said; but she thought it was a good thing that motors didn't eat hay. As it was, she hoped that she was safe. She sat up, ate her four ginger biscuits, and wondered what next.

She could stay where she was for a bit. But in the long run what in the world was she going to do? Mally looked at the question, tossed her head at it, and looked away. And just at that moment she heard a voice upraised in song.

It may be said at once that the voice was not a tuneful one. It was, however, hearty, and burst upon Mally with the loud suddenness of a bass trombone.

"Just a song at twilight," bellowed the voice. There was a loud hammering sound and a pause. Mally suspected that the singer's mouth was performing the more useful office of holding nails. After a moment music again held sway.

"Just a song at twilight,
When the lights are low—*Oh damn!*
And the whispering shadows
Softly come and go.
When the heart is weary, *(this very robustly)*
Sad the day and long,
Then to us at twilight *(bang, bang, thud)*
Comes love's sweet song—*Blast that nail!*—
Love's old swee-ee-eet song."

The hammer dropped with a crash.

Mally jumped up and began to shake the hay off her. The open hatch lay on the right. The sound certainly did not come from there. Half the loft was full of hay, but the rest lay bare and dusty and rather dark.

She crossed into the darkest corner, and saw a door in the long wall facing the hatch. Behind the door there arose the sound of sawing and the sound of song:

"Once in the dear dead days beyond recall
(crunch, creak, buzz)—
When on the—'m—the umpty-umpty-um
Out of the—'m—that umpty-umpty throng,
Low to my heart love sang his old sweet
song—*Oh, drat!*"

Mally turned the handle and pushed very gently. She began doing this whilst the singer was rendering the "umpty-umpty-ums" fortissimo and with a good deal of soulful expression.

Three steps led down from the door into a bright, bare garret with two windows. The room itself contained a carpenter's bench, a heap of scrap iron, a pile of wire netting, a great many odds and ends of wood, tools, shavings, and a very large young man engaged in making something that might have been either a hen-coop or a rabbit-hutch.

Mally surveyed him with interest. She had an entirely irrational feeling that a young man who sang out-of-date sentimental ditties so very loudly, cheerfully, and unmelodiously must be absolutely chockfull of the solid qualities which make you feel that you can trust people even if you have never seen them before.

The young man was very large; the hands that held the saw were an outsize in hands. His hair was black and inclined to stand on end. He had his back to Mally, so that all she saw of him was feet, hands, sunburned neck, black hair, and very old tweeds. A wisp of a furry grey kitten sat on his left shoulder and rubbed its head up and down against his ear. It was doubtless purring, but the tiny sound was swamped by "Love's old sweet song."

Mally came through the door, shut it behind her, stood on the top step, and said, "Who are you?"

The young man stopped sawing, turned slowly, and disclosed a cheerful, ugly, bewildered face. Mally saw that his skin would have been very white if it hadn't been so burned; also that he had grey eyes, a turned-up nose, and a perfectly enormous mouth. He gazed at her, and Mally repeated her question, whilst the kitten stopped purring and arched its back.

"Who are you?"

The young man went on staring. When he saw Mally's foot begin to tap the step, he said hastily:

"Ethan Messenger."

"What?"

"Messenger—Ethan. It gives every one the pip at first, but they get used to it. Er—won't you come in?"

"I am in."

"I mean down—won't you come down?"

Mally came down as though reluctantly. He was so very large. Being three steps up gave one a sort of moral advantage. She understood exactly why the kitten preferred his shoulder to the floor.

Ethan Messenger was not stupid. It had really occurred to him at once that it was he who should have asked, "Who are you?" He looked at Mally and saw her crumpled clothes and the hay that stuck to them. In one hand she held a little black felt hat. Her short brown hair was wildly ruffled and had authentic straws in it. Her eyes reminded him of the kitten on his shoulder before he had made friends with it; they were bright, wary, alert. The kitten at his first advances had spat, scratched, and fled.

He wasn't quite sure whether he dared ask his question. Then it struck him that, under its defiance, this little crumpled creature was most forlornly pale.

"I say, what can I do for you?" he said, and got up.

"I don't know."

The kitten rubbed its head against his ear again. Mally could hear it purring now; and as the kitten rubbed, she saw the big young man with the queer name put up one of those outsized hands and ruffle the little creature's grey fur with an enormous, gentle finger. She had an impulse, and followed it without an instant's hesitation.

"I'm running away from the police," she said. "My name is Mally Lee."

Then she did a thing which it enraged her to think about afterwards. She saw his lips pursed up to whistle; she saw his look of blank dismay—and she burst into tears.

"How dare you!" she said, and sat down on the bottom step.

"I—I didn't do anything."

"You did!" said Mally, groping for a handkerchief.

"Oh, I say, for the Lord's sake don't cry."

"I'm not c-crying." The tears rushed down her cheeks. "I'm not. I never do."

Ethan produced a clean, folded handkerchief, approached cautiously, laid it on Mally's knee, and withdrew to a safe distance.

Mally dried her eyes, pinched herself, dried them again with angry determination, and said:

"Why don't you go and find the police—and give me up—and take me to prison—and—"

"Why should I? I say, how on earth did you get here?"

Mally relaxed a little.

"I came in a car."

"When?"

"In the night. I went to sleep in the back of it—in the garage—in London. And he drove all the way down and never knew I was there." She gave a little laugh, and the wet eyes twinkled. "I don't know who he is, and I don't know where I am. I got into the hay-loft because I was so cold. Who is he, and where am I?"

"You're at Peddling Corner, in Surrey. This is Sir Charles Lennox's place. You must have come down in Marrington's car."

"Who's Marrington?"

"Lawrence Marrington—no end of a big bug—explorer—Aztecs and things. He's staying here. He dined in town last night—some function or another."

"Lennox? But your name isn't Lennox."

He laughed, a loud jolly laugh.

"I'm only a visitor. Lady Lennox is a sort of umpteenth cousin. I'm on leave."

"You don't live here?"

"I don't live anywhere. I say, do you mean that about the police?"

She gave a queer little decided nod; a bright belated tear fell on her dark sleeve.

"I say, why on earth—"

"I d-don't know."

"What on earth have you done?"

Mally's chin came up about an inch. She looked, and said nothing.

"Look here, that's all very well, but what do they think you've done?"

Mally put her chin in her hand. Her expression changed. She said, in quite a different voice, "I don't know—I don't." Then quite suddenly she smiled; her lashes flickered; an imp danced in her eyes. "I'm so frightfully hungry."

"Hungry?"

"I've only had ginger biscuits since yesterday at lunch. I ate the last four when I woke up. I feel dreadfully thin. I expect you'd better go for the police."

Ethan took a banana out of his pocket.

"I've got this. We were going to give it to the rabbit."

"We?"

"Bunty Lennox and I. She got the rabbit yesterday at an awful bazaar, and I said I'd make it a hutch. Why do people have bazaars? D'you know, we were there for two solid hours. And everybody was selling things to everybody else, and then raffling 'em and selling 'em all over again. The rabbit was sold eight times. But when it came to Bunty she howled and froze on it, and went on howling till her mother took her home. And I promised to make it a hutch. She'll be up here as soon as she's done her lessons. The rabbit's in the parrot's cage till I get the hutch done."

Mally finished the banana and laid the skin neatly on the floor, and at that moment somebody laughed outside. The sound floated in through the open window.

Mally gave a gasp. It was impossible. It was quite impossible. But she got to her feet.

"Who's that?" in a breathless undertone.

Ethan Messenger did not answer. He went over to the window and stood there blocking it.

Mally, one hand on his arm, pushed him an inch aside and peeped. He felt, rather than heard her catch her breath.

The window looked out on the vegetable garden. There was a path running up the middle. There were two men walking up the path.

One of them was Mr. Paul Craddock.

Chapter Eighteen

THE APPEARANCE of Mr. Craddock was due neither to coincidence nor miracle. It must be conceded that Paul was efficient, and that not only was he efficient, but that he had the capacity for taking pains which amounts to genius.

Mr. Alfred Dawson had had orders to report at dawn. He found Mr. Craddock extremely disinclined to accept his account of Miss Lee's disappearance. Before he knew where he was, he was being conveyed swiftly to the spot where he had last seen her; and the moment Mr. Craddock set eyes on the red garage door he lost his temper and used language very injurious to Alfred Dawson's self-esteem. Most of what he said was unprintable. And he continued to say it with remarkable fluency and ease during the interval which elapsed whilst the manager of the garage was sending for the young man who had been on duty the night before.

Mr. Craddock went sharply to work with the young man; a large tip, some rapid questions, and he had elicited what he had come to find out.

1. The young man had stepped out to have a breath of air and to look at the weather.
2. It might have been half-past ten, or it might have been elevenish.
3. A gentleman who had left his car there about seven o'clock had come back for it somewhere about midnight.
4. It was a Wolseley four-seater. (Floods of technical details firmly checked.)
5. Yes, he knew the gentleman—recognized him at once—portrait in the *Mail*.
6. It was Mr. Lawrence Marrington, the explorer.
7. No other car had gone out whilst he was on duty.
8. No, he hadn't seen any young lady.

Having turned the young man inside out, Paul Craddock had a few more caustic words for Alfred.

"See the man who came on when this fellow went off. Get particulars of every car that went out. If we don't get on to Miss Lee to-day, we shall take the matter out of the hands of your firm."

Mr. Lawrence Marrington's whereabouts being public property, it will be seen that Mr. Craddock's arrival at Peddling Corner requires no further explanation.

To Mally, looking from the window, it was the sort of thing that doesn't happen unless you are having a bad dream. She pinched Ethan Messenger as hard as she could, and pulled him away from the window.

"Don't, don't let him! Oh, don't!"

Ethan looked at her gravely.

"Who do you mean? Paul Craddock?"

Mally flung out her hands.

"You know him? Oh!" It was a cry of angry despair.

"He's a sort of cousin. As a matter of fact, I loathe him. Look here, it's all right—if you don't want to see him, you shan't. I'm not talking."

Mally breathed an "Oh!" of pure relief. Then she said "S'sh!" ran up the three steps that led to the loft, turned, kissed her hand, and was gone.

The door shut without a sound. On the other side of it she stood and made a plan. She would stay by the door just like this. If any one came up the ladder to the loft, she would slip through into the workshop. If they came through from the workshop, she must dive into the hay. But somehow, *somehow*, she didn't think Ethan would let them come through. He was nice. He was a dear. He was frightfully, *frightfully* strong, and most reassuringly ugly.

She thought of Roger Mooring's handsome features, and rejoiced in the ugliness of Ethan Messenger. Once and for all, Roger had spoiled her for beautiful young men.

Ethan was hammering again, when Sir Charles Lennox flung open the door.

"There's a step, Paul. Ethan, here's Paul Craddock. Quite a surprise visit."

"Er—morning, Craddock. I've nearly done the hutch, sir. What d'you think of it?"

Sir Charles was a kindly man. The kindliness was at this moment obscured by a tendency to fuss. Most extraordinary yarn this of Craddock's—disturbing—annoying—unpleasant. Never had cared much for Craddock—a damned sight too pink and white, too fond of the sound of his own voice, too clever, too full of theories.

He glanced at the hutch, and felt annoyed all over again. Why hadn't Maud been firm about that damn rabbit? Why give way to a child because it cries? Firmness, *firmness* was what was needed. He looked crossly at Ethan, disparagingly at the hutch, and began an aggrieved explanation.

"Paul says he's reason to believe Marrington brought a girl down with him last night. Most unpleasant insinuation—hey, what? Marrington's my guest and a very distinguished man."

"There's no suggestion that Marrington had any idea—"

"Idea? How d'you mean idea? A man doesn't drive a girl down from town—and, hang it all, if he does, he don't give her away. Dashed unpleasant for me, going in and waking the man up, and asking him that sort of personal question in my own house. What can the man do but say he don't know a damn thing about it—hey, what? I suppose he's a gentleman?"

Paul Craddock raised his eyebrows.

"There's really no suggestion that Mr. Marrington suspected that Miss Lee was in his car. It would certainly have been without his knowledge. She might have slipped out and hidden herself."

"Marrington says he locked the garage and came away. If she was in the car, she'd have been locked in too, and Lane 'ud have found her when he went to wash the car this morning. Talk about cock and bull stories—hey, what?"

Ethan Messenger balanced the hutch on one corner. The kitten had scrambled down from his shoulder and was in retreat under a tilted plank; its eyes were green in the shadow, its tiny tail twitched.

"But who is Miss Lee?" said Ethan.

Behind the door Mally held her breath and listened. The blood rushed into her face at the tone of Paul Craddock's answer:

"Miss Lee is a light-fingered young person who, unfortunately, deceived Sir George Peterson into taking her into his house as a governess for Barbara. She lifted a valuable diamond pendant and some papers which we are anxious to recover. She was traced to the garage where Mr. Marrington left his car last night. It occurred to me that she might have stolen a ride."

Ethan Messenger burst into hearty laughter.

"The sleuth upon the trail! From Garage to Gaol! You're wasted as a secretary—fiction's your line, Paul. *The Clue of the Explorer's Car*, by Paul Pry, Private Investigator!"

This light badinage had the same effect on Mr. Craddock as a certain historic anecdote on Queen Victoria—he was not amused. Sir Charles, on the other hand, cheered up visibly. Ethan was an ally. He became more than ever convinced that the whole affair was outrageous nonsense.

"If Marrington didn't see anything, and the men didn't see anything, I don't know what you expect to see," he grumbled.

"One never knows," said Paul Craddock slowly. He was looking at the three steps that led up to the hay-loft, and at a banana skin lying neatly folded over on itself on the floor beside the bottom step.

"Who put that there?" he said, and pointed.

Ethan roared with laughter.

"The super-Sherlock! Height, weight, age, and sex of criminal all deduced from a banana skin."

"Who put it there?" said Paul sharply.

He had lunched a dozen times with Miss Mally Lee and seen her lay a banana skin down like that after eating the fruit. She had a little quick way of doing it, a flick of the fingers.

"Who—" he began; and Ethan interrupted.

He had lounged across the room and picked up the skin. He dangled it between thumb and finger now, and said, "Tut, tut! You mustn't ask the wretched Watson a leading question like that, my dear Holmes. It simply isn't done. It is you who tell us who put it there, with the fullest and most circumstantial details. Remember your little monograph on bananas. There are, I believe, some thirty or more different sorts, and the skin of each kind takes a different length of time to dry. You have, therefore, only to examine this interesting relic in order to give us the past history of the person who ate it, with all particulars."

Craddock turned his back on him.

"Sir Charles, she's been here—I'm ready to swear to it. What exactly did you say to Marrington? Did you tell him it was a matter of my chief's private papers?"

"No, I didn't—hey, what? Why should I?—what's it got to do with him?"

"Nothing, of course. May I ask what you did say?"

Sir Charles did not like being cross-examined; his manner showed it in an extra touch of vexation.

"Say? What should I say? I asked him if he'd noticed anything unusual when he got the car home—any one hanging about, and so forth. And he said no, he hadn't. And there was an end of it. If you want to cross-examine him, you'd better do it yourself."

"I think I will. But I think"—he walked towards the steps—"I think I'll have a look inside that door first."

Mally's heart went bang against her side. Little fool! She ought to have hidden in the hay long ago. Now it was too late. But he would look in the hay—he would look in the hay—he would look everywhere. She had the horrible, horrible trapped feeling that stops thought, and will, and action.

The steps creaked under a heavy foot; a hand fell on the handle. It was mere instinct that sent her cowering into the corner, her face to the wall, her hands, breast-high, pressed flat against the rough boards.

The door swung in towards the workshop. They were coming. There was just a chance that they might not see her. The corner was a yard from the door; they might not look so near at hand. The corner was dark; her coat was dark; the light of the open hatch would be in their eyes.

Mally's hands pressed hard on the wall. It was rough and splintery. They were coming. She mustn't, *mustn't* scream.

When Paul Craddock moved towards the door, Ethan put a large foot on the bottom step. He had heard a faint, faint rustling sound behind him.

"Aren't you going to tell us—" he began.

"I'm going through that door."

"Sleuths shouldn't show temper. It plays the very dickens with the deductive faculties," said Ethan equably.

"Sir Charles!"

"Hey, what? What's all this fooling? Let's get on with it. Let's get done with it."

Ethan stopped laughing.

"All right, sir," he said, and with that took the two steps at a stride and opened the door.

The loft was empty except for hay. Ethan fell back into the corner behind the door and let Paul Craddock and Sir Charles go past. He had his right hand on the jamb of the door. His left went back and fell on Mally's shoulder.

He had been aware of her—strangely, curiously aware. But to touch her like that was rather horrible. The long shudder, and then the stillness—it was what he had felt a hundred times when he had handled some wild thing terrified out of all reason.

His hand pressed her shoulder gently for a moment, felt how tense the muscles were, and drew away. As he stood there, he screened her well enough. Paul was poking in the hay and raising no end of a dust. Sir Charles had begun to sneeze.

"Damn nonsense!" he said and blew his nose. "The girl's not a mouse, I suppose." He sneezed and blew again. "Damn nonsense, I say. Here, better get down this way—it leads into the yard, and if you want to see Lane, he'll be there. You coming, Ethan?"

"The faithful Watson comes."

Ethan reached behind him and gave Mally's shoulder the sort of reassuring pat that he would have given to the kitten. She heard the clatter of feet on the ladder; she heard Ethan cross the floor and follow Sir Charles and Paul; she heard them all talking in the yard outside.

They were gone.

Chapter Nineteen

"OUF!" SAID MALLY with a great breath of relief. "What a frightfully, frightfully, *frightfully* near thing! If it hadn't been for that angel lamb!"

She flung a grateful kiss in the direction of the open hatch and executed a pirouette. Then she picked up her hat, which had fallen in the corner, dusted it, and went back into the workshop. She did not feel as if she would ever really love a hay-loft again.

It was in the workshop, when she was picking a straw or two off her hat, that the little basket brooch attracted her attention. She unpinned it thoughtfully and fastened it on her jumper out of sight. It was pretty, but just the sort of thing that people might notice and remember. Mally had a conviction that the modest, shrinking violet half—or, better still, wholly-hidden from the eye was her rôle. It was not, it may be said, a congenial one.

She looked all round the workshop for a mirror, and looked in vain.

"I must be looking like *absolutely* nothing on earth." Even shrinking violets should be tidy.

She smoothed her hair, took off her coat, shook it, dusted it, and put it on again. Then she powdered her nose and pulled on the black felt hat. She found a bit of oily rag, and got the mud off her shoes. After that she sat down and began to wonder what would happen next.

She must have dozed a little, because the footsteps were on the stair before she heard them, and she had no more than time to jump up before the outer door swung open. With a clatter and a clang there tumbled into the room a large metal cage and a little girl of about six years old. The metal cage contained a half-grown black rabbit, apparently paralyzed with terror.

The little girl was most indubitably the angel child of mid-Victorian fiction—golden curls, blue eyes and apple-blossom complexion complete. She dumped the cage, gazed at Mally without surprise, and said:

"I want Ethan. Where's Ethan? I want him."

"I'm afraid he isn't here."

The angel child frowned. Great masters have painted frowning angels. One in Venice holds a lute; this one held a parrot's cage.

"I want him. He was making a hutch for Dinks. This is Dinks. I got him yesterday in a bazaar, an' Mummy said I couldn't have him because of nowhere to put him, an' I cried right in the middle of the bazaar, with every one saying 'Hush,' until she said I could, an' Ethan said he'd make me a hutch, an' where is he?"

"I don't know. Here's the hutch."

Bunty Lennox flung herself down by it with a shriek. The rabbit twitched one ear; its whiskers trembled slightly.

"It's finished! It's done! Put Dinks into it—put him in quickly!"

"Hadn't we better wait? I think he's frightened."

"Not!"

"He is—really."

Bunty shook her head with great vigour.

"He's a very fierce rabbit. I 'spect he's the fiercest rabbit in the world. He bited my finger, an' he bited cook's finger, an' he'd have bited Mummy, only she wouldn't touch him, an' he bited Daddy, an' Daddy said he was a dam rabbit, an' Mummy said, 'Hush, Charles!' like she does." She paused, and added thoughtfully, "He didn't bite Ethan."

"Then I think we'll let Ethan put him in the hutch."

Bunty displayed a finger with a minute red mark on it.

"I don't mind if he bites me ever so. Ethan said it was brave of me not to mind. I wouldn't mind how fierce he was—not if his whiskers were quite stiff with fierceness, I wouldn't. Ethan said it was very brave of me."

The rabbit snuffed the air with a trembling nose, moved one foot, and then stiffened again.

"I love Ethan," said Bunty. "I'm going to marry him when I am old. He says I may have fifty hundred rabbits and a million guinea-pigs if I like. Mummy hates guinea-pigs quite *dreadful*. She *won't* let me have them. An' she hates rabbits too. But I shrieked, an' howled, an' shrieked till she said I could keep Dinks."

"How awful of you!"

Miss Lennox agreed.

"Yes, *wasn't* it? But I wanted him so as I would have *bit* if they wouldn't of let me have him—an' that's the *very* worst of all."

"What is?"

Bunty gazed at her with angelic candour; her eyes were like bits of blue sky.

"Biting is—the *very* worst. When I bit the butler, Mummy sent me to bed *all* day. Shall we put Dinks in his hutch?"

"No," said Mally firmly. "Ethan shall put him in his hutch."

"Oh! Then shall we play a game? Ethan plays lovely games. What kind of games can you play?"

Mally put her fingers on her lips.

"Ssh! I *am* playing a game—a hiding game. I'm in the middle of it—it's frightfully exciting. Will you help me?"

"U-m-m." There was no doubt of Bunty's heartfelt agreement. "Let me play, too. Who are you hiding from? Are you hiding from Ethan?"

"No, not from Ethan."

Bunty jumped up.

"Are you hiding from Paul? I saw him. Are you hiding from him?"

"Ssh! Yes."

Bunty bobbed up and down.

"Paul is a pig. Mummy says I'm simply not to call him it, but he *is*."

"Bunty," said Mally quickly, "I want to get away without any one seeing me. When do the men go to their dinner? Could I get away then—out of the back somewhere?"

Bunty nodded emphatically.

"U-m-m, you could. Lane's gone to his dinner now. I saw him. His wife makes a nawful fuss if he's the least bit of a minute late, an' she makes him take off his boots in the scullery an' wash. I don't like her *much*, but I like Lane."

"And the other man?"

"Jack goes as soon as Lane goes. Shall I go an' look an' come back an' tell you, an' then I can open the gate on to the down—at least I can open it if you hold me up the teeniest scrap of an inch. Shall I?"

She didn't really wait for an answer, but was gone by way of the hay-loft, and in less than no time came clattering back full of importance and mystery.

"There isn't no one there. Shall we play you're a princess an' Paul is a wicked magician, an' shall we play you've got on a cloak of darkness an' I'm the fairy queen what's helping you, an' shall we play that no one can't see us an' that you've got on seven-league boots?"

"Ssh. Not a word!" Mally bent close to the little pink ear. "Not a single word, or the magic will stop."

Bunty pursed her lips and nodded till all the curls flew. They crossed the loft together.

Paul Craddock meanwhile had had to wait for his interview with the celebrated explorer, who was having a bath and taking an uncommonly long time over it. When he descended at last, he found a fuming host.

"Marrington, I really must apologize—er—this is Mr. Craddock, Sir George Peterson's private secretary—er—he insists—but really I consider the whole thing ridiculous, and, as I say, I apologize."

Mr. Paul Craddock explained himself. He was really very sorry to trouble Mr. Marrington. The fact was Sir George had missed important papers, and the girl who was suspected of having taken them had been traced to the garage where Mr. Marrington had left his car.

"We thought it just possible that she might have concealed herself in one of the cars there. The missing papers are confidential, and Sir George is very much concerned to recover them."

This was Mr. Craddock at his most courteous. Could Mr. Marrington give them any assistance? It appeared that Mr. Marrington could. He was, in fact, very pleasantly frank—wished he had known sooner; was distressed lest Sir George should be inconvenienced by any negligence of his.

"As a matter of fact, I took the girl for an absconding typist or cashier, or something of that sort. There was a paragraph—and the description seemed to fit. I suppose I ought to have handed her over to the police. But it didn't seem to be my business, and—"

"You let her go?"

"I'm afraid I did."

Sir Charles was very properly shocked. He was a J.P. and did not conceive it possible that any guest of his could connive—"Hey, what?" Thought burst into speech:

"My dear sir, you don't mean to say that you let her go?"

"Yes, I'm afraid so." Marrington's slight gesture expressed a bored amusement.

Sir Charles turned purple.

"My dear Marrington, you can't be aware—hey, what? Did you know that you were rendering yourself liable? Good heavens, Marrington, the girl's a common criminal—and you let her go! Hey, what? You're an accessory after the fact—and I'm on the bench, begad!"

Ethan Messenger left them to it. He walked up through the garden in a heavy mood. "The girl's a common criminal—" The words made his mood the heavier. He had shielded Mally on the impulse of the moment. He began to wonder why he had done it. But even as he wondered he knew that he would probably do it again. He had a constitutional dislike to seeing weak things hurt or frightened. When it led him to the rescue of a harried kitten, it was merely an amiable idiosyncrasy; but when it rushed him into aiding and abetting young criminals—what about it?

Ethan was not sure, but he knew very well that he couldn't give Mally away.

He came into the workshop and found Miss Bunty Lennox there, poking Dinks with a straw. She greeted him with a cry of rapture which made the rabbit quiver from nose to tail.

"Put him in his hutch! She said wait for you, so I waited. I wanted her to put him in, but she wouldn't. She said wait an' let *you* put him in."

Ethan knelt down by the parrot's cage and transferred Dinks deftly to the hutch.

"Did he bite you? He bited me."

"That's because you frightened him."

"She said that too," said Bunty, hopping on one leg. "Does he like his hutch?"

"Who is 'she'?"

Bunty came quite close and blew into his ear:

"The hiding princess."

How reassuring is the atmosphere of fairy tales! Ethan put an arm round Bunty.

"I say, Bun, what d'you mean?"

"She said you knew. She said she was hiding, an' we played she was a princess, an' we played no one could see us, an' no one did, because I looked first to see there wasn't no one there, an' I let her out of the back gate, an' she ran away, an' I won't tell no one, only you, because it's a magic secret an' because of Paul being a pig— Oh!" she screamed. "Look, Ethan, look! Dinks is washing his face!"

Chapter Twenty

IN THE LIBRARY Sir Charles Lennox held forth.

"I'll have nothing more to do with the matter. Most irregular— most. No warrant—nothing. If you catch the young woman, what are you going to do with her? You can't lay a finger on her without a warrant—not a finger."

Paul Craddock kept his temper with an effort.

"Sir George is not vindictive," he said. "He doesn't wish to prosecute Miss Lee."

"What's he playing at then? Doesn't wish to prosecute. What does he want?"

"He wants to get his papers back."

Sir Charles walked up and down irritably. Mr. Marrington read *The Times*.

"Papers? What papers? What's the girl doing taking papers?"

"I've no idea. We think she must be unhinged. The papers are of no value except to Sir George. As a matter of fact what she took was a sheet of paper with a cross-word puzzle on it. But I had made some important notes for Sir George on the back of it."

Mr. Marrington turned a sheet of *The Times*.

"Never read a worse weather forecast," he said. "Rain, sleet, snow—"

Paul took no notice.

"May I use the telephone, Sir Charles?"

The instrument was in the library. He had, in fact, to disturb Mr. Marrington to get at it. When the call came through, Sir Charles was still pacing up and down, Lawrence Marrington still reading. Mr. Craddock's conversation was rather limited in its scope. He said:

"Is that you, sir?" And then, "I've traced Miss Lee down here—I am speaking from Peddling Corner—but no one seems to have seen her since the middle of the night."

He heard Sir George's voice rather faint and thin:

"Dawson has just reported. He says she had been traced in town."

Paul Craddock whistled.

"She was here last night. She hid in Mr. Marrington's car. He took her for some one else and let her go. That was between two and three A.M."

Sir George again—the line very poor and interrupted by crackling:

"Plenty of time ... get back to town.... Come back."

"What's that, sir? You want me to come back?"

He listened for a moment longer, then hung up the receiver and announced that he was going back to town. Sir Charles did not press him to stay for lunch.

Mally meanwhile had run away over the down. The ground went on rising. The grass was short and coarse and wet from last night's snow, which had thawed upon it. The sky was a dull lead color. The wind had dropped. The air felt heavy and very cold.

When she reached the top of the rise, she saw the down run sloping away into a mist. There were gorse bushes here and there, and a twisted hawthorn or two. She ran down the slope and came on a wood with a litter of last year's bracken underfoot, and a tangle of thorn, holly and oak overhead. It ran for a quarter of a mile downhill and ended in a hedgerow and a tarred road beyond. Mally went back into the wood and sat down under a holly bush.

When Paul Craddock reached town, it was to be sent off again to follow what Mr. Dawson had described as a very promising clue. He stayed only to telephone to a lady who professed herself very angry at his defection.

"You won't be able to come at *all*?"

"I'm afraid not."

"But the Holmes will be a man short."

"I'm dreadfully sorry."

"It will put their table out—and no time to get any one else. I'm just starting. You *might* have let me know before."

"Candida, I couldn't. You must know how disappointed I am."

"Are you really? Then you won't fail for tomorrow—will you? The dance at Curston—you'll get down to the Holmes' for that?"

"If I possibly can. Candida, you know—"

Miss Candida Long rang off in a temper.

The day went slowly for Mally Lee. She was cold, she was hungry, and she had to struggle hard and hard against the feeling that she could do no more. She began to count up what she might be said to have gained. She was free. She was out of London. No, she wasn't at all sure that this was a gain. London was so full of people, so much easier to lose one's self in. Here in these country lanes, if she passed man, woman, or child, they would remember that they had seen a stranger and wonder who she was. Well, anyhow she was free, and she knew where she was.

She thought of all this country in terms of Curston and the Moorings. Peddling Corner lay on the very edge of what Lady Mooring considered a possible calling distance. She exchanged calls with the Lennoxes, and saw them perhaps once a year. Mally had heard Mrs. Armitage speak of Maud Lennox and Bunty. Well, Curston would not help her, nor any one in the Moorings' circle. They had probably all heard most dreadful things about her by now. Jimmy was the only one who might have helped her, and Jimmy was on the high seas half-way to India.

"Something will turn up," said Mally to herself.

She made up her mind to wait until it was dusk and then take the road away from Peddling Corner. Meanwhile it was cold, most frightfully cold, and dull, most frightfully dull. She pushed her hand down into her pocket, and felt the bundle that Barbara had given her in the dark bedroom. She pulled it out, curious to see what these treasured drawings would be like.

There was quite a thick pile of them. Mally put it on her knee and unfolded it. Her first thought was what a queer collection of different sorts and sizes of paper—foolscap; Silurian; blue linen; a piece of kitchen paper; and the shiny black-edged note-paper affected by Mrs. Craddock. Barbara must have gone about the house picking up a sheet here and a sheet there and hiding them. Little magpie!

Mally spread out the top sheet and found herself looking at a back view of Sir George Peterson—head, shoulders, hands holding a newspaper, all scrawled very rough and large on a piece of foolscap. She was amazed at the likeness, the few bold lines. "Oh, what a shame not to let her draw!" was the first thought; and then, sharp on that, "No one will ever be able to stop her."

She picked up the next sheet, and laughed at the inscription which ran across it in big tumble-down letters: "This is Pinko, and I hate him." It was not a favourable likeness of Mr. Craddock, but it was certainly a likeness. The long neck was made longer, the round cheeks rounder; but no one who had ever seen Mr. Paul Craddock would have had to be told who Pinko was.

Mally went on turning over the loose sheets. She found them quite amusing. Mrs. Craddock, with her knitting all in a tangle and six or seven needles sticking out of it at impossible angles. The pug, Bimbo, with his black lip lifted in a snarl. A less successful attempt at the magnificent orange Persian. Jones, like a ramrod in a tight braided dress. The young footman who had let Mally out. They were all there, on the edge of caricature, but astonishingly recognizable.

The last piece of paper was different from the others. There was no sketch on it, but a cross-word puzzle. Mally did not feel in the mood for cross-word puzzles. She folded all the drawings up and put them back in her pocket.

It was almost dark when she scrambled through the hedgerow and dropped down a bank into the road. It was worth anything to be moving again. But when she began to walk, she did just wonder how far she would be able to go. It was about twenty-six hours since she had had a proper meal; the ginger biscuits appeared to be a portion of the remote past, and even this morning's banana seemed to be a very long way off.

When Mally got as far as this she shook her head vigorously, straightened up, and began to hum to herself as she walked. She hummed her own tune, and presently she was singing the words under her breath:

"They're a' gane east and west"—

It was frightfully appropriate.

"They're a' gane agee."

"*I* should say they'd all gone mad—stark, staring, raving *mad*."

"They're a' gane east, they're a' gane west,
After Mally Lee."

She threw back her head and laughed. As she did so, the lights of a car dazzled about her and she jumped for the hedge. The car came up slowly, ran past her a yard or two, and stopped. A woman leaned out, looked back, and called to Mally:

"Am I right for Peddling Corner?"

Mally came up to the car. The woman was really only a girl. She was alone, and her voice was very plaintive:

"Oh, *can* you tell me?"

"You've passed Peddling Corner—it's behind you. You'll have to turn."

"Oh, but I don't want to go there—I want to go to Menden. And they said I must go right on through Peddling Corner, and now I don't know where I am. And I'm simply hopeless at maps. Deane always reads the maps. I can't do anything but drive, really."

"I can read the map," said Mally.

"Oh, *can* you? How *clever*!"

Mally laughed.

"Where is it?"

"I suppose it's in one of the pockets. I really don't know. Deane always sees to the maps."

Mally found the map, studied it by the light of the side-lamp, and identified the long road over the down.

"It's about eight miles to Menden. This road goes on for about four, and then you turn left, right, and left again." She folded up the map as she spoke, and put it away.

"I shan't remember," said the girl at the wheel. "I suppose you're not going that way?" Her voice brightened. "I could give you a lift if you were."

Mally felt like Cinderella when the pumpkin turned into a coach. She said, "Oh, thank you," and she hoped very much that her voice did not shake. She felt suddenly as though she could not have walked another hundred yards.

"Get in by me. Give the door a good bang. That's splendid." She started the car. "Now you can remember the turnings and look at the map. I was feeling dreadfully lost without Deane."

"Your chauffeur?"

"No, my maid. I can't stick being driven, but I always take Deane. And it's too bad of her, she's just left me *stranded*—and at the last minute, too. I'll never have a maid who's got relations again. Don't you call it the limit for them to go and wire for her absolutely just as I was starting? And it isn't as if I could get any one to maid me down there. I don't know whether you know the Holmes. That's where I'm going. And of course Elizabeth Holmes is a perfect dear, but as for letting her maid do one's hair, one might just as well be a chimpanzee out of the ark and have done with it. And I *can't* do my own."

There seemed to be a good many things that the damsel couldn't do. Mally saw her by the dashboard light—very fair, very fluffy, very pretty, in a scarlet leather coat and cap. She said, "How dreadful!" and tried to keep the laugh out of her voice.

"Of course I can brush and comb it. But I can't *wave* it—and you've no idea what I look like with it straight. I suppose you don't know of a temporary maid? I did ring up an agency, but it was all in a hurry, and you *know* what they are."

"We're coming to the turning," said Mally. Her heart had begun to beat a little faster.

They turned off the tarred road and ran through a patch of woodland—bare trees almost meeting overhead, high sandy banks on either side. Mally looked again at the face of the girl beside her—pretty, foolish, inconsequent.

"Agencies never seem to have jobs for the people who want them. I want one badly enough."

"Do you? What sort of job do you want?"

"Oh, any sort." She pushed herself on. "I'd come as your maid if you'd have me."

"Would you? Would you really? Do you know anything about it? Hair—that's the chief thing—I do look so awful if mine isn't right."

"I'm frightfully good at hair—I really am—it's my strong suit. I did every one's hair whenever we got up plays."

"How enormously clever of you!"

"I haven't any *things*," said Mally.

"I can lend you some, I expect. Deane packed, and she always puts in plenty. Look here, my name's Candida Long. But I don't know yours—and where *are* your things?"

"Turn to the right," said Mally.

"How did you remember?" Miss Candida Long spoke admiringly. She negotiated the corner. "What did you say your name was?"

"Marion," said Mally slowly—"Marion Brown."

"Is it?" Candida looked sideways, and Mally gave a little desperate laugh.

"No, it isn't. Miss Long, you asked me where my things were. Some of them are in London, and some of them are at Curston not very far from here, but—but I don't want the Moorings to know where I am or what I'm doing."

Candida looked sideways again.

"Is that why you're Marion Brown?"

"Yes. Would you like to put me down here?"

"No, I shouldn't. My dear girl, what does it matter to me whether you're Brown or Jones or Montmorency? Funny your knowing the Moorings. I'm going to a dance there to-morrow. That's really what I've come down for. It ought to be rather a good show. Dominos and masks to start with, and fancy dress after midnight. I've got a ripping black and silver domino. And my dress—you just wait till you see it! It's really rather dinky. I won't tell you about it—I'll just let it burst on you. It was Paul Craddock's idea. Have you ever come across him? I think he knows the Moorings. He's rather a friend of mine. As a matter of fact, he was coming down with me to-night, and he rang me up half an hour before I started and said his stuffy old chief had a job for him in town, but he'd try and get down to-morrow for the Curston show. Wasn't it the limit? First Deane, and then Paul. I very nearly telegraphed Elizabeth to say I was *dead*." She giggled. "She's so literal she'd probably have sent me a wreath."

"Turn to the left," said Mally. "It's about a hundred yards along this lane, I think."

She remembered Menden Place, and she had seen Mrs. Holmes once in the distance. She hoped with a good deal of earnestness that Mrs. Holmes had not seen her.

Chapter Twenty-One

"I SAY, you do look tired!" said Candida when she came up to dress. "Are you all right?"

Mally held on to the back of the chair she had been sitting in. She had unpacked Miss Long's suitcases and laid out the contents of a very expensive dressing-case. Then she had sat down by the cheerful fire and fallen into a doze. She blinked now at the lights, and said with engaging frankness:

"It's nothing—I'm just hungry."

"Didn't they give you any tea?"

Mally shook her head.

"I came straight up here."

"That was stupid of you—I'll wear that emerald and silver rag. There's some chocolate in my dressing-case. I say, when *did* you have a meal?"

"Lunch yesterday." Mally laughed shakily. "There *were* some ginger biscuits and a banana, but—"

"How *idiotic* of you! Here!" Candida threw a packet of chocolate at her. "Sit down and eat as much of that as you can. And for the Lord's sake, don't start waving my hair till you're sure you're not going to fall on top of me with the tongs."

The chocolate was a great success. So was the hair. Candida talked all the time it was being done.

"It's quite a jolly party. And fortunately they had a man over, so that Paul not coming won't put the table out. There's Colonel Moulton, a priceless old dear—pays lovely compliments that take about twenty minutes each; and Janet Elliot, who's an awfully good sort; and her brother Willie, a very cheery soul; and Ambrose Medhurst—I suppose Elizabeth's asked him for Janet. Why did you jump? You nearly burned me."

Mally had jumped because she knew Mr. Medhurst's name. Jimmy's friend—it must be the same one. Jimmy Lake had talked about him, said he was a topping chap and frightfully in love with a girl who had pots of money, so of course he couldn't ever tell her about it. Mally remembered saying, "I don't see why." Now she said, "I'm *so* sorry," and then, "Is Miss Elliot an heiress?"

Candida went off into a peal of laughter.

"Janet? Good Lord, no! She's a church mouse—a ripping little church mouse. Her father's the parson here, and there are about umpteen of them—a frightfully cheery crowd. Now I'm ready for my dress."

She slipped it on and stood looking at herself.

Candida in green and silver was really a very pretty creature. It was quite obvious that she thought so herself. She turned from the long glass with a flirt of the short, flaring skirt.

"Not bad—am I? Now, Brown, tell the truth. Would you say that a man—" She stopped, frowned, and tapped with a silver foot. "Isn't it *beastly* if a girl's got money—the foul way people talk, I mean, as if any man who made love to her only wanted her money? What would you say about it—*honestly*?"

"I should say it depended on the man."

Candida Long laughed rather consciously.

"Oh, the man's Paul Craddock, and he hasn't a bean. I've got five thousand a year, and sometimes I wish it was all at the bottom of the sea. Other times, of course, I don't, because I have a frightfully good time. But you girls who have to earn your own living have got no end of a pull when it comes to marriage. You do know whether a man wants you for yourself or not. All right, you needn't sit up. Eat a good supper and go to bed. I say, I haven't told any one that I picked you up on the road. Elizabeth's rather Victorian—she'd probably fuss. So don't you say anything either."

She turned for a moment by the door.

"Take a nighty and anything else you want. I don't *care* for Paul, you know. But I'd like to know whether he cares for me. He's awfully ambitious. If he married me, he'd go to the top of the tree in politics. That's what he'd *like*. And sometimes I think it would be pretty good fun having a *salon* and all that. And sometimes I think it would be a most infernal bore. What do you think about it?"

Mally repeated her previous answer.

"I think it would all depend on the man," she said.

When the door had shut on Candida Long, Mally busied herself with putting things away. Then she sat down by the fire again and began to think.

If only Paul Craddock were not coming to-morrow. She poked the fire and watched the flames go roaring up the chimney. Delicious warmth. She shut her eyes for a moment and called up the picture of the wet, cold wood and the black holly bush that had been her shelter only a few hours before. With a little quick shiver she opened them again and looked at the nice old-fashioned room with its low ceiling and dark, shining furniture. The carpet was old and faded, the pattern on the wall paper was dimmed to a pleasant blur; but there were new gay chintzes—the shiny white sort with parrots and roses and long-tailed birds of paradise. The curtains were lined with rose color, and there was a bedspread of thin rose-colored silk. Mally thought it was a very nice room.

If she could only tide over the next two days. Perhaps Paul Craddock wouldn't come. She put her chin in her hand and stared at the fire. Even if he came, why should he see her? A guest arriving for a dance and going away next day—why should he come across Miss Long's maid? If he came at all, it would only be for the masked ball at Curston; and next day Candida Long was going abroad for a month. It was really a splendid chance.

By the time the housemaid came to call her to supper, Mally was quite sure that Paul would not come, or, alternatively, that if he came, she would be able to dodge him. In either case she would go abroad with Candida Long and they would have a simply ripping time.

Paul Craddock came down next day. Mr. Alfred Dawson's clue had led him on a wild-goose chase. He found Sir George Peterson very much in favour of his going to Curston; there was an off-chance of picking up information there, and it was just as well to keep up appearances and not to seem over-anxious about Miss Lee and the papers she had gone off with.

He arrived in time to dress. Mally, coming round a corner, almost ran into him. She drew back quickly, and he passed without looking at her. The corner was dark, her dress was dark; he had gone straight on.

Mally put the lights on in Miss Long's room, and told herself that she was a perfect fool to be so frightened.

Paul Craddock, meanwhile, went to the end of the passage, turned the corner, waited a minute, and then retraced his steps and went downstairs again. He knew the house, and was pretty sure of getting the study to himself at this hour. He closed the door, went straight to the telephone, and gave Sir George Peterson's London number. The call came through almost at once and, to his relief, it was Sir George himself who said "Hallo!"

Paul Craddock began to speak in Portuguese. Post-office employees do not as a rule know Portuguese, and he found it a useful medium for private conversations with his chief.

"She is here."

"Where?" Sir George was sharply incredulous.

"Here in this house. I've just seen her."

"Does she know you've seen her?"

"No, I should say not. She came round the corner in a dark passage, and I walked straight on."

"What are you going to do?"

"We daren't let her go again; and we can't touch her without a warrant. I think you ought to apply for one."

"Your reasons?"

"I've been thinking. I'm sure we were wrong in suspecting that she had any purpose—I mean I feel sure she wasn't planted in the house, as we thought at first."

"Go on."

"If she'd known what she was taking, or if she'd been sent to take it, she'd never have left London. She'd have gone straight to a certain quarter. I think it's safe enough to have her arrested. If she's got any papers on her, you claim them—they're your private affair. If she hasn't any papers, she does time for taking the diamond and is sufficiently discredited to be negligible in future. If she knows anything, she doesn't know where to take her information. But it's my belief that she doesn't know anything."

There was a moment's silence, and then Sir George said, "Yes, I think you're right. I feel that way myself. I'll get the warrant and have some one sent down as soon as possible. I don't know if they'll do anything to-night."

"All right."

Mr. Craddock rang off and went to dress.

"Brown," said Miss Candida Long, "I've had an absolutely splendid brain-wave."

"Oh!" said Mally. "Don't twist like that! I very nearly burned you." She was waving Candida's thick, fair hair.

"All right—no harm done. Listen, my good girl, and for Heaven's sake don't singe me."

"I won't if you keep still."

"You're not listening. Didn't you say you'd left some things at Curston?"

"Yes, I did."

Mally began to wish she had held her tongue; even a very short acquaintance with Candida made her view with suspicion anything that she described as a brain-wave.

"Well, listen. *Are* you listening? It's an idea—it really is. I'll take you over with me, and you shall fetch your things. I was rather thinking of taking you anyhow, because I do simply hate driving alone."

"But you wouldn't be alone. There's the rest of the house-party and—Mr. Craddock."

"Brown, you're not being intelligent. I want to be an absolutely deadly secret. That's why I told you not to open the box with my domino. I want to be quite, quite, *quite* sure that nobody knows me until I unmask—and especially I don't want Paul Craddock to know. I shall just take you along, and you can get your things. I'm going to slip away from here as soon as dinner's over. So you'll be all ready—won't you? And *now* we'll open that box. Prepare to have your breath taken away."

Mally was certainly a little taken aback. The dress which Miss Long proposed to wear under her domino was calculated to cause a sensation at Curston. Mally pictured Lady Mooring's face, and very nearly burst into disrespectful laughter.

"It's a silver-fish," said Candida, picking up the glittering tights. "Isn't the tail dinky? It was Paul's idea. We agreed that I hadn't quite enough money to be a goldfish—it would run to five figures, and I've only four. Oh, I say! It *is* rather nice—isn't it?"

Silver shoes; silver stockings; silver tights with the fish scales picked out in glittering diamond points; and the little three-cornered diamond tail, which Candida had described as dinky—it was all as revealing as a bathing-dress, if rather more becoming.

Candida's silver-flaxen hair stood out like a halo. She rose on the tips of her silver shoes and twirled in front of the glass.

"Oh, I do hate to take it off! But I can't go down to dinner in it. I'd love to see Elizabeth's face if I did. She told me once quite seriously that it took her years to get used to ankles. 'And now, my dear,' she said, 'nobody minds what they show.' I say, I do look nice—don't I? Here, give me that black thing to go down to dinner in—and hide this with my domino—and don't breathe a word to a soul, or I'll kill you and dump the corpse in the loneliest wood between here and Curston."

Downstairs Miss Long was greeted with cries of "Not dressed?"; "I say, Candida, you're not going like that?"; and "My dear, what about your fancy dress? Hasn't it come?"

Candida kissed her fingers to them all.

"It's come—it's upstairs. No, Elizabeth darling, I shan't make any one late, because I'm going to drive myself *by* myself, and I'm absolutely the deadliest secret that ever was, and nobody's going to see me till I take off my domino at supper. No, no one's going to know my domino either. I've just told my maid I'll kill her if she tells. You wouldn't like a murder in the house, would you, Elizabeth?"

"My dear!" Mrs. Holmes was rather shocked. She was a large lady, squarely built to take plain tweeds, and looking frankly out of her element in a frightful magenta satin, which she had bought because her dressmaker urged her to. She had bright hair of a shade between red and gold, and a skin like brick-dust. She said "My dear!" and Candida laughed.

"Yes, darling, I *said* you wouldn't like it. Who do I go in with? Ambrose? All right—Come along, old dear."

She linked arms with a handsome, dark-eyed boy and whispered to him as they went through the hall:

"I'm not telling every one, but I don't mind giving you the tip. Look out for a violet domino—p'raps she'll give you three and five. Mind, I don't promise."

She had Paul Craddock on her left at dinner, and as soon as the fish came round, she told Ambrose to play with Janet Elliot on his other side, and turned to Paul.

"Well," she said. "I don't suppose I've any dances left for you."

"How are you going to be an absolutely dead secret if you book dances ahead?"

"Perhaps I'm not an absolutely dead secret to every one."

"Must you be one to me? After all, I gave you the idea for your dress, and I haven't told a soul, so I deserve something."

"We don't always get what we deserve. Think of all the lovely things I should have if we did."

He looked at her with an expression which she could not interpret.

"Have you really anything left to wish for?"

"My *dear* Paul! What a question! Why, only yesterday I'd the most fiendish bit of luck. You know I'm off to Florence, to the Hallidays, to-morrow. And yesterday, after you rang up, if that miserable, abominable *fiend* of a Deane didn't go off at a moment's notice, just because her sister had had twins—twins!"

"Poor Candida! So you're maidless?"

She dropped her voice.

"No, I'm *not*—that's the extraordinary thing. I suppose I *am* rather lucky after all. I don't mind telling you, but for goodness gracious mercy's sake don't let on about it here. It's the sort of thing Elizabeth would have a fit over."

"What have you done?" said Paul, smiling at her. "Go on—confess! I won't give you away. What have you done?"

Candida opened her pale eyes in a look of injured innocence.

"I? *Nothing*. She was absolutely dropped in my path."

"She?" His tone sharpened just a little.

Candida bent nearer him, nodding.

"Ssh! Not a word! Elizabeth would have ten thousand fits."

She sat up and helped herself to an entrée. Paul let it pass him, and she shook her head reproachfully.

"It's frightfully good. You ought to have some. I don't know what it is—it's a mystery like me!"

"Or your maid. How did you say you got her?"

Candida hesitated.

"*Swear* you won't tell—*absolutely*? All right. I picked her up on the road, just out of Peddling Corner."

"You *didn't*."

"I *did*. And she's pounds better at doing hair than Deane ever was. So I really am lucky."

Paul appeared to feel no further interest in the picked-up maid. He gazed tenderly at Candida and said in a low voice:

"And am I to be lucky, too? Are you going to promise me some dances?"

"How can I? I'm a *secret*."

"Must you be a secret from me?"

She dropped her eyelashes.

"Do you want to know frightfully?"

"Of course I do."

"Well—then—you won't tell any one? *Swear*?"

Mr. Paul Craddock swore.

Candida looked over her shoulder. Ambrose was telling Janet Elliot in full detail why he had taken nine to the fourteenth hole that morning. It was quite safe. She turned back to Paul and whispered.

"What did you say your favourite colour was?"

Paul was not sure that he had a favorite colour, but he knew, or thought he knew, where Miss Long's own preference lay.

He said, "Pale blue," and looked suitably eager and devoted.

"How *clever* of you!"

"Is it pale blue?"

She laughed.

"A pale-blue domino *might* be there and give you seven and ten."

Candida came upstairs in a state of reprehensible mirth.

"Lightning quick, Brown! I want to get away before the others. It is going to be fun. You haven't said a word to a soul, have you? No, there's no fastening—it's elastic. Pull! Pull like the dickens! Yes, that's got it. Tophole, isn't it? My good Brown, I've told Ambrose Medhurst that my domino is violet in *strict* confidence. And I've told Paul that it's pale blue—absolutely exclusive information. And Willie Elliot thinks it's white and gold. And Colonel Moulton caught me in the hall, and I just breathed in his ear that I was going to be a she devil in scarlet. Now, let's have the real article!"

Mally held up a black and silver domino. It was more silver than black really.

Candida pulled the hood close down over her hair and put on the mask with its deep lace fall.

"Now my fur coat to hide the domino—and that scarlet chiffon to put over my head! Are you ready? Come along then!"

Just at the head of the stairs they met Mr. Craddock standing on guard. Mally had on her dark-blue coat, and she had turned down the brim of her black felt hat, the better to hide her face. She went by, following Candida, and felt Paul Craddock's eyes.

Chapter Twenty-Two

THE CAR SLID through the dark lanes. Mally loved driving at night; there was something magical about the enclosing dark and the white beam that cut through it and made a road for them. To-night there was a touch of strangeness on everything. It had snowed a little, and tree, bush and hedgerow were like silver ghosts watching the black lanes.

Candida Long drove very well. She talked nearly all the time. But Mally had only a surface attention to give her. She was finding the situation quite extraordinarily exciting; with the excitement there was a touch of terror, a touch of amusement. The ball at Curston had been planned in her honour, it was her ball; and she was going to it in the double character of a fugitive from justice and Candida Long's maid.

Upstairs in the box-room at Curston was the trunk that she had left behind, her old school-box; and in the box was the domino that she had made to wear to-night. Roger had quarrelled with her because she would not tell him what the domino was like. Like Candida, she had meant it to be an absolutely dead secret, and she had bought the stuff in London one day when Roger had driven her up, and had sewed at it in her own room with the door locked.

It was at this point that the great idea came to her. It came just as Candida said in a commiserating tone:

"It'll be most awfully dull for you all those hours. But I suppose you know some of the people in the house, and they'll look after you—the housekeeper or some one."

"Oh, I shan't be dull." Mally suppressed a funny little laugh. "I—I shall be perfectly all right."

"Well, mind you have some supper," said Miss Long. "And meet me in the cloak-room when people begin to go. I say, we got away rather neatly—didn't we? I don't see how any one can have the least idea of who I am. I mean to have simply the most priceless time."

Mally said, "'M," which was all that was required of her. It was her ball, and she was going to it as Candida Long's maid. She could just see the stiff pride that had made the Moorings go on with it in the face of the broken engagement. She wondered whether every one knew. It seemed about a thousand years since she had flung her ring at Roger and cut his cheek, but really and truly it was only forty-eight hours ago.

Something inside Mally's mind said "Nonsense!" with such insistent loudness that she had to count up on her fingers to convince herself. It was between eight and nine o'clock in the evening that she had banged the door on Roger and her engagement. Then there had been a night divided between a garage, a car, and a hay-loft—a night that had felt about three weeks long; and a second night on a hard little bed in an attic room at Menden, where she had slept without moving. It was now just a quarter past nine, so that it was really only forty-eight hours and three-quarters of an hour since she had smashed Lady Catherine Cray's collection and run away from Roger, who deserved everything, every single thing she had done, and *more*. Of course he might have sat down straight away to write one of those devastatingly discreet announcements which one sees in the papers:

"The marriage arranged between Mr. Dash and Miss Asterisk will not take place."

Mally was sure that he wouldn't lose any time in letting everybody know that he wasn't engaged to a girl who might be arrested at any moment.

"So you see," said Candida, finishing a long speech of which Mally had not heard a single word. "So you see, I shall *know*, shan't I? Of course I don't care twopence for him, and I don't intend to until I'm *sure*—Hallo! Here we are! Last time I came here I'd only just learned to drive, and I went slap into the middle of Lady Mooring's pet rose-bed. And that stiff Roger was polite about it— *polite!* I've hated him ever since, because he had 'damns' simply sticking out all over him the whole time, and it would have been so *much* more comfortable to have a good old row. If he'd said, 'My good girl, you can't drive for nuts! Why on earth do they let you out without a nursemaid?' and I'd said, 'You're simply the most odious, cross pig I've ever met!' we might have got it off our chests and been friends, whereas now we loathe each other."

The worst moment was coming out of the dark into the lighted hall. Mally kept her head down and made for the back stairs. They were early, but a fairly big party had arrived just before them, so that the hall was not empty.

Once through the swing door, Mally took a very long breath of relief. The worst was over. She ran up the stairs, just missed one of the housemaids on the first landing, and then found the rest of the way quite clear.

She shut the box-room door behind her, switched on the light, and looked about her for her box. It stood on the top of another one about a yard away, a dreadful, shabby old thing with the canvas coming through one of the broken leather corners. It was simply years since the lock had functioned, and for this she had cause to be devoutly thankful. She tugged at the straps and threw back the lid. The domino was tied up in a paper parcel down in the left-hand corner. She pulled it out, opened the paper, and took stock of its contents. First the domino, rose-red with a little gold pattern on it and a dull-gold fringe; then the black velvet mask—a really wide one with a deep lace fall—the gold and silver shoes, and the light stockings, which she had been saving for this ball—"Only I never, never, never thought I'd have to dress in the box-room."

She was out of her coat and slipping off skirt and jumper. She must have something to wear under the domino. She rummaged for a very old gold tissue slip which she had worn for some school theatricals. It went on, and the domino over it. As she slid the elastic of the mask over her hair and pulled up the rose-red hood, a most beautiful feeling of safety came over her. She was here, at her very own ball. She was safe. She was going to enjoy herself.

When she had put on the silver stockings and the gold and silver shoes, she rolled up a change of linen, and all the things she had taken off, inside her out-door coat, and fastened the bundle with a couple of safety pins. Then she ran downstairs.

The hall was now quite full. She slipped through the crowd, out at the front door, and round to the right to where Candida had parked her car. It was turning frightfully cold. She pushed her bundle into the car and ran back to the house. She edged her way to the big open fire-place, where a huge fire of logs was blazing, and whilst she warmed herself, the rest of the party from Menden arrived.

Mally knew from the other maids that Mrs. Holmes was going to wear a purple velvet domino, and Janet Elliot emerald-green. Of the men, Paul Craddock was easy to recognize on account of his height. He wore a bright-red domino lined with black. Colonel Moulton and Ambrose Medhurst were about the same height; but Colonel Moulton had a forward tilt of the head, and she decided without difficulty that he was the brown, and Ambrose the yellow domino.

She was rather pleased with herself as she passed down the corridor with a crowd of other people and came out into the ballroom, where Lady Mooring in black velvet and pearls stood, saying alternately: "How d'you do," and "I haven't an *idea* who you are." She said "I haven't an idea" to Mally, and Mally passed on with just one backward look at the three rows of milky, iridescent pearls that were to have been her own on the day that she married Roger.

She put up one hand and touched her smooth bare throat. Roger had shown her the pearls and made her put them on. She remembered the feel of them, and once more she looked back and saw them on Lady Mooring, one row tight up under the double chin, one just reaching the Honiton lace tucker, and the third falling down over the black velvet to the ample waist.

"They must be worth hundreds and hundreds and hundreds of pounds. How comic—how *frightfully* comic! And I've only three and ninepence farthing in the world!"

It pleased her a good deal to think that it was she who had whistled Roger, and Curston, and three rows of pearls down the wind.

The first dance had just begun, when the yellow domino from Menden stopped in front of her and said, in the high, squeaky voice affected by masks:

"Er—may I have the pleasure?"

Mally had decided on a husky whisper as a better disguise than a squeak. Not that Ambrose Medhurst would know her voice, but the room was certainly full of people who had come here to see her act only three weeks ago, and some of them might have good memories. She swung into the dance with Ambrose and said:

"You're very formal. Perhaps we know each other very well—or perhaps we don't know each other at all. So we needn't bother about being polite."

"You dance like a dream," squeaked the yellow domino.

"Yes, I know I do. It's my one consuming passion. Let's dance, and talk afterwards. I'm sure you can't go on squeaking like that—it sounds frightfully uncomfortable."

When the music stopped, they found a couple of chairs in an alcove, and Mally gave indiscretion the rein:

"Shall I tell you who you are, and all the horrid secrets of your past? I will if you like."

"Who are you?"

"Some one who knows *all*."

"What on earth—"

"Did you ever play 'I love my love'?" said Mally on a thrilling note of mystery. "It goes like this, you know: 'I love my love with a C because she is Charming. I hate her with a C because—' Why do you hate her, yellow domino?"

"Who on earth—who are you—what are you driving at?" Mr. Medhurst rather forgot his squeak.

"You won't say why you hate her. All right, we'll pass that. Perhaps you don't hate her at all. And it goes on like this: 'I took her to Curston and gave her Compliments and Chaff. Her name is Candida and she's going on the Continent.'"

There was a little pause. Mally had seen Ambrose Medhurst look at Candida when Candida was looking away. It had also occurred to her that Miss Long, who would talk by the hour about Paul Craddock, not only changed the subject when Mr. Medhurst was mentioned, but actually changed color too. The maid hears a good deal of talk between women as she lays out clothes or puts them away.

After that little pause, the yellow domino said:

"Who are you? Candida?"

"Supposing I said 'No'?"

"I should say you were not playing the game."

Mally laughed, a little whispering laugh.

"Supposing I said 'Yes'?"

"I shouldn't believe you," said Ambrose Medhurst in his natural voice.

The music struck up, and they went back to the ballroom. He had turned away, when he felt himself pushed a little and heard a faint, laughing thread of sound:

"I wouldn't be frightened of her *money*. She's just a girl."

Mally slipped away before he could turn round. She was looking on at the dancing, her foot tapping a little, when an arm went round her waist and she felt herself swung into the stream without so much as a "With your leave" or "By your leave."

The new partner was several sizes larger than Ambrose. He wore a black domino lined with red, and for a dreadful moment she wondered if Mr. Craddock had turned his coat. It was only for a moment, for the wildest imagination would have failed to picture Paul Craddock in a rollicking mood.

The black domino was a very rollicking partner, who swung Mally right off her feet in the best Russian Ballet style, and announced in a horrible growling voice that he was Foxtrotski, the Bounding Bolshevist from Brixton, adding that his friend Bombemoff was proposing to wind up the proceedings with a grand gala display of exploded guests.

Mally enjoyed her dance with him very much. It was about half-way through it that she found something astonishingly familiar about the big hand that was holding hers, and recognized Ethan Messenger. It was strange what a feeling of reassurance came over her; and before she could bridle her tongue, she gave a warm little excited laugh and said:

"How is Dinks?"

The Bounding Bolshevist had answered "Top-hole!" before he realized the revealing nature of this question. He broke off and said, "Hallo—'allo—'allo! Good Lord! Who are you?"

"Cinderella," said Mally—"or the Beggar Maid—I'm not quite sure which, but I think it's Cinderella. You don't really belong to either of the stories, so it's simply a frightful ana—what's-his name for us to be dancing together."

"Do you mean anachronism?"

"I expect so. Anyhow it's frightfully improper. But you haven't told me about Dinks. Did he bite you?"

For one surprising moment the impossibility of reconciling a queerly vivid memory of Mally Lee, with straws sticking all over her and a smudge on one cheek, with the rose-red elegance in his arms struck Ethan dumb.

Mally rattled on:

"I took good care he didn't bite *me*. I never thought rabbits were ferocious before. Bunty wanted me to put him in his hutch, and I told her you'd do it ever so much better. I *do* like Bunty—don't you?"

Ethan took no notice of this question.

"So it's you!" he said.

Mally shook her head vigorously.

"I'm not me, and you're not you. I'm a rose-colored domino, and you're a black one. And we haven't got any faces—we've only got masks. Nothing's ever happened to us till to-night, and nothing's ever going to happen to us again. We're just going to dance and have a frightfully good time until your friend Bombemoff blows us all right out of our fairy tale."

Ethan swung her round with a laugh.

"I mustn't ask how you got here, then?"

"Certainly *not*!"

"Or anything?"

She shook her head again. A moment later, she caught sight of Candida's black and silver, just clear of the dancers at the edge of the room. Without any warning she twisted away from Ethan and came up to Candida, laughing.

"Shall I tell you a secret?" she whispered.

Miss Long's partner, a white domino, did not seem pleased, but Mally went on whispering:

"I can tell you something worth knowing."

The silver hood and black mask turned towards her.

"What can you tell me?"

Mally decided that Candida really had no notion of how to disguise her voice. If she couldn't do better than this, she might just as well not wear a mask at all.

"I can tell you that the red domino lined with black would like a rich wife. And the yellow domino is so afraid of money that he'll let the girl he cares for go to a man who doesn't care for her."

Candida stamped a silver foot.

"How dare you! Who are you?" And then, rather breathlessly: "How do you know, and who do you mean?"

"Won't you dance?" The white domino was getting impatient; but Candida just flung him a "No" and came closer to Mally.

"*What* did you mean? *Who* did you mean?"

Mally put a finger on the lace fall that hid her lips.

"S'sh," she said. Then she pointed. "There's the yellow domino. He's too proud to tell you that he cares—I don't think he'll ever tell you unless you make him."

"Who is he? What nonsense you talk! You can't know who he is."

"Perhaps I can't—perhaps I can,

For he's a most particularly proud young man."

Mally hummed the doggerel on the lowest note she could reach. Then she went on inconsequently: "His name reminds me of amber in the middle of a wood."

"What *nonsense*!" Candida gasped a little.

"Yes, isn't it? And the *very* tall red and black domino coming down the room now has the same initials as police courts and privy councillors. And *he* isn't proud at all—he can swallow a fortune as well as most men."

Mally gave Candida a little twirl and went chasseing down the room by herself. She really was enjoying herself very much indeed.

She went on dancing with Ethan Messenger, who had apparently been waiting for her. Presently she saw Candida and the yellow domino go by together.

"I know what I am," she said.

"A witch?"

"*Certainly* not! Witches are all perfectly hideous, and at least a hundred. No, it burst on me just now—I'm not Cinderella, and I'm not the Beggar Maid; I'm an absolutely up-to-date fairy godmother."

She went on enjoying herself.

Chapter Twenty-Three

"How DID YOU know me?" said Ethan suddenly.

They were sitting out together in a little alcove bounded by screens, and palms in pots.

Mally took up his left hand, which was nearest to her, straightened the fingers in a brisk, matter-of-fact way, and pointed at the top joint of the forefinger.

"That's where you'd just hammered yourself when I opened the door."

"What a romantic memory!"

"Yes, isn't it? You said 'Damn!' and I opened the door, and there we were."

"You had straws in your hair."

"So would you if you had slept in a hay-loft. It's warm, but it *does* prick. O-o-o-oh!"

Ethan's hand was pinched rather hard. From the other side of the screen on their right a voice said, "Mally Lee?" It was a woman's voice; what Mally would have described as a dowagery voice—the sort that goes with chins and diamonds.

"Oh, yes," said another woman. There were sounds as of two comfortably proportioned ladies settling themselves for conversation.

Mally went on pinching Ethan's hand. What on earth were they going to say?

"You don't mean to say she isn't here to-night!" This was the first voice.

The other had a sharper tone:

"My dear Louisa, you don't mean to say you haven't heard!"

"Not a word. Is there anything to hear?"

"Oh, *yes.*" The sharp-voiced lady threw a good deal of zest into the words. "Oh, *yes.* Why it's all off."

"Not *really!* Are you sure?"

"Of course I'm sure. Really, Louisa! As if I should say such a thing unless I had it on quite unimpeachable authority!"

"And you have?"

"Lady Mooring rang me up this morning to tell us. Poor thing, I'm sure it's a relief to her; for I happen to know she was most unhappy about the engagement. And really you can't be surprised—a little nobody from nowhere without a penny piece. You know she was Maud Emson's governess, and managed to catch Roger when he was staying there. Most annoying for both families, because of course it was an open secret that he and Blanche were meant for each other. And such a name too—Mally Lee! Mally!— out of some old song that she made herself ridiculous by singing at those theatricals they had! I know Lady Mooring felt that very much. Such a thing to do!"

Ethan's right hand came down and covered the little cold fingers that were pinching him. Mally stopped pinching, and her hand began to tremble under his hand.

"I heard she sang charmingly," said the comfortable, fat voice.

The other lady sniffed.

"A great deal too theatrical. All very well for the stage—but not for one's daughter-in-law. Lady Mooring was dreadfully upset about it."

"Well, well, she needn't be upset now. What happened?"

"I don't know exactly. But she did say—only don't repeat it."

"No, no, of course not."

The sharp voice sank lower.

"Well, she did say that she could never be thankful enough that Roger had found out the girl's true character in time."

Mally pulled her hand away from Ethan and stood up. Her face burned behind her mask, and her eyes stung. How *dared* they? Oh, how *dared* they?

Ethan caught her arm and followed her out of the alcove and down the passage. Where the last pair of chairs stood, his grasp tightened. The place was empty, for the music of the next dance had begun.

"Come in here," he said. "Why should you mind what a spiteful old woman says?"

Mally turned to face him.

"I *do* mind—I do!" she said, and backed away from him until she stood against the wall between the two chairs.

"Were they talking about you?"

"Yes, they were. You heard them."

"Then you were engaged to Roger Mooring?" Ethan's voice was slow and altered.

"Yes, I was."

"And he broke it off? What a swab!"

Mally brought her hands together with a sharp, exasperated sound.

"No, he didn't, he didn't, he *didn't*! Every one will say that he did. But *you're* not to say it—you're not to think it. He *didn't* break it off—I did it. Do you hear? I did it."

Her hood had fallen back. She put up a shaking hand and snatched off her mask. Ethan looked at her gravely.

"Why did you?"

"Because I chose to—because he didn't care for me, or know me, or understand anything at all. How dared he make love to me when he didn't care for me?"

"Are you sure?"

Mally laughed, a very hurt, angry laugh.

"Yes, I'm quite, quite, *quite* sure. He believed everything that odious, hypocritical Peterson said to him—he believed I'd stolen Mrs. Craddock's diamonds. People who care for you don't believe things like that—they *don't*."

Ethan gave a long whistle of dismay. What sort of mess had this child got herself into?

"Why should any one believe such a thing?"

The anger and the defiance went out of Mally; she felt frightfully helpless and alone. She put the backs of her hands to her eyes like a little girl, and said in a low, trembling voice:

"I don't know."

And then suddenly—voices, laughter, a dozen couples looking for a place to sit out in. The intimate, passionate moment was over before Ethan knew what it was that he would have said or done. Mally's hood was up, and her mask on again; her hand rested on his arm conventionally.

"Don't let's stay here. Let's go into the ballroom and guess at who everybody is. I hate dark corners—don't you?"

Half-way down the corridor Mally saw Candida's black and silver. As she passed, Miss Long caught her by the arm and pulled her aside, all very imperiously.

"I've been looking for you everywhere. I *must* speak to you. Why did you say those things to me? Who are you?"

"One who knows," said Mally in a whispering voice.

"I don't believe a word of it. How can you know? How can any one know? That's the curse of money—you can't be sure. Look here, you've got to tell me who you are."

"Can't you guess?"

"No, I can't. What made you say those things? What do you know? Do you really know anything?"

Mally dropped the disguising whisper.

"Jimmy Lake's a great friend of mine. He's a great friend of Mr. Medhurst's, too. He told me Mr. Medhurst was in love with an awfully nice girl with a lot of money, but that he was much too proud to ask her to marry him."

"Oh!" said Candida with a catch in her breath. "Is that true?"

Mally nodded.

"You're *Brown*! How on earth—"

"I'm not any one—I'm a rose-colored mask."

"Brown!"

Mally laughed.

"No—rose-color."

She ran away, still laughing. As she came out into the ballroom, she heard herself addressed in the correct squeak.

"Will you give me the next dance?"

Mally had noticed the handsome purple domino and remarked that he danced well. She made a mute curtsey. A new partner would give her time to recover. A furious shyness of Ethan Messenger had come down on her. She looked back, and wondered at her emotion. He was a stranger; he was nothing to her. But the anger and the emotion that had swept her off her balance were on his account. If he had not been there, she would not have minded what any one said. Her cheeks burned again. She had not justified herself to Roger Mooring, but she had come perilously near trying to justify herself to Ethan Messenger.

The music of the next dance broke in on her abstraction. She had not given the purple domino a thought; but they had not gone the length of the room before a most dreadful conviction came over her. "Idiot! Why didn't you guess *in time*? Idiot—idiot—*idiot*!" If she hadn't been wool-gathering, surely something would have warned her that this was Roger Mooring. Suspicion lasted for a moment only, and then became certainty. She had danced too often with Roger not to know his step, the way he held her.

It was when they were going round the second time that they both heard Mally's name.

"Mally Lee?"—it was a girl's hard, penetrating voice—"Oh, that's all off. Didn't you know?"

Roger steered for the middle of the room, his hand a little stiffer on Mally's, and the rest of the dance passed silently. When it was over, he gave her his arm and crossed the hall to the study. It was in Mally's mind to draw back, to plead a torn anything. But when it came to the point she was dumb.

Roger shut the door on them, pushed back his peaked hood, and lifted his mask, disclosing a pale and gloomy countenance. He gazed at Mally in the way that had always annoyed her and said, "Why did you come?"

Mally put her hands behind her and took hold of the handle of the door. She was very angry because her heart would beat so fast. Why should it? Why did it? It was only Roger in one of his glumps.

"Why did you come?"

It couldn't be Roger who was making her feel so frightened; she had never, never, never dreamed of being frightened of Roger.

"Why did you come?" said Roger. "It was cruel."

All at once Mally knew that it was her own conscience that was making her afraid. She had cut Roger's cheek; she had broken a lot of lovely things that had never done her any harm; and she had been glad because she was angry with Roger. She looked at him, and something began to hurt her. He looked unhappy—not just gloomy, but unhappy, and hurt, and hungry.

Then suddenly he said "Mally!"; and Mally twisted the handle she was holding and called out quickly.

"No, Roger—*please*."

"Where have you been?" he said in a harsh, jealous voice. "Who's looking after you? How did you come here to-night?"

Mally pushed up her mask half impatiently. This was a mood that she knew and could deal with; Roger had been jealous so often. In the old days she would have said, "Pouf! Mind your own business." But she did not want to flirt with Roger now. She felt remorseful, angry with herself for having come. For once in her life she didn't know what to say.

Roger came nearer.

"Why don't you speak?"

"I don't know," said Mally in a small voice.

Roger caught her hands. His own were very hot and dry.

"Don't! No, Roger!"

She tried to pull her hands away.

"Roger, let me go! I oughtn't to have come. Let me go—and let's part friends."

"Friends! We've never been friends—we never shall be. I don't want to be *friends* with you. I'm mad about you."

"I can't think why. Roger, do let me go. It's no use."

"I can't think why either." He spoke with gloomy ferocity. "Look here, Mally, you're in the devil of a mess. That man Peterson's got his knife into you. I don't know what you've done, or why you did it—and I've got to the point where I don't care. I want you, and I'm prepared to stick to you."

Mally stared at him. Was this the prudent, conventional Roger? She did not know him.

Roger Mooring did not know himself. For forty-eight hours he had been telling himself how well rid he was of Mally Lee; and all the time the memory of her furious contempt was playing havoc with his self-esteem. To change that contempt into admiration he was ready to go to unheard-of lengths.

"Roger, let me go!"

"I'll never let you go. Don't you see that I'm the only person who can really help you? No, listen—you *must* listen! Supper's due in half an hour, and every one will unmask. There's half the county here to-night. You go in with me, and when we unmask, I announce the date of our wedding. I can square Peterson. He's going to stand for Parliament, and he wouldn't have a dog's chance if he made trouble over my wife. I can get a pull on him through the Armitages, too."

The color came quick and bright to Mally's cheeks. In her eyes Roger saw what he had been looking for—the surprised admiration which was to restore his own lost picture of himself. A sense of triumph came over him. And then Mally said:

"Oh, Roger, how frightfully nice of you! But I can't!"

"You can't? You must. I don't understand. We were engaged."

Mally nodded.

"*Were*," she said, and lifted her chin. Then she added quickly, "Roger, you must please let me go. I'm sorry I broke all that nice glass. I—I was angry. And it's frightfully nice of you to want to marry me and all that. But it's no earthly use. I can't. Only I'll never forget that you wanted to. And—and—let's part friends."

She pulled her hands away and turned to open the door. If Roger had had a momentary spasm of relief, it was instantly swallowed up in a sense of angry loss. He was not going to be called upon to make his fine gesture of self-sacrifice; he was going to lose Mally.

As the handle turned, he caught her violently in his arms.

"You can't go—you can't! Mally! Mally!"

Mally did not struggle. She stood stiff and still, and said in a little cold voice, "It's no good, Roger."

"Mally, I love you!"

She shook her head. She was full of a sudden wisdom.

"No, you only want me." And then as his arms dropped, she got the door open and ran away across the hall pulling down her mask as she went.

Chapter Twenty-Four

CANDIDA LONG watched Mally disappear.

"Brown!" She laughed, and a wave of excitement swept over her. "*Brown!* Now who on *earth* is Brown when she's not playing at being my maid?"

She went back to the yellow domino, who was waiting for her. They went into the little alcove where Mally had talked with Ethan. Candida sat down, leaned back in her chair, and took off her mask.

When her partner made no sign she said:

"So you knew me all the time. I thought you did."

"Why?"

"I just thought so."

"And when did you recognize me?"

"Oh, I knew you at once." Then after a pause, "I wonder how many other people are playing at cross-purposes to-night."

"I don't know. A good show—isn't it?"

Candida took no notice. Her voice sounded dreamy.

"You were pretending about me, and I was pretending about you."

There was a silence—one of those silences which it seems very difficult to break. At last Candida said, "I think I'm tired of pretending. Look here, Ambrose, we're pretty good pals, aren't we?"

Ambrose Medhurst sat forward. He had been an absolute fool to come and sit out with her like this. He could see the silver of her hood, the pale gold of her hair; the dusk was full of glamour. He was a first-class fool. He ought to have started talking about golf, or cars, or something, right away, instead of letting the silence close in upon them both like this. He ought to say something now, but for the life of him he couldn't think of anything to say except her name. And before he knew, he had said it:

"Candida,"—just like that.

"Look here, Ambrose, I want to ask you something; and I want the sort of straight answer you'd give to another man. I want you to remember we're pals, and let me have it dead straight."

He found he was saying her name again:

"Candida!"

"I want to ask you a question. I want to ask you if you're in love with any one."

The hand that was lying on his knee closed with a jerk.

"Why do you want to ask me that, Candida?"

He had found his voice now; but it was a voice that Candida hardly knew. She felt a little frightened.

"Aren't you going to tell me?"

"No, I'm not going to tell you."

"Ambrose—why?"

"I've got my reasons."

Candida leaned forward too.

"Ambrose, you've got to tell me." With feminine mendacity: "You *promised*."

"I think not."

Candida threw up her head and laughed.

"If you weren't in love with any one, you'd say so like a shot. So the answer is 'Yes.' Who is it? Is it Janet?"

He remained dumb.

"Ambrose, you promised—you really did. You said you'd give me a straight answer, and I think you're being simply beastly. Do you suppose I *want* to ask you all these questions? Do you suppose I wouldn't m-m-much rather be proposed to p-p-properly?"

Ambrose pushed back his chair and got up.

"For the Lord's sake, Candida!"

Candida put her hands over her face.

"If you don't care for me, go right away! Go now—go at once!"

A most frightfully long minute went by. Then Candida sprang to her feet.

"Why don't you go? Why don't you?"

He made a sort of half step away from her, and then turned back.

"If you care," said Candida. "If you care, and if you go away just because of my horrible money, I—I'll never speak to you again."

Ambrose Medhurst was human. Candida's voice shaking like that—He found that his arms were round her without any very clear idea on his part as to how it had happened. With Candida in his arms, her money didn't seem to matter. He wanted to kiss her, but she held him off.

"You haven't answered. You haven't told me. If you're not in love with me, you're to go away."

"Don't be an idiot!" said Ambrose. "I'm in love with you all right. I wish I wasn't."

"Oh!"

Ambrose let go of her with a good deal of suddenness.

"What's the good of my being in love with you?" His voice was cross and jerky.

"I don't know," said Candida. Then she added with a shade of defiance, "Do you want me to marry Paul Craddock? Because I shall if you go on like this. I think you're being a p-p-perfect beast."

Ambrose ran his hands through his hair.

"It makes no difference to me who you marry. But Paul Craddock! Why in Heaven's name Paul Craddock?"

"He wants me to."

Ambrose laughed.

"That seems a pretty poor reason. Of course I don't want to bias you; and, as I said before, it's no affair of mine—"

"Oh!" said Candida suddenly. "I hate you, Ambrose!" She stamped her foot. "I won't be preached at. Do you hear? And I won't be told it's no affair of yours. And I'll marry a dozen people if I like. And—and—what's it got to do with you anyhow? You don't care— you don't care a *damn* what happens to me."

Ambrose glared.

"That's a lie!"

"It's not!"

"It is."

"Then why are you being a perfect fiend to me?"

"Because—Look here, Candida, I haven't got a bean besides my pay, and I never shall have. And if you think I'm going to dangle round after a rich wife, I'm not—and there's an end of it."

There was a silence. Candida pulled down her mask.

"All right. Paul won't mind." Her voice shook a little. "Every one doesn't think such a lot about money as you do."

"I don't."

"Don't you? You never stop thinking about it. I don't matter— and you don't matter—and our both being unhappy doesn't matter. Nothing matters to you except my money."

She straightened her hood and moved away from him into the corridor. Before he realized that she was going, she had gone.

Ambrose did not follow her.

Candida came out into the ballroom just as a new dance was beginning. She looked all round for the red and black domino, and saw him on the far side of the room alone. A moment later she was saying, "Don't you dance?" and the red and black domino was offering her his arm.

As they slipped into the stream of dancers, Candida hoped that Ambrose saw her, and that he knew who her partner was. After the first half-turn she made no attempt to disguise her voice, and a man with a much lower opinion of himself than Paul Craddock might have found her manner encouraging. Paul was certainly more than ready to respond. By the time the dance was over and they were sitting out, his manner had become tenderly confidential, and Candida was experiencing a slight sense of reaction. Quite definitely she did not want Paul to propose to her to-night. Ambrose had behaved like a fiend, but she hadn't finished with him yet. And then, quite suddenly, Paul was leaning closer, and saying in a very carefully lowered voice:

"I'm so glad of this opportunity. I was afraid I might have to wait until after supper. I simply had to see you to-night. I didn't think it would be fair to let it all come on you without any warning. Anyhow, I'm afraid, it's bound to be a shock."

Was it a proposal? A *shock*? What on earth did he mean?

She sat up and said, in a voice calculated to discourage sentiment:

"What do you mean? Who's going to have a shock?"

"You are."

"How do you know? Suppose I simply won't?"

Mr. Craddock waved this flippancy away with an earnest gesture.

"I'm afraid it's bound to be a shock. It's about your maid."

"About *Brown*?"

"About your maid. Her name is not Brown."

"No, of course it isn't. If that's your shock, I'm bearing up quite nicely, thank you."

"My dear Candida, I'm only trying to spare you." His voice hinted a tender reproach. "I don't know what you know about the girl, but it's the unpleasant fact that she's a thief. A warrant for her arrest has been issued, and she'll be taken into custody to-morrow."

"Nonsense!" said Miss Long with a good deal of vigour.

"I wish it were. It's most unpleasant for you—I quite see that. And I felt that, at all costs, you must be prepared."

"I don't believe it."

"It's most unfortunately true. She was little Barbara Peterson's nursery governess, and she took a very valuable diamond brooch belonging to my aunt."

"There must be some mistake."

"The brooch was actually found on her. After that she went off with some papers. Sir George thinks she may be unhinged."

"Oh," said Miss Candida Long.

She looked down at the point of a silver shoe, and then quickly up to Paul Craddock's face. He had taken off his mask, and as far as she could see in the dim light, he wore an expression of concern. For some reason this had an irritating effect upon her. She said quite crossly:

"What on earth makes you think that your nursery governess is the same as my maid? Why should she be?"

Paul began to explain patiently:

"The nursery governess was traced to Peddling Corner. As soon as you told me you had picked up a strange girl on the road just beyond, I naturally began to put two and two together."

"People who put two and two together generally finish up with being at sixes and sevens." Candida tossed her head as she spoke.

"My dear Candida, I saw her go downstairs with you this evening. By the way, why did she have a hat on?" The point had only just struck him, and there was alarm in his voice.

Candida felt so cross that she could hardly speak. When Paul Craddock called her "My dear Candida," it roused her worst passions. And if it was true about Brown—"Oh Lord, what fuss Elizabeth'll make!" What on earth did Paul want to rake up all this for? Such a fuss! Going abroad without a maid—*impossible*! And she liked Brown—she liked her awfully.

"Why was she wearing a hat?"

"Because she was going out. Maids do go out, you know."

"Where was she going?"

"Really, Paul, I'm her employer, not her chaperon."

Paul awoke to the fact that he was not being diplomatic.

"Don't be vexed," he said. "I'm dreadfully put out about the whole business. You know I'd do anything I could to save you a moment's annoyance. You know—you must know—exactly what you mean in my life."

"Do I?" said Candida in a very dry voice. "H'm—let's go back and dance."

Mr. Craddock was not sensitive, but it occurred to him that this was not a propitious moment for courtship.

Chapter Twenty-Five

MALLY WAS DANCING again with Ethan Messenger.

"This is the last," she said regretfully. "It's ten minutes to twelve by the clock in the hall and I'm Cinderella—I can't face midnight."

"I thought you were the fairy godmother."

"So did I"—Mally's tone was mournful—"I thought so, but I'm not. I'm just Cinderella's ghost wandering through the palace and bound to disappear when the clock strikes twelve."

"What about the Prince?" said Ethan.

She shook her head; her voice became more mournful still:

"There isn't any Prince in this story—or any happy ending. It's all frightfully modern and up-to-date. Happy endings aren't done. I'm just a ghost who doesn't know where to go. It's all hundreds of years afterwards, and the palace is a ruin, and Cinderella nothing but a little cold wreath of mist."

"I say, *don't!*" said Ethan. Then he laughed. "Do you know, you made me feel quite creepy. I should think you'd be an awfully good actress."

"I am." Mally's voice stopped being mournful and became full of modest pride.

They both laughed.

"I *did* do it awfully well—didn't I? But you know, it's partly true. In three and a half minutes I'm going to vanish away, and you'll never see me again."

"Why on earth not?"

"Because you won't." There was a pause, and then she added, most reprehensibly, "Do you *want* to?" Her voice was very soft; there was a little tremble in it. It might have been due to laughter, or it might have been due to tears.

"Why shouldn't I see you again?" said Ethan.

He was almost sure she was laughing at him—almost, but not quite. The doubt plucked at his heart.

"Why should you?"

"Because I should like to. I've left Peddling Corner, you know. I'm only about four miles away, staying with two of my father's sisters. Of course, I don't know where you're staying—but I don't see why you shouldn't tell me."

Mally laughed. And when she laughed he could have sworn she was on the edge of tears.

"I don't stay anywhere. I run away. And when I can't run any more I sleep in a hay-loft, and a kind person gives me a banana. And then I run away again."

"I say, where *are* you staying? You might tell me. I—I'm not fooling. I'd like to come and see you. There might be something I could do, you know. You can't go on like this."

Before Mally could answer, her arm was touched. She looked over her shoulder and saw a black and silver domino receding.

"Some one wants to speak to me," she said quickly. "Get me out of this crush, will you?"

They came to a standstill by door leading into the hall, and a moment later Candida Long came up with them. She was alone. She spoke rather breathlessly in Mally's ear:

"I've sent Paul for a brooch I didn't drop. Don't wait a minute, but go and get into the car! I'll come."

She melted into the crowd and was gone.

Ethan Messenger had moved a step away when Candida began to whisper. He stood and watched the dancers until he saw her pass by. Then he turned back to Mally. But Mally was gone. There was no rose-red domino by his side or anywhere else in the ballroom. The hall was empty.

As he stood in the doorway looking about him, the big clock on the other side of the hall began to strike. It was midnight, and Mally Lee was gone.

It was quite extraordinarily cold out of doors. Mally ran all the way to the car, and was glad to shut herself in. Her bundle lay on the back seat. She unrolled it, pulled off her domino, and slipped back into the navy jumper and skirt which she had been wearing when she came. She had just changed her shoes and stockings and put on her coat and hat, when there was a sound of running feet and Candida pulled open the door by the driver's seat and jumped in.

"Are you there, Brown? Are you there?"

"Yes. What is it?"

"Get into the front seat by me. I've got to talk to you. But we must get away first. I hope to goodness she starts without a fuss—it's most awfully cold."

The car started up nobly. They ran down the long drive under thickly arching trees and came out upon a perfectly white road. Snow had been falling steadily whilst they danced, and before they had gone half a mile it began to come down again in small, wavering flakes that fell into the glare of the headlights and floated there.

They ran for about two miles, and then Candida slowed down and pulled up by the side of the road.

"What a poisonous night! Look here, I've got to talk to you, but I don't know what to say."

She was bare-headed and her mask had fallen as she ran through the snow to the car.

"What is it?" said Mally.

"I expect you know. If half Paul Craddock says is true, you *must* know."

"I shouldn't think any of it was true." Mally's voice was composed and scornful.

Candida caught her arm and shook it.

"I've known him for three years, and I've known you for about three minutes. I've actually thought of marrying him. Why should I believe that he's telling me lies?"

"I don't know—except that he probably is."

"You don't know what he told me yet."

"I can guess."

"Well?"

Mally sat up very straight. One cold hand pinched the other cold hand very hard.

"He told you I'd stolen a diamond pendant belonging to his aunt. And I don't mind betting he said how distressed Sir George was, and a lovely piece about their not wanting to prosecute if only I'd give back some paper which they pretend I've got, and which I don't know a single thing about."

"But why?"

"I think they're mad—no, I don't. I'll tell you what I do think. I think there's something awfully fishy somewhere. But I don't know what it is—I don't know a bit what it is."

Candida sat with her hands laid loosely on the wheel. She looked round quickly at Mally.

"Paul Craddock told me there was a warrant out for your arrest, and that you'd be arrested to-morrow morning."

Mally did not speak, or make any sound, or look at Candida.

"Oh!" said Candida Long, "Oh, do say something! I don't know what to do—I don't indeed—and you just sit there—and I don't know what to do—I *don't really*. I'd have asked Ambrose to help if he weren't being a perfect fiend. Only I did find out for certain that he cared, so I owe you something for that, because he'd never have said so if I hadn't made him. And I'd like to help you, only I don't know what on earth to do."

Mally began to speak with a little jerk; her mouth felt rather stiff.

"Did he know—did Mr. Craddock know I was there to-night?"

"No, he didn't. He saw you go downstairs with me at Menden, and he fussed to know why you had a hat on. And I told him you had a hat on because you were going out."

"Does he know you've come away?"

"No," said Candida quickly. "And he mustn't know—nobody must. I must get back. That's the horrible part—I must get back, and I don't know what to do with you. You can't stay at Curston, and you can't go to Menden—and where *can* you go at this time of night? You see, I must get back."

"Yes, I see."

Mally sat quite still for a moment. They had come about two miles down the road. It was frightfully difficult to judge distances at night. She didn't think they had passed the turning to Peaslea station, but she wasn't sure—that is, she wasn't quite sure. Anyhow the turning must be quite near, and the station was only half a mile down the lane. She turned to Candida and said:

"It'll be all right—I'll get out here."

"You *can't*!"

Mally laughed.

"Of course I can. Good-by, and thank you most, most awfully. You've been a brick."

"Oh, you can't!"

"I shall be perfectly all right," said Mally firmly.

She pushed open the door beside her, squeezed Candida's arm somewhere up near the shoulder, caught up her bundle, and jumped out. The door shut with a slam. To Candida, in the light, Mally had become just one of the shadows on the snowy road.

She put her hand on the starter and winked away a little stinging rush of tears. Something in her cried and said, "I can't!" and something else never stopped saying, "You must!" She ran into the mouth of a narrow lane and turned.

As she ran back along the way that they had come, the light fell on Mally standing pressed close up against the hedge. All the snow-furred twigs glittered in the dazzle. Mally looked very black against the whiteness; only the rose-red domino, clutched together in a bundle, made a brilliant spot of color against her dark coat.

Chapter Twenty-Six

MALLY STOOD AGAINST the snowy hedge and saw the car go away from her. The white light swept her and was gone. She watched the red tail-light get smaller and smaller until it was like the smallest spark in the world. Then it too was gone and everything was most frightfully dark and still.

She waited for her eyes to get accustomed to the darkness. It was silly of her really to have watched the lights for so long. She shut her eyes for a little, and then opened them again. She looked up and could see nothing but a formless gloom which seemed to move as she looked at it, slipping down upon her in a thick, stinging fall of snow. She looked down, and the snow made a sort of twilight about her feet. It was odd to have the light—if you could call it light—coming from below like that. She could see the hedge against which she was standing, but she could not see the other side of the road, and the continual movement of the falling snow was very confusing.

She had to get to Peaslea station. Well, Candida had turned the car where a lane ran into the road only a few yards away. That would be the lane that led to the station. She had only to walk along it for about half a mile. She stamped her foot in the snow and felt how hard the ground had frozen. "What a mug I am! What a perfectly idiotic mug! Of course the station will be shut!" It was a most sobering and depressing thought.

Mally could not remember exactly when the last train stopped at Peaslea, but it was somewhat short of ten o'clock. It was now between midnight and the half-hour, and the first train in the morning was just before six.

She began to count on her fingers: Half-past one—half-past two—half-past three—half-past four—half-past five. She reached her thumb with dismay. Five hours at the very least before the station would open—five black, icy, snowy hours, from a January midnight to a January dawn. Only it wouldn't be dawn even then.

A horrid panic of cold loneliness came down on her. It was just like the closing of a trap. The minute before, she had been shivering and wondering what on earth she was going to do, but quite free, quite able to think and plan and do: and then with a snap the terror closed on her and shut her in. She spun half round and caught at the hedge, at something, anything that she could touch and hold to. Her bundle dropped in the snow at her feet and her bare hands closed convulsively on sharp thorny twigs with ice that melted and ran between her fingers in a cold trickle. Some of it went down her sleeve. She shivered, let go, and shook the water from her: her left-hand sleeve was wet. She looked for a handkerchief, and could not find one. And all in a minute the trap was open again and the terror gone.

She picked up her bundle, shook the snow from it, and began to walk briskly down the lane. As she walked, she thought what she would do. First she would find the station, and then she would walk to and fro between the station and the road until the early train was due. Of course she might be lucky; there might be a shed or something at the station, shelter of some kind where she could sit for a while and get out of the wind. Her spirits began to rise at the thought. Of course there would be a shed or, at any rate, a truck or something. Even a coal truck would be better than having to face this poisonous wind all night.

She went on walking, and the lane went on being a lane, with fields on either side of it, and little stubbly hedges that had been cut to the bone. After about twenty minutes Mally began to get anxious. There ought to be cottages, and a farm, and Peaslea church, if not now, at least very soon. But still there was only the lane and the hedges.

In another ten minutes she knew that she must have taken the wrong lane; this one was quite evidently not going to arrive at Peaslea. She turned round and began to walk back.

Half an hour later she was still walking, but she had not reached the road. She was in another lane with high banks. It wasn't the lane by which she had come. She stood still, and realized that she had no idea where she was. In the dark she must have got off the road into a branching lane which she had not noticed. She turned again and went back, but with shaken confidence and a complete loss of her sense of direction. She began to feel drowsy. Between these high banks there was not much wind, and only old nursery stories about people going to sleep in the snow and never waking up again saved her from sitting down under the lee of the hedge and falling into a doze.

She must have turned again without knowing it, for presently she was on a wide, flat road with no hedges. The wind drove across it with great gusts; it felt like floods of icy water breaking in waves of cold. There was not a light anywhere, or a sound, except the sound of the wind, and the horrible pale light of the snow, which wasn't light at all but a sort of ghostly darkness.

She went on walking. But she was getting very much confused. Twice she found herself off the highroad on rough, tussocky grass. Then after a long time she was feeling in front of her with her bare right hand, touching something. Her hand went up and down, backwards and forwards. She was touching something that felt familiar; only she was so shaky that she could not tell what it was. There was a queer smell too, queer and strong—the sort of smell that one knew perfectly well when one wasn't asleep. Something sharp pricked her. She drew her hand back, and then put it out again, rousing a little. It was a paling; she was touching a paling. The smell was tar; it was a newly tarred paling. She roused a little more. If there was a paling, perhaps there was a house.

She began to feel along the fence until she came to a gap. She went through the gap with the wind behind her. It seemed to push her on, and she saw a large, vague lumpy blackness blotting out the even pallor of the snow. The wind pushed her and she went on, coming nearer to the blackness with her hand out before her, feeling all the time. Only her hand was so cold that she could not really feel. Suddenly she touched the wall of the house and stood still. Mally must really have known that the blackness was a house, because she was not at all surprised when she touched it. She drew her fingers down over the brick with a sort of stroking movement, and then she began to feel for the door. She thought that the door would be opposite the gap in the fence.

Finding the house had waked her up, and she had begun to think again. A step up into the porch. The door must be just in front of her then. She moved forward, feeling for it, and found the doorpost. She meant to knock on the door until somebody came, and she put out her hand to feel for the knocker. Her hand went on, right through the place where the door ought to be. There wasn't any door.

Chapter Twenty-Seven

MALLY CAUGHT the doorpost and held on to it. Why wasn't there any door? She did wish she could think properly. It had given her a curious sort of shock to put her hand out into that dark emptiness. Then it came to her that the house wasn't finished. That was why there was a gap in the fence; that was why the fence smelled of tar; that was why there was no door.

The wind pushed her, and she went through the empty doorway and felt her way to the wall. It was pitch-dark inside the house. The wall was damp and cold. She felt along it and found a doorway, groped past it, and touched the wall again. It was vaguely in her mind that the wind was blowing in on this side, and that she wanted to get away from the wind.

Keeping to the left-hand wall, she came to a second doorway. Here she turned at right angles and came into the room, still feeling along the wall. When she had taken about half a dozen steps, her foot struck something soft. She stood still at once, not frightened, but puzzled, her frozen thoughts moving very, very slowly.

It was a full minute before she lifted her foot. Then she stooped. There was a pile of sacking lying against the wall. It was the sacking that had felt soft to her foot. She let her bundle drop, and pulled at the sacking. It was heavy and harsh to the touch. She went on pulling rather feebly until she got it back into the corner by the doorway. It came unfolded as she pulled. She put a piece of it on the ground right in the corner and, kneeling on it, pulled all the rest of it up round her and over her. Then, half crouching, half lying, she leaned back against the sacking and the wall and slipped into a strange, deep sleep.

It was many hours before she woke. A dream that she could not remember melted like a mist, and she opened her eyes. The sun was shining right into them, and as she moved and pushed at the heap of sacks, she became quite awake. She got up stiffly and looked about her.

She was in a small square room; the walls of dark, unplastered brick; no door, but the windows were glazed, thank goodness. Each pane had a round white splash in the middle of it, and the sun, very bright and red, shone through the glass and made a level beam which had little dusty motes dancing in it. It was most frightfully nice to see the sun.

She went to the window and looked out. There must have been quite a lot of snow in the night. Well, at any rate, no one would find her footsteps; that was one good thing. It looked as if it might snow again before night. A great bank of fog rose well above the horizon. Where the low sun had cleared the mist, there was a space of purest turquoise; but away to the right there were heavy lead-coloured clouds.

Mally thought it must be about ten o'clock, and dismay took hold of her. The early train from Peaslea had gone without her hours and hours ago. She ought to have gone by it; she ought to have got away before she was missed at Menden. It would be very, very risky to walk to Peaslea now; and yet she must do it. And oh, how ragingly hungry she was!

"It's not the slightest use your being hungry," she began in her severest manner. And then she remembered that she hadn't eaten all Candida's chocolate the night before—no, it wasn't the night before but the night before that, ages and ages and ages ago. She had put half of it in her jumper pocket, and half of it was worth having. She could eat it all too, because as soon as she got to London she could get food—No, she *couldn't*; she wouldn't have any money. She wasn't really sure whether she had enough money to pay her fare.

She put her hand into her coat pocket for her purse. Surely— *surely* she had put it in the right-hand pocket with Barbara's drawings. It wasn't there. She felt the left-hand pocket, and it wasn't there either. She shook her coat, she turned the pockets inside out. She shook herself, and rummaged in her bundle. The purse was gone.

Mally sat down on the new boarded floor, still thick with sawdust and shavings, and said out loud to the damp brick walls, "Oh, Lord, I'm beat!"

The purse must have fallen out in the attic when she changed, or in the car. She was a perfect idiot to have left it in the pocket of a coat which had been turned upside down and inside out and used to roll things up into a bundle with.

"I'm an absolute, first-class, utter, prize, born fool!" said Mally firmly. Then she stuck her chin in the air and laughed. "Thank goodness the chocolate didn't drop out too!" She undid it and divided it into three. "Breakfast—lunch—tea. Something's bound to turn up before the evening, so it's no use glooming."

She ate "breakfast," and put away "lunch" and "tea" in her jumper pockets. Then she went outside, quenched her thirst with snow, washed her face and hands, and dried them with her handkerchief. All the interminable hours of the day stretched before her. She went back into the sunny room, sat down on the pile of sacks, and tried hard to make a plan.

Half an hour later she had not thought of a plan, but she had remembered that there was a cross-word puzzle amongst Barbara's drawings. It would be something to do. Plans won't always come when you try to make them come. But sometimes, if you stop bothering and think of something else, a really good plan just drops down on you ready-made.

Mally pulled out the bundle of papers and unfolded it. The crossword puzzle was at the bottom of the pile. She laid it on the top of the drawings and began to read the clues: "Lady Bird"; "A Swift Curler Of Old Times"; "New Child's Holiday Invention"; "Old Hats for New"; "Hard Amber"... She stared at the words. The person who had made the puzzle must have had a passion for capitals; nearly all the words had capital letters.

There were a lot more clues, and they all looked most frightfully difficult. One, farther on, that caught her eye was "An Elephant's Height In Nowgong." And right across the top of the paper was written, "Heliogabulus was never emperor in Constantinople."

She frowned at the page and turned it so as to get a better light. The sun must have gone behind a cloud; it seemed to have got much darker just in the last ten minutes. The thought of how much darker it had got edged itself into Mally's mind and suddenly had all her attention. She got up and went to the window.

The bank of fog stood no higher than it had done when she awoke. The space of sky above it was a clear thin blue line tinged with green. The sun was gone. She looked, and could not believe her eyes; went on looking, and had to believe them. The sun was really gone. The wind last night—the wind that had pushed her into the house—had been northeast if she had ever felt a northeast wind in her life. This room on the other side of the house must face southwest, and it was the setting, not the rising sun that had waked her. If she was going to get anywhere at all to-day, it behooved her to make a start and at least reach a main road before the dark closed down and she was lost in it as she had been lost last night.

The shock of her discovery braced her. She felt more awake, more alive, better able to think; and the plan that had eluded her when she racked her brains for it came to her now. She couldn't stay here, and she couldn't freeze in the open, and since she had no money, she could not travel by train; she must just find Ethan Messenger and get him to help her. He was staying with aunts four miles from Curston. It wasn't much to go on, but it was all she had. He had said "my father's sisters," so they were probably

Miss Messengers—no one spoke of married aunts like that. Of course four miles from Curston might be four miles in the opposite direction, "in which case I'm done." Well, the first thing was to find some human habitation and just ask for Miss Messenger's house. It was risky, but Mally had come to the place where she was bound to take risks or just sit down and starve with cold and hunger.

She went out into the hall, which had become startling dark, and climbed the ladder which led to the upper story. If there were a light anywhere within sight, she would make for that. She went into every room and looked through every window. Trees, fields, snow; but not a twinkle of kindly light anywhere until she came to the last small room and saw from the window a faint, far spark. She very nearly cried out in her relief.

"Even if it's a policeman's house and he arrests me the very first minute he sets eyes on me, I don't care," said Mally vehemently to herself. "I don't care. Do you hear? I don't *care*. I want to see people, and hear people, and not be alone in this horrible, cold, empty place—*Oh! What's that?*"

It was exactly as if some wicked fairy had been listening and had flung Mally her wish with a horrid, mocking laugh. Mally, half-way between the window and the door of the little upstairs room, heard a heavy, stumbling footstep that came nearer and nearer—a man's footstep—, and then a man's voice, hoarse and unpleasant, calling out. For a moment Mally thought that he was calling to her, and all the dreadful stories she had ever heard in her life came into her mind and paralyzed her with terror. It was only for a moment, because another voice called back.

There were two men. They were both horrible. They used dreadful words and they had dreadful voices. She put her fingers in her ears so as not to hear them, and then took them out again quickly, because if she couldn't hear, she wouldn't be able to tell whether they were coming upstairs or not.

"Thank *goodness*, there aren't any stairs! They sound as if they were drunk. Drunken men won't try and climb ladders. At least"—

Mally gasped—"At least I—I shouldn't think they would. Oh, don't let them—don't let them—don't *let* them!"

She heard their footsteps go into the room where she had been. She tried to remember whether she had left anything there. The papers had gone back into her pocket. She had left her bundle just by the foot of the ladder. They'd find it in a minute if they looked.

"Don't let them look. Please, *please* don't let them look. It's dark—it's getting darker every minute. They needn't see it—they really, really needn't see it. Oh, *please* don't let them!"

Mally did not say these things out loud, but she said them very fervently in her own mind. She stood with her hands clenched under her chin, and her lips moved stiffly without making any sound. She could hear a match struck. She could hear the sacks being dragged about. She could hear the men's voices, but not what they were saying. The smell of coarse tobacco floated up to her.

After a while the tension relaxed. Mally was a very resilient creature. She passed quickly from an extremity of terror lest the men should come upstairs to a cheerful conviction that they would not come upstairs. She gave herself a little shake and tiptoed back to the window from which she could see that one friendly spark of light. Presently the men would go to sleep, and she would crawl down the ladder and get away. Meanwhile, lunch-time and tea-time both being past, she ate all the rest of her chocolate and felt better.

It was a long, long, weary wait. The last faint gleams of daylight followed the sun, and a very black darkness came down upon the dusk and blotted it out. It got colder and colder and colder. The men downstairs talked intermittently. As a matter of fact, they were playing cards by the light of a filched candle-end, though Mally was not to know that. Presently they quarrelled, and Mally felt terror come leaping back at the sound of their raucous shouts.

At long, long last there was silence.

Chapter Twenty-Eight

WHILST MALLY WAS sleeping the dark morning hours away on a pile of sacks in the back room of an empty house, Ethan Messenger was having breakfast with the younger of his two aunts.

Some fifty-five years before, Ethan's grandmother, enraptured with her twin daughters, had cast about her for names which should express her emotions. She considered her ultimate choice of Serena and Angela "very sweet indeed." Angel Messenger; Serene Messenger—what could be more beautiful and inspiring? Most of her friends and relatives made appropriate response with, "What, indeed?" Only her mother-in-law, a tough old lady who would have liked one at least of the children to be named Martha after herself, had something unpleasant to say:

"Angela—Serena. H'm, my dear Annie, the Messenger women are apt to be plain, and I'd advise you to give the girls good plain names that won't shame them. If Martha's good enough for me, and Annie for you, I should have thought it might be good enough for the next generation."

Ethan's grandmother was a gentle creature and an obstinate. She said nothing, but she pressed her lips together; and at the font the babies received the names which she had meant them to receive.

Angela and Serena were plain babies, plain children, plain young girls. Now, at fifty-five, they were no plainer than a great many other people, and every one they knew had got used to their names.

On this snowy morning Miss Serena had gone to town, and Miss Angela was giving Ethan his breakfast and hearing in full detail all about last night's ball at Curston.

"It must have been quite a sight. Of course, dear boy, Lady Mooring asked us both; though I suppose she knew that we should not come. At least she would have known that Serena would not come. No one could possibly expect your Aunt Serena to have time for balls—I'm sure the number of committee meetings she attends is quite bewildering. But I sometimes think that perhaps it was rather a mistake—for me, I mean, to give up society in the way I did."

Ethan looked kindly at his little aunt. She was small, and peaked of feature, with a good deal of wispy hair that had once been monotonously flaxen and was now a yellowish grey. The tip of her nose was always a little pink, and she had a habit of shutting first one eye and then the other, in order to look sideways at it, so that she might see just how pink it was. If it was very pink, she felt depressed; if the light flattered it, her spirits rose and she was capable of mild coquetry. Her small grey eyes were kind, and her smile, when not worried, very sweet indeed.

"Why did you give up society?" asked Ethan.

"Oh, I don't know. Serena didn't care for it. But then, of course, she has all those committees. I can't think how she remembers which is which—but she's so strong-minded. I did like going out. Only there was the war, and of course we're not as well off as we used to be."

"What committee is it to-day?"

"My dear boy, I'm not sure. I think it's the N.Z.U.K., or else the P.S.T.W.—or perhaps both. Yes, I think she's going to two at least, because it's the second one that may make her miss the last train, in which case Margaret Gooding will put her up. It's so tiresome all our trains being so early. But if she isn't in by half-past ten, I always know she isn't coming. It used to worry me, but I've got accustomed to it. Your Aunt Serena is so strong-minded."

"Oh, but Aunt Angel, I didn't know you were going to be all by yourself to-night, or I wouldn't have said I'd dine with the Holmeses. Look here, let me ring Mrs. Holmes up. She'd be delighted to have you too—I'm sure she would."

Miss Angela flushed.

"Dear boy! Oh, no—I couldn't. Why, I haven't got a dress I can dine out in."

Ethan grinned.

"Mrs. Holmes wouldn't know what you had on. They all rag her about her own clothes, and she only laughs."

Miss Angela looked at the tip of her nose, and brightened.

"I was at her wedding," she said in a pleased, reminiscent voice. "She was a fine, fresh-coloured girl, but no beauty. And if you'll believe me, she came up the aisle with her wreath crooked and her veil all over one shoulder. Well, it's turned out very happily in spite of Mr. Holmes being twenty years older and never going anywhere—like me."

"Come to the Holmeses."

"No, no, I'd rather not. I feel it's rather dreadful of me, but in a way—if you understand what I mean—I quite enjoy an evening to myself. Serena's so political, you know, and she likes me to try and keep up with her. And of course I can't play the piano when she's busy with her reports. And she doesn't really approve of novels. So to-night I thought I'd go through all my old songs. And I've got a novel—it's—it's rather modern, I'm afraid, and—" Miss Angela hesitated and lowered her voice. "My dear boy, now I wonder—I mean there's something I should like to ask you."

Ethan had visions of being asked to explain the "modern" novel. He blenched. But Miss Angela went on hurriedly:

"You go about so much, I thought I could ask you. It—it's rather *delicate* of course."

He wondered what on earth was coming.

"You see, I can't ask Serena, and I don't like to ask any one else; but I thought that you—" She dropped her voice still lower. "It's about my hair."

"Your hair?"

"S'sh! Grace doesn't listen at doors, but she might be passing."

"But—your hair?"

"S'sh. Yes, *whether I should shingle it.*" This in the very smallest possible whisper. "Oh, dear boy, what d'you think? Could I?"

"I don't see why not."

Ethan looked at the wispy ends of hair, the jutting hairpins, and tried to picture Aunt Angel with a smooth, neat head, and some little curls over her ears. (Miss Mally Lee wore her hair that way.)

"I don't see why not," he repeated, and was rewarded with a rapturous smile.

"Don't you let Aunt Serena bully you. You have it off if you want to. Look here, I'll tell you what, you go and pin it up in what's-his-names at the sides, and we'll see what it looks like. And if you like it, I'll run you into Guildford to-morrow, and you shall have it off."

"Oh, dear boy! Oh, I couldn't!" Miss Angela was very much flushed. She stole a look at her nose, and felt discouraged. "Oh, no, I couldn't really."

Ethan supplied suitable encouragement. He spent the entire day in being nice to his Aunt Angel, of whom he was really very fond. They walked in the snow, and Miss Angela found occasion to visit most of the shops. There was a time-honoured formula to which Ethan was so used that it no longer made him smile: "My dear boy, I think I really must go in here—if you wouldn't mind too much." And once in, a pleasant interchange of compliments would follow: "I see you've got your nephew with you again, miss—and I hope in good health," whereupon Miss Angela would become pleasantly fluttered and turn to Ethan with a "Mrs. Jones, whom you will remember," or "Miss Wright, whom I'm sure you haven't forgotten."

Once, Miss Serena, loud-voiced and aggressive, had taken it upon herself to tell her sister roundly that no young man could be expected to put up with being dragged round all the shops in a one-horse place, tied to an old maid's apron-strings. Miss Angela looked struck to the heart, and Ethan had a really satisfying row with his Aunt Serena.

After tea all the old songs were produced, and he listened to Miss Angela enjoying herself very much in a faint, small voice over such classics as "Whisper and I shall hear," "Pray, Sweet, for me," and "The Lost Chord." He even joined in the refrains, deriving a special pleasure from "Whisper, and I shall hear," delivered in a stentorian roar which the lady of the ballad could certainly not have avoided hearing.

When he had departed for dinner at Menden, Miss Angela felt that she had the most delightful day to look back upon and a pleasant evening still in store. Her conscience pricked her a little as she reflected that the house did seem more peaceful when Serena wasn't there, and she reminded herself instantly of how clever, how energetic, and how admirable in every way Serena really was.

She had her supper on a tray by the drawing-room fire, a thing which always made her feel rather dissipated, and then she read the "modern" novel until close on ten o'clock, when she turned the lamp down and went up to her room. Grace had retired half an hour ago, and somehow Miss Angela never cared to stay alone on the ground floor for very long.

She went up to her room, put on a dressing-gown, and began to try experiments with her hair, pinning it so as to get the effect of its being cut short. Presently she looked at her watch. Serena could not be coming back, or she would have been here by now.

With trembling fingers Miss Angela took from the very back of her drawer an aged pair of curling tongs and held them over the lamp. They got very black, and they did not get very hot; but in the end she succeeded in curling the side bits of her hair and peered timidly at the result. As she stood there, her eyes bright and rather alarmed, she bore an extraordinary resemblance to a mouse just peeping from a hole, its whiskers all a-tremble lest the cat should be about.

Miss Angela touched the little grey curls with a nervous finger. Did they make her nose look pinker, or did they not? Was it really so very pink? She shut her left eye and looked sideways at it with her right. It did seem pink—yes, it really did. And perhaps the curls were too juvenile. She opened the left eye and shut the right one. They might be juvenile, but she did think that they were becoming. She touched the curls again, a little more hopefully this time; and as she did so, she heard the click of the gate, and footsteps coming slowly up to the front door. Her heart gave a terrified jump.

"Serena! Oh, dear—and my hair like this! Oh *dear*!"

She ran to the door and locked it, then to the window and raised the sash with trembling hands.

Serena was knocking. Miss Angela leaned from the window and called to her in a soft, breathless voice:

"The key is under the mat. And there's coffee on the stove, and plenty of hot water if you want a bath. The dear boy's not in yet. I—I won't come down. Good-night, dear."

She shut the window.

Chapter Twenty-Nine

MALLY HAD LOST COUNT of time; she had no idea how long it was since she had slipped down the ladder and fled, clasping her bundle, from the dark, closed-in place which was no longer a shelter. The sound of horrible heavy breathing seemed to follow her, and she ran from it until she pulled up gasping and could run no more.

It was after that she lost count of time. There was a cottage where a woman talked to her from the window, but wouldn't open the door. It was the woman who told her that there were two Miss Messengers living in Weyford, and that Weyford was "just a piece along the road."

It was a long piece, or else she had missed her way. She began to have the feeling that she was being blown along by the wind like a leaf, and that presently, like a leaf, she would be all dry and withered and brown. Once she slipped into something like a dream, and woke from it to find herself leaning up against a thorny hedge.

It was the pricking of the thorns that waked her, and it was soon after that she met a vaguely strolling couple with arms entwined. They told her that the Miss Messengers' house was right in Weyford High Street—"third house after you pass the church, and you can't miss it, because it stands back from the road like."

Mally felt curiously comforted by the confident way in which the young man asserted that she could not miss the house. It was the third house after the church, on the left. It had a white gate. She couldn't miss it. She went on saying these things over and over to herself as she struggled along that last half-mile into Weyford. She went on because she had to go on—and for other reasons.

Presently the darkness was pricked with little points of light. If Mally had still been capable of emotion, the first lamp-post in

Weyford would have brought tears to her eyes. She found herself leaning against it, touching it almost incredulously. And standing there, she could see, just ahead, the square, black tower of Weyford Church. Three doors beyond the church a white gate. She couldn't miss it. She went on, and came very slowly past the church, holding to the low stone wall which shut it in.

Where the wall ended there was a lane, and then a square house, black with ivy, and next to it a little dumpy, low cottage with shuttered windows flush with the pavement. Mally went past blind shutters, and saw a white gate and a flagged path that ran back to a little white house. "It stands back from the road—you can't miss it." She hadn't missed it.

She lifted the latch and went up the flagged path to the front door. It was all like the end of a dream. The house was to be found, and she had found it. Nothing felt real except the cold—and it was very cold.

She put up her hand and knocked on the door, and immediately there was a sound overhead. A window opened above her on the left, and a fluttered, anxious voice called down to her in a whisper:

"The key is under the mat. And there's coffee on the stove, and plenty of hot water if you want a bath. The dear boy's not in yet. I—I won't come down. Good-night, dear."

The window was shut.

Mally stood leaning against the door. Her hand had slipped from the ice-cold knocker to the smooth painted panel below it. It rested there, open, all her weight upon it. She felt very odd, very detached, as if this were happening to somebody else, some one in a fairy tale. It wasn't Cinderella now, but Red Riding-hood. "Lift up the latch and the bobbin will fall"—yes, that was how it went—"Lift up the latch and the bobbin will fall"—"The key is under the mat."

She stooped down, turned up the mat, and picked up the key. It moved in the lock without a sound. The door swung in, and Mally came into a little square hall lighted by an oil-lamp hung from the ceiling by a brass chain. She shut the door, and felt a blessed warmth and stillness. On the left a half-open door showed a dimly lighted room. On the right there was an oak chest on which were set two bedroom candlesticks. The passage ran right through the house, with the stairs going up on the left beyond the half-lit room.

Mally put down her bundle and lighted one of the candles. The voice had said "coffee on the stove." She went down the passage and found the kitchen at the end of it, neat as a new pin and warm with a warmth which she had almost forgotten. The fire was not quite out, and the coffee was in a double saucepan on the hot-plate. At one end of the kitchen table there was a tray with a home-made cake, two cups, an *egg* on a plate, and a spirit-lamp on which stood a saucepan half full of water. It was exactly like the best fairy tales.

She boiled the egg, and discovered brown bread and butter between two plates. She boiled the coffee, and drank two large, steaming cups of it. When she had finished the egg and bread and butter, she ate about half of the home-made cake. It was one of the nice damp sort, with little bits of ginger in it, and very fat sultanas.

All this time the house was as still as any house could be—still, not with the dead, uncanny stillness that makes you wish for any sound, however dreadful, but peacefully, gently, sleepily still, as a virtuous house should be at such an hour. Grace in her attic-room slept as she was accustomed to sleep, the immovable, dreamless sleep that no sound would penetrate until her alarm went off at half-past six. Miss Angela had made haste to put out the light and cover the incriminating curls with the bedclothes. She had not unlocked her door. She hoped that she would be asleep when Serena came upstairs. She hoped that it would not be very wicked if she pretended to be asleep. She began to think about her curls and her nose, and slipped insensibly into a dream.

Mally found the bathroom half-way up the stairs. "Plenty of hot water if you want a bath"—how delicious that sounded! She took a long, long time over that bath, and in the end only left it because she was afraid of going to sleep. She put on the clean clothes she had brought from Curston, and then looked with repugnance at her dark jumper and skirt. Not for any one in this world would she go out again that night. She put on her rose-red domino and went on round the turn of the stairs, walking very softly in her gold and silver slippers.

The first door was on her right. This was the room from which the voice had spoken. She went past it, holding her candle with a steady hand. She was past caring about anything. She opened the next door an inch at a time and looked in. There was no one there; but the bed was turned down, with a crimson eiderdown lying folded at the foot of it.

Mally made a step forward and saw a suit-case. It was a brown leather suit-case, and it had the initials E. M. stamped on it in black. She looked across at the dressing-table and saw a man's brushes, a safety-razor. She made a snatch at the crimson eiderdown, whisked it over her arm, and fled noiselessly down the stairs.

The E. M. stood for Ethan Messenger—and Ethan Messenger was the "dear boy" who hadn't come in yet.

"Ethan is the 'dear boy'; but who in all the world am I?" said Mally as she came to a standstill in the hall. She put the key back under the mat, rolled up the things she had taken off, and brought them down from the bathroom so as to be handy in case she had to run away again—"But not tonight—*nothing* will induce me to run anywhere to-night."

She went into the room on the left of the hall door, and found a lamp turned low and the remnants of a fire. The room was a drawing-room, with prim, light chintzes on the chairs and a rose-patterned carpet on the floor. There was a piano. There was a glass-fronted cupboard with old china in it. There was a white woolly sheepskin mat on the hearth.

Mally put two bits of coal on the fire without so much as a tremor of conscience. Then she curled herself up in the largest chair and went fast asleep under the comforting folds of the crimson eiderdown.

Chapter Thirty

ETHAN MESSENGER came home from Menden in a rather preoccupied mood. It was just on the hither side of midnight and as cold as the wind could make it. It had been a jolly evening—in some ways. He liked Mrs. Holmes and he liked Janet Elliot; but it was not of either Janet or Elizabeth that he was thinking as he drove through the icy lanes. His mind was entirely taken up with Candida Long, whom he had met for the first time that evening. Was it the first time? That was the question which he debated.

The first sound of Candida's voice had called up a vivid picture of the ballroom at Curston. He was sure, or he was almost sure, that it was Candida who had touched Mally on the arm just before the clock struck twelve. He tried very hard to piece his disjointed scraps of knowledge together.

Item one:—Mally had disappeared.

Item two:—Miss Long had meant to cross to France to-day, and had put off going because she said she couldn't travel without a maid.

Item three:—Some one—was it Janet?—had said that Candida's maid had vanished into the blue whilst they were all at Curston.

Item four:—Willie Elliot had begun to say something about Paul Craddock.

Item five:—Elizabeth Holmes had said "Hush," and changed the subject in an extremely masterful manner.

It was all extremely disjointed. Candida Long—Mally Lee—Where *was* Mally Lee? He thought that he would like to see Candida Long again, and alone. Vague plans for doing so floated through his mind. They were still unformulated when he ran his car into a vacant stall in the Vicar's stable and, having locked the door on it, came past the church to the house with the white gate.

He took the key from under the mat, opened the door, and passed, as Mally had done, into the square lighted hall. On the chest to his right stood two bedroom candlesticks. But instead of being arranged neatly side by side, one of them stood on the very edge of the chest, and the candle in it had burned right down. On his left the drawing-room door stood ajar. He pushed it a little wider and saw, between the firelight and the turned-down lamp, Mally Lee lying very fast asleep in his Aunt Serena's large armchair.

Ethan stood on the threshold and experienced the most extraordinary sensations. He felt exactly as if some one had hit him. That was the first of it. Then, as he braced himself, there came incredulity, conviction, and an extraordinary feeling of pleasurable relief.

The fire burned brighter than the lamp. Mally lay curled up with her head on her arm. Her short, tossed hair was still damp; it looked very dark against the light-coloured chintz. She had pushed down the crimson eiderdown, and he saw that she was wearing the rose-red domino she had worn at Curston. His heart contracted. Good Lord! She hadn't been wandering about like that ever since!

He came a step inside the door, staring at her with horrified eyes. She was most awfully white; there were blue smudges under her eyes. She looked like a child.

He came nearer, and as he moved, Mally began to dream. Her mind had been quite still, quite empty; but there came into it now the black picture of the house from which she had fled. She was upstairs again in the dead dark, groping her way to the ladder, whilst from below there came up to her the sound of heavy breathing and the sound of stumbling feet. A wave of the utmost terror broke on her. The men were coming—they would find her. They were coming up the ladder—and they would find her. She couldn't get away. She gave a very little, piteous cry and began to whisper in her sleep.

Ethan saw her shiver and start as the cold wave struck her. Her lips parted over stumbling, broken words: "Don't let them. No—no—*no*!" She shuddered and threw out her hand. "No—no—don't let them come! *Don't* let them!" Her voice broke in a frightened sob.

Ethan made a stride towards the lamp. His heart was wrung. If he turned up the light, it ought to wake her. She ought to be waked.

He heard her cry out behind him, and turned vigorously at the screw of the lamp with instant, horrifying effect. The flame shot up, making everything look unnaturally large, and then died suddenly, utterly, completely, leaving the room in a darkness which seemed deeper than it really was. A coal had fallen in the fire, and the flame had died there too.

Mally woke with a gasp to a black room and the sound of some one moving behind her in the blackness. The soft, smothering folds of the eiderdown were across her knees. She thought she was in a drift of snow. She thought it was holding her down. She thought she was in the dark house of her dreams. She cried out, choking, and sprang up, stumbling over the eiderdown. She put out her hands to save herself and pitched forward against Ethan.

There was an awful, endless moment, in which he held her, and all the horror in the world seemed to come crashing down. Then he said, "Mally! Mally, darling! Oh, for the Lord's sake, don't! Mally—it's only me."

Mally caught at him with both hands and began to be shaken with a flood of tears. She cried away the fear, the cold, and the loneliness. She cried away her courage and she cried away her pride. She was five years old again, crying in the dark and clinging to the strong, safe arms that held her tight.

Ethan let her cry. At intervals he said, "Mally!" or, "Poor little kid!"

She felt so small in his arms, so light, so shaken, such a little, frightened thing.

"It's only me. You're quite safe. Mally, darling, it's only Ethan. Don't cry so!"

"Ethan—Ethan—Ethan!" She said his name on a whisper of sobbing breath.

"It's all right, Mally, it's all right."

"Don't let them—don't let them come! Oh, please don't let them come!"

"There's no one here. I've got you. You're quite safe."

He put his face down to hers, comforting her, very much as he would have comforted little Bunty Lennox; and for a moment Mally clung to him and let herself be comforted. Then, with extraordinary suddenness, she pushed him away and said in a choking voice:

"Oh—oh—I hate you! Go away! I haven't got a handkerchief!"

Ethan was staggered.

"I—I'm sorry."

"You're not—you know you're not!"

"I'm *frightfully* sorry. I meant to turn the light up, but it went out. I—I must have given you an awful fright. Mally, don't cry any more."

"I—I'm not c-crying." The last word ended in a shuddering sob.

"I'll light the lamp. And—and—here's a handkerchief. Where have you got to?"

The handkerchief was snatched from his extended hand, and by the time that he had lighted the lamp and turned the wick—the right way this time—Mally had made some progress towards recovering her self-control. She was sitting on the arm of the big chair, her domino clutched about her, Ethan's handkerchief on her lap.

"You frightened me dreadfully. You frightened me so that I didn't know what I was doing."

She looked at him accusingly and dabbed her eyes very hard.

"I'm most dreadfully sorry. I was a perfect fool."

"Yes, you *were*. I didn't know what I was doing. I thought I was back in that horrible house. And the men—the men—" She put out her hand with a groping gesture and turned painfully white.

Ethan took the hand very gently. The little cold fingers clung to his.

"What men, Mally?"

"Tramps." Her teeth chattered. "Dreadful! I thought they'd got up." She looked at him strangely. "You don't know. It was a house—it wasn't finished—I went in to get out of the wind."

He held her hand tight.

"When?"

"A long time ago. It was dark, and the wind was so cold. I found some sacks, and I went to sleep. And when I woke up, I thought it was morning. But it wasn't. The sun was going down, and it got dark. And then the men came."

She had caught his wrist with her other hand and he could feel her shaking.

"Mally! They didn't hurt you?"

She shook her head.

"They didn't find me. There were no stairs in the house. There was a ladder—I went up it. Then the men came, and I couldn't come down."

He bent and kissed her hands.

"You're quite safe. You're quite, *quite* safe."

Mally caught her breath.

"I dreamed that I was back in the house. And then I woke up, and I heard you, and—and *of course* I thought it was those horrible men."

"But, Mally, how did you get here? You haven't been wandering about ever since night before last in those flimsy things?"

Mally pulled her hands away.

"Yes, I have. I had a coat and a j-jumper suit. I ran away."

"When the clock struck twelve. Mally, why did you?"

"Because I *had* to. Candida Long helped me. She's a brick. She told me I was going to be arrested in the morning, and she got me away from the ball."

"And then?"

"I walked about, and I lost myself, and I came to that horrible house."

"And after that?"

"I remembered about your aunts, and I crawled down the ladder when the men were asleep. And when I'd walked for weeks and weeks and weeks, I came here. And I knocked on the door, and some one put their head out of the window and said, 'Lift up the latch and the bobbin will fall.'"

The corner of Mally's little pale mouth twitched very slightly; her eyes remained fixed on Ethan's face in a mournfully accusing stare. He began to have a very proper feeling that in some unexplained way all these things that had happened to Mally were his fault.

She gave a little nod.

"So I came in and lit somebody else's candle, and had somebody else's supper and somebody else's bath. They were lovely!"

This time a quite definite dimple showed for an instant. Between the look in Mally's eyes and the quiver of Mally's lips something happened to Ethan. He said, "Oh, Mally!" and he kissed her.

It was entirely indefensible; and if for an instant Mally did not draw back, it was, of course, only because she was so completely taken by surprise. She said "Oh!" and she would, no doubt, have said a great deal more if somebody else had not said "Oh!" too.

This second "Oh!" was a very faint one, but at the sound of it Ethan swung round, and Mally slid down from the arm of the chair. They both looked at the door. It had been pushed wide open, and on the threshold stood Miss Angela Messenger in a pink flannel dressing-gown with a scalloped edge. The new grey curls bobbed unregarded on either side of her horrified little face. The tip of her nose was as pink as her dressing-gown. She said in a little dry voice.

"My *dear* boy! My dear *boy!*"

Chapter Thirty-One

SHEER COLD RAGE drove every vestige of colour from Mally's cheeks. She stiffened her neck, stuck her chin in the air, and looked at Ethan Messenger. If she had been angry a little sooner, she would not have been so angry now. She looked at him, and waited. If he failed now, she would never forgive him or herself.

Ethan took his Aunt Angel by the pink flannel sleeve and thanked Heaven that she was not his Aunt Serena.

"Aunt Angel—" His voice achieved a creditable firmness and loudness—"Aunt Angel, this is Miss Lee—Miss Mally Lee. She lost her way in the snow, and—and I'm afraid I frightened her."

"Idiot!" said Mally to herself. She looked at Miss Angela, because she felt that if she looked at Ethan any longer, she would begin to tell him exactly what she thought of the way in which he had behaved.

"In the snow? My dear boy—my dear Miss Lee—how dreadful! Really lost?" She felt bewildered and as if she did not know what she was saying.

"Absolutely," said Ethan.

"Oh, my dear!" She turned to Mally. "In those clothes? Are you frozen?"

Mally's chin came down a little. The concern in Miss Angela's voice was nice. Miss Angela was nice; she was kind. A warm friendly feeling melted away the angry pride that had stiffened her. She took a step forward and put an impulsive hand on the other pink flannel sleeve.

"You won't be angry—will you? I *was* lost—*really*. And it was so dark and so cold. And when you said, 'L-lift up the latch and the b-bobbin will fall,' I just came in, and I took the egg, and the bread and butter, and the coffee, and—and thank you so very much for them. You won't be angry—will you?"

Miss Angela became more bewildered every moment. Ethan on one side of her, and this appealing creature on the other—and a latch—and a bobbin—and coffee, and egg, and bread and butter.

"My dear, of course not—I mean of course—no, of course *not*—I mean—What was that about a bobbin and a latch, my dear? Did you say, 'Lift up the latch and the bobbin will fall'? It—it sounds like a fairy tale."

Ethan had his arm about her. He tried to catch Mally's eye, but she was looking down at the pink flannel sleeve and stroking it.

"Yes—*doesn't* it? Dear Miss Messenger, it was dreadful of me. But you're too kind to be angry. The egg and the coffee were lovely. I'd forgotten what things to eat tasted like. And I haven't told you the very worst. I did have a bath too, because you know you said, 'There's lots of hot water if you want a bath.'"

A very faint light began to break upon Miss Angela. She turned to Ethan.

"Where's Serena? Oh dear! I thought it was Serena. Hasn't she come at all?"

"I don't know. Has she, Mally?"

"It was me," said Mally. "It wasn't any one else—it was only me. I—I couldn't help it when she said about the coffee and the bath." To her horror, the tears began to run down her cheeks again. "I—I—I—" She caught at Miss Angela's arm with shaking hands. "Oh, make him go away! Do—do make him go away!"

Here was something that Miss Angela could understand very well. "Poor child—quite overwrought," she said to herself; and then, aloud, "Poor *child*! Dear boy, I think you'd better—Yes, yes, my dear, he's going. Sit down and dry your eyes. There, there, now, it is really quite all right—you are just overdone. No, no one's angry. And you shall have my sister's room. And when you've had a good sleep, you'll feel a great deal better, poor child."

Mally found herself crying on Miss Angela's shoulder, quite gently and enjoyably. And presently Miss Angela was tucking her up in Miss Serena's bed.

"The sheets were clean this morning. And now, my dear, you must just go to sleep and forget all about everything. And Grace shall bring you a nice cup of tea in the morning."

"'M," said Mally, very, very sleepily. She snuggled her head down into the pillow, and felt Miss Angela's hand just touch her hair. With a little drowsy movement she turned so as to rub her cheek against it; and almost as she did so, she fell asleep.

Miss Angela looked over the banisters, saw that the light was still on in the hall, and went down. She was in a flutter of importance, interest, and romance. A much-indulged conscience strove to cast a cloud over this mood by a sharply pricking assertion that it was very wicked indeed to feel that dear Serena's absence was a thing for which to be profoundly grateful.

She found Ethan in the drawing-room.

"Well, dear boy, she's gone to sleep, and—and—you won't think me inquisitive, but I'm afraid I don't really understand how she came to lose her way or—or anything. And what made her think of coming here? Are you—my dear boy, are you engaged?" Miss Angela was plainly palpitating with curiosity.

"Oh, Lord! She *did* see me kiss her!" thought Ethan. He groaned inwardly. In Miss Angela's romantic world only engaged couples kissed one another.

"We're not engaged," he said rather gruffly. Then he ran his fingers through his hair. "I'd no business to kiss her. She'll probably never forgive me. I—she—well, I don't suppose I could ever make you understand how it was."

Miss Angela put her head on one side. She looked like a brightly intelligent but rather timid bird.

"My dear boy, but I think I do understand. I—I wanted to kiss her myself. I—I did kiss her. There's something extraordinarily engaging about the way she looks at you. Don't you think so?"

Ethan thought there was; but he didn't say so. He was wondering whether he had kissed Mally because she looked at him through her eyelashes, or because of the way in which the corners of her mouth turned up. He told his Aunt Angela that it was time they were both in bed.

Mally slept till ten o'clock next day. She awoke with a start to the unfamiliar room, with its old bow-fronted chest of drawers, heavy mahogany wardrobe, and dark-blue curtains. For a moment she wondered where she was. And then she remembered. It was like remembering a dream. She had slept very deeply, and everything that had happened to her on the farther side of that deep sleep felt strange and unreal. She had wandered in the snow. She had been most dreadfully frightened. She had come to a fairy-tale house in the dark. Ethan Messenger had kissed her.

Mally sat up and tossed the hair out of her eyes. She was awake; she was quite awake. She ought to be boiling with rage. Why wasn't she? When Paul Craddock kissed her—or tried to kiss her—she had boiled furiously. Why wasn't she boiling now? "How dared he? I *will* be angry—I *am* angry—I—I'm furious," said Mally. "I *am*."

She began to think of what she ought to have said. "Only there wasn't time to say anything. And anyhow, I was too sleepy. That's why it was so awfully mean of him—the wretch!"

At this moment the door was opened very softly and slowly. Miss Angela peeped round it.

"Oh, my dear—you're awake!"

Mally nodded.

"I've had such a lovely, lovely sleep."

Miss Angela ran away.

"Grace! Grace! Miss Lee's ready for her breakfast!"

Then she came running back.

"You slept so peacefully that I couldn't wake you. Do you like eggs? Grace is boiling you an egg. And I thought tea, not coffee—and some toast and marmalade, and a banana."

Mally blew her three kisses very quickly and lightly.

"Scrumptious!" she said.

"And when you've had your breakfast"—Miss Angela was a little flustered by the kisses—"Ethan wants to see you—I mean when you're dressed. And Grace is lighting the drawing-room fire, and—in fact—I told him I'd give you his message and say he wanted to see you most particularly."

Mally reminded herself that she was very angry indeed with Ethan Messenger.

Miss Angela went on talking.

"This is my sister Serena's room, and I just wanted to say how pleased I should be if you could stay until to-morrow. Of course I don't know what your plans are; but Serena has just telephoned to say she won't be back to-day. She missed her train last night, and as she had to stay the night in town, she thought she would make it two nights and go to a lecture on—let me see—is there such a word as incidence, my dear?"

"I expect so."

"Well, then, that was it—the incidence of taxation in—in—well, my dear, I'm not quite sure where. One of those new countries. Yugo-Slovakia? No, that doesn't sound quite right. I got a geography prize when I was at school, but none of it seems to be any good to one now. So restless! I mean one had hardly got accustomed to saying Petrograd instead of St. Petersburg, when they started calling it something else. None of the names seem to be the same as they were when I was a girl."

Mally had her breakfast to the accompaniment of a pleasantly continuous ripple of conversation. By the time she had reached the banana, Miss Angela was earnestly asking her advice as to shingling. She had brushed out the grey curls—"I don't know if you noticed them last night, my dear. No, of course not"—and wore her hair in its accustomed tight but straggly braid.

"Oh, I did notice them—of course I did—I *loved* them. You *must* have darling little corkscrews. I adore them."

Miss Angela looked swiftly at her nose, and found it pale. She decided that Mally was a very engaging girl—very, very engaging—and that *of course* the dear boy was in love with her.

Mally came into the drawing-room and found Mr. Ethan Messenger picking out the tune of "Sing Me to Sleep" with one finger. He was frowning horribly at the old yellow piano-keys, and the whole effect was mournful in the extreme.

"So he ought to be mournful," said Mally to herself. "I'm frightfully angry with him."

She advanced with cold dignity, and Ethan sprang up.

"Oh, I say, are you all right? Did you sleep all right?"

She inclined her head very slightly.

"Yes, thank you." The ice in her voice very sensibly reduced the temperature of the room.

Ethan gazed at her in dismay. She was angry, she was horribly angry. He had put his foot into it like anything. She would probably never forgive him. Oh, Lord! How funny she looked when she stuck her chin in the air and wrinkled her little nose like that—how funny, and how dear! A curious warm feeling blotted out his dismay. And, quite suddenly, an odd thing happened.

We go through the world with an impalpable something which separates us one from the other. Once in a while this unseen wall of separation melts and is not; thought, feeling, consciousness, can pass unhindered, can pass and blend.

Ethan looked at Mally playing at icy dignity—and this strange thing happened to him. The barrier went down, and nothing would ever put it up again. She wasn't some one whom he had offended, some one on whom he would like to make a good impression; she was just his funny little dear—his little Mally—his. The most extraordinary part of the whole thing was that it all felt quite natural. There was no shock, no disturbance; it was as easy and natural as breathing.

With commendable self-control Ethan kept his new and astonishing feelings to himself. He said, "Er," and then stuck, whereupon Mally felt a most dreadful desire to laugh. He saw her eyelashes flicker, and pulled himself together with what was really a very creditable effort. He pushed forward a chair and said in quite a natural voice:

"Let's sit down and talk. Do you mind? I think we ought to get things straightened out a bit."

Chapter Thirty-Two

MALLY LOOKED AT the chair and shook her head.

"What do you want to talk about?"

"You," said Ethan.

"Why?"

"Why? Because I think it's about time some one did talk about you. I think it's about time something was done. You can't go on running away, and not having anything to eat, and losing yourself in the snow."

"Why can't I?"

"Well, you can if you like. But do you really want to? Do you?"

Mally looked at Ethan, and her lashes flickered again. There was something different about him, something high-handed and impenitent. Quite suddenly her mood changed, melted. He was *friendly*. She wanted some one to be friendly—she *did*. She gave a little nod and said, in tones of modest pride.

"There's a warrant out for my arrest."

"Nonsense!"

"There is. That horrible Paul Craddock told Candida Long."

"What on earth for? Look here, Mally, you must tell me all about it. That is, you must tell some one, and—and—"

"I don't mind telling you." She sat on the arm of the chair and swung her legs. "I don't mind telling any one."

She darted a repressive glance, and then, for no reason at all, changed color a little.

"Begin at the beginning."

Mally began. It wasn't really very easy to know where to begin. She skipped Roger Mooring, and landed in the middle of the Peterson household.

"I thought they were nice—all except that loathsome Paul. I thought they were just nice, ordinary people. I danced with Sir George, and he was ever so nice to me. And then all of a sudden he began to behave like a nightmare—they all did—and—and—drug my coffee—and hide diamond brooches in the hem of my skirt—and swear I'd taken frightfully valuable papers—and please would I give them back, and then they wouldn't say any more about the diamonds."

Ethan came and sat on the arm of the other chair.

"Look here, Mally," he said in a new voice, "I can't get the hang of it this way. You must be serious and tell me about it properly."

Mally jerked her head up.

"What's the good? I think they're mad—I think they must be mad. But you'll only think *I'm* mad, or else you'll think I took the diamonds."

"Shall I?"

Mally looked at him defiantly. Then she looked away.

"I'll tell you. Only I don't see why any one should believe me."
She began to speak quickly and quite seriously: "Mrs. Craddock lost
her brooch, and we all looked for it. And next day, when Barbara
was hiding in the study, I went in to get her; and Mr. Craddock was
there telephoning. He saw me come in, and I went and got Barbara;
but he didn't see us come out, because he'd turned round a bit.
And I don't think he knew Barbara was there at all. I think now—I
do think—that Barbara took the paper that they missed. She was
always wanting to draw, and they wouldn't let her. I didn't think of
it at the time, because I was so taken by surprise. But now I'm sure
that Barbara took a paper off Mr. Craddock's table. It—it's *queer*—a
sort of cross-word puzzle thing. I don't know why they should make
such a fuss about it."

"What sort of fuss did they make?"

"They drugged my coffee. Oh, yes, they *did*. And whilst I was
asleep they put the diamond pendant—it wasn't a brooch really—
into the hem of my skirt." Mally clasped her hands very tightly and
turned rather pale. "It's horrible. That's what they did—I've had lots
of time to think it out. Then they brought in Mrs. Craddock and
her maid." Mally's breath caught; she stopped and dashed away an
angry tear. "I don't want to talk about it—I *don't*!" she cried in a
breaking voice.

Ethan caught her hands in his.

"My poor little dear! It's only me—it's only Ethan. Tell me."

Mally pinched him very hard indeed.

"The maid found the diamond," she said in a thread of a voice.
"And they said they wouldn't send me to prison if I would give them
back the paper. They really thought I'd taken it—I can see that now,
but at the time, I hadn't the least, faintest scrap of an idea of what
they were driving at."

"Go on."

Mally went on talking. She also went on pinching him.

"They shut me up in a room, and I climbed out of the window
and got in on the next floor, and got my hat and things, and got
away. And Barbara gave me all her drawings because she thought

they'd tear them up. And I found the cross-word puzzle thing in the middle of the drawings. Only I don't believe it's a real cross-word puzzle at all. Look at it."

She pulled away her right hand, dived into a jumper pocket, and thrust a folded paper at Ethan. He unfolded it, and saw what Mally had seen in the empty house.

The paper was a half-sheet of foolscap. Right across the top of it ran an odd statement:

"Heliogabalus was never emperor in Constantinople."

Below this, on the left, was the square of a cross-word puzzle, and all the rest of the paper was taken up with the clues. There appeared to be twenty-eight of them. Thus:

▓	▓	1			2			3	▓	▓
4	5		▓	▓	11	▓	▓	6	7	8
9		10	12		13	14				
15				▓	16					
▓		▓	17		18			▓		▓
▓	▓	19							▓	
▓	20	▓	21					▓	22	▓
23		24		▓	25		26			27
28										
29			▓	▓		▓	▓	30		
▓	▓	31							▓	▓

ACROSS.

1. Lady Bird.

4. A Swift Curler Of Old Times.

6. New Child's Holiday Invention.

9. Old Hats for New.

15. Hard Amber.

16. A House of Archaic Outline In Highgate.

17. Imperial Tokay Bought New.

19. Army Architecture turned Awry on the Nevsky.

21. Half Shoes of Antique Type Non-inflammable.

23. New Solid Light Tractor.

25. Seven Old Indians.

28. A New Army Invention.

DOWN.

4. An Elephant's Height In Nowgong.

5. A Nest of Owls New Caught.

7. Name Old Light Balloon About Sixteenth Century.

8. Olive Oil.

10. The Next High Tree (South Africa or Nigeria).

12. Old Obvious Things Invented New.

13. Obsidian Never Twisted.

14. London News Circulation Carefully Improved On A Liberal Hypothesis.

18. Try Our Oatmeal And Then Buy.

20. Corners Of An Oval Octagonal Oolite.

22. Amber Satin Hose of Innate Novelty.

24. High Arbours Of Orange Leafery.

Ethan looked at the paper, and Mally looked at Ethan.

"It's odd, isn't it? When I first looked at it, I thought it was odd. But I was much, much too hungry and too cold to care. I looked at it again this morning, just for a moment, and it seemed odder than ever. Do you think it's really a cross-word puzzle? If it is, why should they make such a fuss about it? Do you think it is? Do you?" Mally's voice thrilled and her eyes sparkled.

Ethan said, "'M."

He was reading number fourteen:

"London News Circulation Carefully Improved On A Liberal Hypothesis."

He glided to number twenty:

"Corners Of An Oval Octagonal Oolite."

Then he emitted a long whistle.

"It's either made up by a lunatic with a passion for O's, or it's a cipher. I think it's a cipher."

"Yes—yes!" said Mally. "A cipher? How clever of you!"

Ethan felt a good deal uplifted.

"If it's a cipher—"

"I'm *sure* it's a cipher."

"If it's a cipher, the O's ought to be E's, as there are such a lot of them. That's the way you start unravelling a cipher—with the E's. Now supposing these O's—No, where's a bit of paper? Never mind, I'll double this over."

He doubled it over, and said, "Oh!" very sharply and in a different voice.

"What is it?"

He dragged his chair nearer, put the paper on Mally's lap, and leaned over, pointing.

"We shan't have to bother. It's decoded on this side. It's a cipher all right, and whoever got it had been decoding it—"

"It's Paul Craddock's writing. It is!"

"It's practically all decoded. How on earth did you miss it?"

"I don't know. I never looked on that side. It was frightfully cold, and I hadn't anything to eat for years and years and years. Oh, it does look funny! What does it mean?"

Right across the paper ran the words:

```
H.E.L.I.O.G.A.B.A.L.U.S.
a.b.c.d.e.f.g.h.i.j.k.1.
C.O.N.S.T.A.N.T.I.N.O.P.L.E.
m.n.o.p.q.r.s.t.u.v.w.x.y.z.
```

"That's the key. Look!" said Ethan. He put a large thumb on the C of Constantinople. "Twenty-six letters in the two words—look! And the alphabet running along underneath. No wonder there are such a lot of O's. E is O all right. But so are N and W. And I and R are both A. I say, look here! It's rather like Hawaiian—isn't it?"

There was a line drawn under the alphabet, and below that came a string of letters:

```
LBASCOOTN/CHIO/HN/HAAHOAOI/
HITBNAATAON/HSOAT/NINSOLT/
SOIAN/AIAE/HINANO/ON/CNAO/
LBASCOOTN/HT/SAONOOT/IN/ONT/
LNCCIOALHTO/OATB/CO/AO/
OOASHOI/NHAOOL/
```

"What is it? What does it mean?" asked Mally breathlessly.

Ethan turned back to the other side of the paper.

"'Lady Bird,'" he read, "'A Swift Curler Of Old Times.'" Then he turned back again: "'L-B-A-S-C-O-O-T.' Yes, that's it; the cipher is in the capital letters of the clues, and Heliogabalus Constantinople is the key. I expect the square is just a blind."

"What does it *mean*?" said Mally.

"This is the bit that he's decoded." He slipped his finger down the page and read: "'Shipments made as arranged. Authorities alert. Suspect Pedro Ruiz. Advise no more shipments at present. Do not communicate with me....' Then there are two blanks and 'Varney.'"

"What does it mean?"

Ethan whistled.

"Something pretty fishy, I should say."

Mally was rather pale.

"Oh," she said, "I don't like it." She pushed the paper away and jumped down off the arm of the chair. "There's a perfectly horrible feeling about it." She paused for a moment, and then said in a whisper, "Is that all?"

"'M." Ethan had a pencil in his hand. He frowned at the paper, and his pencil dabbed to and fro between the cipher and its key.

"'M—hold on a minute—I'm filling in the blanks. 'I—N—E—N—G—L—A—N—D.' Yes, that's it—'Do not communicate with me in England. Varney.' Now I wonder who Varney is."

"Is that all?" said Mally again.

She had backed against the piano, and she did not look at Ethan as she spoke. She looked instead out of the window and saw, without seeing, the flagged path with the frost-bitten standard roses on either side of it, and the high, stiff gate that her frozen hands had fumbled at in the dark.

"Is that all?" she repeated, and felt a loathing for the paper and all that it contained. She hated to feel that she had carried it in her pocket.

Ethan looked at her stern little profile with surprise.

"There's a drawing of a man's head under the word Varney," he began; and the next instant everything changed, broke up.

Mally gave a sharp cry, jumped back a yard, and ran to him, catching at his arm with hard, shaking fingers.

"A policeman!" she gasped. "A f-fat policeman! He's just come in at the gate!"

Chapter Thirty-Three

WHEN MALLY SAID, "A f-fat policeman," Ethan put his arm round her waist. With his other hand he shoved the cross-word puzzle into his pocket. Then he must have opened the door, because before Mally had finished saying "in at the gate," she was being whisked down the passage that ran right through the house.

They passed the stairs and heard Miss Angela talking to Grace in one of the bedrooms. They checked for an instant by the row of pegs which lurked in the shadow beyond, whilst Ethan gathered an armful of coats. Then they had burst into the kitchen and shut the door behind them. The kitchen was empty.

Ethan dropped his bundle on the floor, picked out a thick fleece-lined coat, crammed it on Mally, pushed a tweed cap into her hand, and struggled into a Burberry. They heard the thud of the front door knocker, and in an instant, Ethan had Mally by the elbow and was running her through the scullery, out at the back door, and down the flagged path, where the frozen snow slipped beneath their running feet.

The path cut the garden in two and ended at a door in the boundary wall. They were through the door and had it slammed behind them just as Miss Angela felt obliged to interrupt Grace's voluble account of a niece's wedding with a reluctant, "Grace, surely—I think—yes, there *is* some one at the front door!"

The door in the boundary wall gave upon a little lane. The Vicar's stables opened into it. The door stood open, and they were both in the car before Grace was half-way down the stairs. Ethan had put in an hour in the garage that morning, and as he had run the engine, it was warm enough to start up easily. They came out into the lane, where they had to back to take the turn. They slid down the narrow alley which ran between the Vicarage and the high church wall. Ethan turned to the right, left the church and a half-dozen scattered cottages behind, and filled his lungs with a huge breath of relief.

"We're off!"

He began to sing loudly, untunefully, and in a variety of keys:

"From the desert I come to thee on my Arab shod with fire,
And the winds are left behind in the umty tumty tum—"

"I say that's a ripping song—isn't it? Sort of thing you can really let out on!"

He let out:

"At thy window I sta-a-and, and the something hears my cry.
I love thee, I love but thee, with a love that shall not die
Till the sun is co-o-old—"

"I say, that's beastly appropriate—isn't it? I don't know that I ever struck a day when the sun was colder."

Mally went off into a fit of helpless, gurgling laughter.

"We're mad," she said. "We're both quite mad. We must be, or this sort of thing wouldn't happen to us."

Ethan slipped his left arm round her waist and gave her a hug.

"It's rather jolly being mad together. I say, that was a good get-away—wasn't it?"

He hugged her again. Mally caught sight of herself in the glass screen, formless in Ethan's bulging coat, with the peak of a tweed cap hanging over one eye. She fell weakly against Ethan's shoulder, and Ethan kissed the corner of her mouth where the deepest dimple came and went. They very nearly went into the ditch, because the kiss was a long one; and it ended because Mally gave a sudden choking sob and hid her face against the sleeve of the aged Burberry. Fortunately the road was empty.

Ethan continued to drive at thirty miles an hour with his arm round Mally's waist.

"You're not angry—Mally—darling?"

Mally burrowed her nose into the Burberry and sniffed.

"I couldn't help it. I shall never be able to help it when you look at me like that. Were you frightfully angry when I did it last night? Were you?"

Mally sniffed again.

They left the highroad and swung to the right. The tweed cap fell off. Mally sat suddenly bolt upright and crammed it on again. Her mouth was trembling and she was very pale.

"Where are we going?"

"To London, I think. You ought to see a solicitor. This warrant business is all nonsense. I'm not going to have you arrested. I'm going to take you to my cousin, Mansell Messenger. He's a good old sort. He's the senior partner in a fearfully respectable firm of solicitors with no end of a comic name—Worple, Worple, Worple and Wigginson. The last Worple died in the eighteenth century, and I don't believe there ever was a Wigginson. Mansell runs the show. He's a clever old bird, and well in with Scotland Yard. His wife is a sister of Sir Julian Le Mesurier, the chief of the C.I.D., so he'd be quite a useful man to get on to."

"Suppose he w-won't," said Mally.

"He will, like a shot. Besides, I shall tell him we're engaged. We are, aren't we?"

"N-no, we're n-not. You m-mustn't."

Mally looked straight ahead of her and felt a tear run hot and salt into the corner of her mouth.

"You little darling idiot!"

"I'm n-not."

Ethan burst into a great roar of laughter.

"Mally, you're so funny! You really are! I shall drive slap into a hedge if you make me laugh like this."

"You oughtn't to laugh," said Mally in a small, obstinate voice. "It's very serious. I shall be sent to prison for years and years and years. And you can't possibly be engaged to a girl in a p-p-prison— you know you can't."

Ethan jammed on his brakes. The car skidded and stopped. Mally said, "Oh!" and felt Ethan's hands come down very hard on her shoulders. He pulled her round to face him and gave her a little shake.

"You're not to talk like that! Do you hear? I won't have it. I don't like it. You're not to do it. No, I'm quite serious. We are engaged, and we're going to stay engaged until we're married—and we're going to get married as soon as possible."

Mally cocked her left eyebrow at him.

"'M," she said.

"No!" said Ethan loudly. "No! Mally, you're an imp of darkness. But for the Lord's sake be good—at any rate until we've finished running away. I can't really drive the car with one hand and shake you with the other—and we've got to push along. I can't risk going through Weyford or Guildford, so we've got to go round and strike London road beyond Ripley. I think we've got a sporting chance; but we certainly haven't got any time to waste."

He started the engine, and they began to do a rather perilous thirty-five miles an hour along very narrow winding lanes, where the snow had turned to ice. They came out on the London road half an hour later, and mended their pace.

Mally sat hunched up in the big coat. She had not spoken for a long time, when she suddenly giggled and said:

"If there's a police trap on this road, you'll be the one to be arrested. And then, perhaps, *I* won't marry *you*."

"There isn't a trap," said Ethan sternly.

Next moment, as a small car passed them, she clutched his arm.

"Ethan! That's Candida Long! It is! Oh, it is! Oh, I want to speak to her—she was such a brick to me! Catch them up! Catch them up quickly! I must speak to her!"

Ethan caught them up. Mally stuck her cap out of the flap of the side screen and waved it. Ethan hooted. Miss Long's companion shouted something unintelligible. Miss Long herself glared, exclaimed, and applied her brakes. Both cars came to a standstill, and in a moment Mally had whisked out into the road.

"It's me!" she said. She hitched up Ethan's coat and climbed on the step. "I got away—I wanted to tell you. You *were* a brick. Oh! It's Mr. Medhurst!"

Ambrose Medhurst opened the door on the other side and got out. He was a sensitive young man, and it seemed to him that he was *de trop*.

"Oh!" said Mally. "Has he? Are you?"

Candida leaned over the side. She said, "S'sh! Not exactly." Then she put her lips close to Mally's ear and whispered, "You were quite right. He *does*—but he *won't*."

They could hear Ethan and Ambrose talking.

"Why won't he?" said Mally, bobbing on the step.

"My beastly money. But I believe I've lost a lot of it. And if I have, he will."

"Ouf! How good of him!"

Mally's eyes danced. So did Candida's.

"Yes—*isn't it*? What are you doing? Are you all right? Paul was *wild*. I say, are you sure you're all right? Because I should simply hate them to get you now. What *are* you doing?"

"I'm still escaping. I'm escaping with Ethan. Do you know Ethan? He says we're engaged. And I'm much too frightened of him to say we're not."

Candida began to laugh; and as she did so, Ethan and Ambrose came round the car. Candida turned, with her hands out.

"Ambrose, I've had a brain-wave! Let's change cars."

Mr. Medhurst's fine dark eyes took on a bewildered look. He said, "Change cars?" And Candida said, *"Change cars."* And then Ethan pushed forward, very large and frowning.

"Miss Long—I say—do you really mean that?"

Candida jumped out.

"Of course I mean it. Are they after you? Are you being chased? Would it really be a help? Do you think they'll chase us instead? Oh, *what* a lark!"

Ethan seemed in doubt as to how many of Miss Long's questions really required an answer.

"I'm *sure* we're being chased," said Mally from the step of the car. Ethan's coat trailed from her shoulders to the ground; she clutched his cap in her bare hand.

"As a matter of fact," said Ethan, "we had to bolt by one door whilst the local policeman was being let in by the other. And as everybody in Weyford knows the number of my car, I don't think we've a frightfully good chance of getting to London. I want to get to my cousin, Mansell Messenger. He's a solicitor and can advise us."

"Then take my car, and we'll have yours. Come along, Ambrose, you shall drive. And we'll get off the main road and see how long we can keep going before we're taken up. I've never been arrested! It's the chance of a life-time. What a jest! Bless you, my children!"

She kissed her fingers to Mally and ran laughing to Ethan's car, dragging Ambrose with her.

"She *is* a brick!" said Mally. "Come along, slow-coach!" She jumped in, trailing the coat behind her. "I know where her garage is, so that's all right."

"How do you know?"

"Because she told me—and because I'm so frightfully clever."

"Now then," said Ethan warningly.

Mally dimpled at him. With a sudden movement she rubbed her head against his shoulder and said, "Didums?" Then she began to laugh softly. "We're really, really, *really* going to get away. I didn't think we could—but we're going to!"

Chapter Thirty-Four

MR. MANSELL MESSENGER was a brisk little grig of a man with rosy cheeks, grey hair that rumpled easily, and very lively hazel eyes. He allowed the eyes to dart some searching glances at Miss Mally Lee as she sat in one of his big leather armchairs and told her story.

She told it all through from the beginning, and it did not escape him that a good deal of it was news to his cousin Ethan. He held a pencil in his hand and drummed against his lips with it. Every now and then he made a note of something. And then the eyes were scanning Mally again, from the short, rumpled dark hair to the shabby house shoes in which she had walked so many weary miles. The big muffling coat lay over the arm of the chair.

Mally, in her short skirt and jumper, was extraordinarily small and young. She sat up straight, and she told her story well, but not too well. Mr. Mansell Messenger had a well-founded distrust of the too glib tale. Mally was not glib; she was natural. He liked her voice, and the set of her head, and the way she looked at him. He liked the way in which she spoke of the Peterson household; there was no rancour, no sharp-voiced resentment. She was puzzled, and she had been frightened; and she was plucky—not the sort to be frightened for nothing.

When she had done, he asked her questions:

"Had any one in the house any grudge against you?"

Mally lifted her head a little.

"I didn't like Mr. Craddock."

"Had you quarrelled?"

"Oh, no. We weren't *friends*. He knew I didn't like him."

"May I ask how he knew?"

Mally stuck her chin in the air.

"I s-slapped his face."

"Just so," said Mr. Messenger—"just so. I'm sure he deserved it. But perhaps you'll just tell us why you found it necessary to slap him?"

"It was my own fault," said Mally. "I ought to have known he was a slug and that you can't trust slugs. I came home late and he offered me sandwiches, and I said 'Yes' because I was hungry—dancing always makes me hungry. And then he tried to kiss me, and I slapped him frightfully hard and ran away."

Ethan, standing propped against the mantelpiece, was understood to mutter something of an imprecatory nature.

"Just so," said Mr. Mansell. "And when did all this happen?"

"The night before."

"The brooch was already lost then?"

"Yes, we'd been looking for it all the afternoon."

"And it was next day after lunch that they searched you and found it?"

"Yes, it was."

"Just so. And when did you first hear about the lost paper?"

"After they searched me, I *think*."

"You're not sure?"

"Not quite sure. It was all so horrid—I didn't seem to be able to think. They sent the maid away, and then they went on, and on, and on about the paper. They said they knew I'd got it; and they said if I'd give it up, they wouldn't say any more about the diamond and they wouldn't send me to prison."

Mr. Mansell bit the end of his pencil.

"And you say you had no knowledge of any paper?"

"I hadn't then."

"But you had subsequently?"

"Barbara gave me her drawings. She loved them frightfully, and she said her father and Paul Craddock would burn them. She gave them to me after I climbed out of the window—I told you—and I put them in my pocket and forgot all about them until I was sitting under a holly bush in the wood at Peddling Corner waiting for something to turn up."

"And then?" said Mr. Mansell Messenger.

"I looked at the drawings to pass the time, and I found a paper with a cross-word puzzle on it. But I wasn't feeling like cross-word puzzles, so I put it back in my pocket and didn't worry about it. Only when I was in that empty house I told you about, I looked at the paper again, and I thought it was *odd*—"

"You thought it was odd. In what way did you think it was odd?"

Mally met his eyes very engagingly.

"Just odd," she said with a little wave of her hand. "I didn't worry about it much—I was too cold and hungry. But this morning I showed it to Ethan. And first we both thought it wasn't a cross-word puzzle at all; and then we wondered what it was. And then—" She turned towards the hearth. "Ethan, you've got it. Show him."

Ethan came forward with the paper in his hand. He leaned across his cousin and laid it on the writing-table.

"It's a cipher," he said. "I tumbled to that at once. But when I started to work it out I found that it was practically all decoded on the other side of the paper. Have a look at it yourself and you'll see."

Mansell Messenger swung his chair about and positively pounced on the paper.

"Heliogabalus—Constantinople," he read aloud, and stabbed the blotting-paper with the point of his pencil.

"The key words," prompted Ethan; and Mansell said, "Just so," and ran his finger along the next line, where the alphabet stood letter for letter beneath the two key-words.

Ethan went on explaining.

"They've taken the initial letters of the clues to make the cipher. Here it is, decoded." He pointed lower down. "These two words—'In England'—I worked out with the key. The rest was already decoded, including the signature. It's Paul Craddock's writing, Mally says."

"That so?" said Mansell, looking sharply round at Mally. "Don't say you're sure if you're not. Don't say anything unless you're sure."

"But I *am* sure—I'm *quite* sure."

"Very well."

He proceeded to read the decoded message over in an undertone. "Shipments made as arranged. Authorities alert. Suspect Pedro Ruiz. Advise no more shipments at present. Do not communicate with me in England. Varney." He read it over twice, and stabbed at his blotting-paper all the time. Then there was a silence.

It seemed a long time before he made a quick movement and jerked a question at Mally:

"Any idea what this means?"

"N-no," said Mally.

"No idea what shipments are referred to?"

She shook her head.

"Ever heard of Pedro Ruiz or Varney?"

"N-no."

"But you're sure this is Mr. Paul Craddock's handwriting?"

"Yes, I'm quite sure."

Mansell Messenger went on looking at her for about half a minute. Then he pushed back his chair and got up.

"I'm going to ask you both to go into the next room. Wait a moment whilst I tell you what I'm going to do. I'm going to telephone to Sir Julian Le Mesurier and ask him if he will see you. I think it possible that he may be interested in this cipher, and I should advise you to tell him everything you know quite unreservedly. If you are not willing to do so, I don't think I can help you very much. But if you will be guided by me—"

"Oh!" said Mally, a little overpowered. "But we *will*. That's why we came here—didn't we, Ethan? We *want* to be guided by you, so please don't say you won't help us." She looked at him very appealingly indeed.

"I don't say anything of the sort." Mr. Messenger took her by the arm, patted it, and propelled her gently towards the outer room. "Run along and talk to Ethan."

The outer room was empty. As soon as Mansell had gone back into his office, Ethan picked Mally up and hugged her.

"You're not to be frightened," he whispered in her ear.

"I'm n-not."

"You are. And I won't have it. Do you hear? I simply won't have it. You're all shaking and cold like a little frozen bird. You're not to do it."

"S'sh!" said Mally. "S'sh! He's left the door ajar. I want to listen."

They stood quite still, and heard Mansell's voice a little raised.

"That you, Piggy? Yes, Mansell speaking. Hallo! Are you there? Yes, that's better now. Can you hear me all right? It's rather important. Look here, you remember our conversation last night after dinner…. Yes, the very confidential part of it…. She's here now…. Yes, that's what I said—*Here*—H for horse, E for Edward, R for ructions and E for emergency … A warrant? Yes, I know—so she says. I'd like you to see her. And I've a document that I think will interest you—Hallo, the door's open! Wait a minute while I shut it."

The door shut with a click this time, and Mally fairly flung herself into Ethan's arms.

"Ethan—don't let them take me to prison! I c-couldn't bear it! I *am* frightened—I'm dreadfully, dreadfully frightened. Oh, I *am*!"

Ethan held her very tight indeed. She was shaking from head to foot, clinging to him with all her might and sobbing as a child will sob when it has cried all its tears away.

Presently Mally stopped shaking. Ethan was a very comfortable person—very large, and solid, and unshakeable. In a most irrational manner Mally began to feel a firm conviction that she would not be sent to prison. Ethan wouldn't let her.

Having arrived at this comforting conclusion, she rubbed her cheek against Ethan's arm and said in a little quick, eager voice, "I w-want to tell you about Roger."

From the standpoint of the reasonable sex, this was certainly the last remark that any one would have expected her to make. Not only was Ethan taken aback, but he also experienced an extreme disinclination to be told anything at all about Roger Mooring. The fellow was a swab who had let Mally down. He was back history. And, quite frankly, he gave Ethan the pip.

"I don't want to hear about him," he said. "Why should I?"

As he spoke, the outer door was pushed open. Ethan took a step back towards the window, Mally whisked about, fixing an earnest gaze upon an engraving of Queen Victoria, and there came in at the door a very tall, portly lady with a highly coloured face and rather a wild black hat.

"I don't care if he's engaged or not—I've got to see him." The lady looked back over her shoulder and addressed a flurried clerk after the manner of a politician replying to a heckler. At the first sound of her ringing voice, Ethan murmured:

"Oh, my hat!"

The door shut. The portly lady turned, and, exclaiming, "My dear boy!" advanced and kissed Ethan in a firm and businesslike manner.

"Er—Aunt Serena," said Ethan. "Er—may I introduce Miss Lee?"

Mally stopped looking at Queen Victoria and lifted limpid eyes to Miss Serena's hat. Her lashes were still a little wet.

"Lee?" said Miss Serena. "Did you say Lee, Ethan?"

She took Mally's hand in a very hard, hot clasp.

"Are you related to Ernestine Wotherspoon Lee?"

"Who is she?" said Mally.

"You surprise me! I thought that every woman in the country knew the name and could feel thankful for the labours of Ernestine Wotherspoon Lee."

"What did she do?"

"What did she *not* do? Ernestine by name, and earnest by nature. What did not her single-minded efforts accomplish for the Cause?"

Mally was just going to say, "What cause?" when Ethan saved her.

"Aunt Serena, Mally and I are engaged."

Miss Serena Messenger was so much taken aback that she dropped Mally's hand and became for the moment a mere aunt.

"My dear boy, not really? How—how very unexpected!" She began to recover. "I—I—No, my dear boy, it would be against my principles to congratulate either of you. Miss Lee and I must have a little talk. I disapprove of marriage. I consider it a barbarous and degrading form of slavery, as you know. And I hope that perhaps I may induce Miss Lee to see things as I do, in the dawn-light of the new era which ushers in Woman as supreme. As your gifted relative Ernestine Wotherspoon Lee remarked last week in her address on 'Woman Dominant'—"

The door of the inner room flew open, and Mr. Mansell Messenger appeared upon the threshold. If his first impulse was to shut the door and run away, he concealed it heroically.

"Ah! Serena!" he said; and then as he took her hand, "But I'm busy—terribly busy. Can't see you without an appointment, you know."

"Now, Mansell! What's the good of talking like that? I'm here, and you've got to see me."

"But I can't. No, Serena, I really can't."

Miss Serena took him by the arm and began to walk resolutely towards the door.

"I shan't keep you for ten minutes," she said in her loud ringing voice. "I just want to consult you on a point that has arisen in connection with our Z.K.W. work."

They disappeared together, and Miss Serena shut the door.

"Oh, Ethan!" said Mally.

"I know."

"Is she always?"

"Pretty much of a muchness. I'm used to her."

Mally pressed close to him.

"Ethan, don't let her—please!"

"Don't let her what?"

"T-talk to me about being a degraded slave."

He burst into a roar of laughter.

"Oh, Mally—you funny little thing! Yes, you are. Never mind, you shall be my degraded slave, and I'll be your degraded slave, and we'll both cock snooks at Aunt Serena and live happy ever after."

Mally made a horrible face at the closed door.

"Yes, we w-will," she said.

She put out her tongue and dropped an impish curtsey.

Chapter Thirty-Five

"WHAT A ROMANTIC MIND you've got, Mansell!" said Sir Julian Le Mesurier pleasantly. He leaned back in his office chair as he spoke and smiled with an indulgence which infuriated his brother-in-law.

"I? A romantic mind? What next?"

"Inveterately romantic. Oh, there's nothing half so sweet in life as love's young dream. And the lad Ethan only a subaltern, too! Well grown—but a mere child. Fie, Mansell, fie!"

"He's expecting his step any day. The well-grown child, my dear Piggy, is nearly thirty. Anyhow it's nothing to do with me, except professionally. I approach you on behalf of a client—*a client*, Piggy."

Sir Julian waved a large fat hand.

"Then there's nothing doing—absolutely nothing. This is a pleasant family chat, far, far removed from the sordid associations of the criminal law. Beautiful things, family ties—nearly as beautiful as love's young dream. Er—have you got this alleged cipher on you?"

"Miss Lee has it."

"There's a warrant out against her," said Sir Julian irrelevantly.

"So she said. She's a frank young thing. Are you going to see her?"

"Not my job. The excellent Murgatroyd has the case in hand. But, as a matter of fact, I think—yes, I think I'd like to meet her—er—socially, you know. Have you got her with you?"

"Yes."

Sir Julian touched a bell and spoke into a telephone. Then he drew forward a clean sheet of paper and began to enliven it with a frieze of sleeping cats with folded paws and neatly curled-up tails. Outside the door of the room Mally gave Ethan a last desperate pinch. Then she let go of his arm, stuck her head well in the air, and walked in.

"Er—how do you do, Miss Lee?" said Sir Julian. His little light eyes met Mally's and for a moment held them.

Then Ethan came in and shut the door, and Mr. Mansell Messenger gave her a chair. And then she had to begin all over again and tell this big, queer, fat man how it was that she had come to be Barbara Peterson's governess and just what had happened from that minute to this present one. All the time that she was talking, the big man fidgeted with his pencil. Sometimes he appeared to be engrossed in drawing cats; sometimes he looked at her. And when he looked at her, Mally felt as if she were made of very thin, transparent glass.

Oddly enough, this did not frighten her at all. If she had had anything to hide, it would have frightened her dreadfully; but as it was, she only felt sure that the big man would understand. He did not say a single word until she had finished. Then he held out his hand.

"Let me see this cross-word puzzle."

She took it out of her pocket and passed it across the table. Sir Julian spread it out, looked at it for some moments in silence, and then turned it over. Mansell came round and stood beside him, pointing, explaining; and Sir Julian said, "Yes, yes," and tapped the paper with his pencil.

"Ethan decoded these two words 'in England.' The rest was done already."

"Yes, yes," said Sir Julian.

He read the message through to himself. Mally knew it by heart. She watched him as he read, and found the big face blank.

Shipments made as arranged. Authorities alert. Suspect Pedro Ruiz. Advise no more shipments at present. Do not communicate with me in England. Varney.

The paper was folded in two where the message ended. Sir Julian lifted it, unfolded it, and looked suddenly and quickly at Mally Lee.

"There's a drawing of a man's head here."

"Is there?"

"Haven't you seen it?"

"No. I looked at the other side, and then Ethan had it." She hesitated.

"Well?"

"I remember he did say there was a drawing. Barbara must have done it. That's why she took the paper—to draw on, and perhaps because she thought that it would vex Paul Craddock."

"Barbara did it?"

"She must have done it—it was with her other drawings."

"How old is she?"

"About eight and a half."

"Have you got those other drawings you speak of?"

She shook her head.

"They're in my coat pocket. I just brought this one down to show Ethan, and then the policeman came up the path and we had to run away."

"You didn't make this drawing yourself?"

"Oh no. I can't draw."

"And you haven't seen it? You're sure you haven't seen it?"

"No, I haven't—really."

Mally felt a queer rising sense of excitement. She wasn't frightened, but she felt breathless.

"This message is signed, 'Varney'—'Varney.' Does that convey anything to you?"

"No, it doesn't!"

"Never heard the name before?"

Mally's brows drew together.

"In—a—book," she said slowly. "*Scott*—the one about Amy Robsart. He—he was the villain, wasn't he?"

Piggy looked at her, very intent. She looked back at him a little eagerly, with the color rising in her cheeks; her eyes were wide and clear.

"I can't remember what it's called," she said.

"'Kenilworth,'" said Sir Julian affably. "Yes, I think 'Kenilworth' is what you mean. And Varney is the villain. The name doesn't suggest—er—any younger villainy than that—something a little more recently criminal?"

"No, it doesn't?"

He turned the paper and pushed it over the table. In the right-hand bottom corner was a man's scrawled profile, and under it, in Barbara's tumble-down writing, the faintly pencilled words: "Varney. I *hate* him."

Mally stared at the face, and she stared at the words. Her eyes saw a sheet of paper—a white sheet of paper with a pencil scrawl on it; but her mind held a much more vivid picture—the dark stable; the flashlight; the man's profile, seen for a moment, and for a moment only.

"Oh!" she said. "Oh!"

She took the edge of the table in a hard little grip and stood up.

"You know the face?" said Sir Julian.

"Yes, it's the man—the man in the stable. I saw him."

"Steady, Miss Lee! What man?"

"Ethan knows. It was where he was staying. I hid in his car—the man's car—and when I woke up, we were in the stable at Peddling Corner. I saw him just for a moment. I don't know his name. Ethan knows."

Sir Julian turned to Ethan with the paper in his hand.

"Oh, Lord!" said Ethan. "It's impossible!"

"Only a very few things are impossible. I'm afraid this isn't one of them. You recognize this 'sketch?'"

"There isn't enough of it to recognize—is there?"

"Whom does it remind you of?"

"I'd rather not *say.*"

"In whose car did Miss Lee come down from town? Perhaps you'll answer that."

"Ethan!" said Mansell Messenger.

Ethan looked profoundly uncomfortable.

"She came down in Lawrence Marrington's car."

Mally looked from one to the other.

"Who is Lawrence Marrington?"

Sir Julian laid down the paper with the sketch on it.

"Miss Barbara Peterson says that he is Varney," he observed in a quiet, detached voice. "It will fall to the excellent Murgatroyd to discover whether she is speaking the truth."

Chapter Thirty-Six

Mally held on to the edge of the table.

"What does it all mean? There's something horrid." She drew a long, shivering breath and fixed her eyes on Sir Julian. "There *is*—isn't there?"

"Yes."

There was a pause. Then Sir Julian rang his bell again.

"I'm going to ask you to wait for a few minutes."

He turned to his brother-in-law.

"Where is Miss Lee staying? Murgatroyd will want to see her."

Mally looked at him seriously.

"Are you going to send me to prison?" she said in a little faint voice.

Ethan made a movement But Piggy held out his hand.

"Not this time. But we shall want your evidence. Where do you say she is staying, Mansell?"

"I'm not staying anywhere," said Mally.

"I thought"—Mansell's voice was low and confidential—"I thought—I hoped that Miss Lee would give us the pleasure. Janet, I know, will be delighted." He turned to Mally. "My wife and I hope that you will stay with us."

"Oh!" said Mally. She took his hand in both of hers and squeezed it. "Oh, you *are* a brick! I'm going to cry—I know I am. You—you're *both* such nice bricks!"

She looked round at Sir Julian, winked away two big tears, and ran out of the room. Ethan followed her.

"Well?" said Mansell rather slowly. "Well?"

"Engaging damsel," said Piggy. "Not pretty exactly, but undeniably heart-smiting. The lad Ethan is pretty far gone, I observe. A bit of a thruster—eh, Mansell?"

"What does it all mean?" said Mansell.

"Something pretty nasty. Murgatroyd will be delighted with the cross-word puzzle."

"What's it all about? Or mustn't I ask?"

"Yes, you can ask. The answer's only for you at present. Not a word even to Janet, please." He paused and tapped the paper on his desk. "Dry stuff to damn a man, isn't it? 'Shipments made as arranged.' Shipments"—his voice hardened—"the shipments are cocaine, Mansell. And this dry message in the handwriting of Peterson's secretary is going to damn Peterson. It's just a link in a chain, but it's the link we've wanted. And, now we've got it, I'm remembering that Peterson and I were at school together and that he used to be a very decent sort."

"How on earth?"

"Oh, easily enough. It's easy enough to slip into Avernus. Ten years ago, I suppose, he'd have been quick enough with his 'Is thy servant a dog that he should do this thing?' and to-day, apart from the risk, I don't suppose it keeps him from his sleep. I know just when it took him. He was smashed, Mansell. The war left him smashed, and then this easy way of making money was pushed at him—shoved right under his nose by Varney, who was already an old hand. He had to do so little. There were his ships; he had only to afford facilities for the stuff to be concealed. It was easier then than it is now. And Varney—now there's another queer bit of human nature for you—Varney is Lawrence Marrington. He was at this game in China twenty years ago. But mind you, it's all in the sacred cause of science. The man's a mad keen enthusiast—a fanatic. He lives for his researches, and he must have money to carry them out; so he's head over ears in this rotten business."

"And Craddock?"

"Ambitious young pup with a taste for politics. Depressing business, Mansell—a very depressing business. Murgatroyd'll be pleased—that's one bright spot. And the heart-smiting damsel's another. Plucky kid! I don't know whether trying to stick her with a mean charge of theft isn't about the dirtiest bit of the whole business.

They were scared stiff, of course, when they missed the paper. But if they hadn't run amuck and started trumped-up accusations against Miss Mally Lee, this particular bit of evidence would never have come into our hands. One could write a tract about it."

"How important is it?"

"Well, just a useful link. Pedro Ruiz has made a statement which we got; but Pedro Ruiz is the sort of gentleman whose statements require corroboration. Here we get Varney, who is Lawrence Marrington, warning Peterson's secretary about Pedro. It fits in, you see—it fits in."

He pushed back his chair, got up, and stretched himself.

"Take your damsel errant away and keep her out of sight and mischief till we've called the warrant off. So long, Mansell."

Chapter Thirty-Seven

MR. PAUL CRADDOCK came quickly out of the telephone room on the half-way landing of Sir George Peterson's house and ran down the broad flight of stairs past the marble bust which had frightened Mally on her first arrival.

He came into the study, shut the door, and said in a hurried undertone:

"They've got her!"

Sir George Peterson looked up from the letter he was writing. He frowned slightly as he said, "You're losing your nerve, Paul. If you can't pull yourself together, get out!"

"They've got her!"

"And any one who heard you run down the stairs and burst in here has been informed that you've just had—shall we say—interesting news, and that you're in a great hurry to tell me what it is." His manner changed a little. "By her, I suppose, you mean Miss Lee."

"Of course. They came up with the car in Sutton, and she's been brought here to be charged. They want one of us to go and identify her. Shall I go?"

"Yes, I think so. If the paper's there, get it. But don't stress anything. I think the line you should take is that you think you made a memorandum on the back of a puzzle sent you by a friend— Yes, I think that's the line to take. I wish now that we'd left the whole thing alone."

"Why now—just when we're out of the wood?"

Sir George raised his eyebrows.

"Are we out of it?" He paused, and added, "I'm so sure we're not that—" He broke off, pushed back his chair, and got up. "Go along and identify her. Be very careful what you say, and avoid the slightest appearance of being vindictive. We're sorry for the girl, and we don't want to be hard on her."

Paul Craddock went uneasily from the house. He took a taxi, and occupied himself with some very unquiet thoughts. There had been a note in Sir George Peterson's voice which he did not like. There was something in his manner which he liked still less. He began very heartily to curse the day that had brought Miss Mally Lee into the Peterson household.

At the police station he subdued his frown to a look of concern, and came from the outside dusk into a brightly lighted room, where a police inspector sat writing at a table.

Mr. Craddock found himself nervously anxious to get the business over, and nervously impatient of such formalities as having to give his name and address, and to submit to being told how seasonable the weather was. He wanted to have done with the whole thing and to get away. He wanted to see that accursed cross-word puzzle of Varney's burn to a powder of fine white ash. He found it difficult to keep up his look of concern. And then an inner door was opening, and there came through it the very last person whom he was expecting to see—Candida Long, her pale-gold hair shining under a close, dark hat, and her cheeks bright with indignant color.

He exclaimed, "Candida!" and the inspector turned a puzzled face.

Candida Long laughed an angry little laugh.

"Perhaps you'll tell these people who I am, Mr. Craddock. I must say it's the limit when one can't drive up to town without being arrested. Why, I've driven thousands and thousands of miles, and I've never even been fined. And then to be arrested—absolutely arrested! And we were crawling—*positively crawling*—in case any one should be mean enough to be timing us! Perhaps you'll tell this gentleman"—here she looked blue fire at the inspector—"perhaps you'll tell him that you've often driven with me and that you can answer for my being one of the safest, steadiest, and most reliable drivers on the road. And what's more, Ambrose had just looked at the speedometer, and he's prepared to swear we were only doing nine and a half. He's gone to see a solicitor about it this minute. Why I've never heard of any one being arrested unless they'd run some one down—not even in Sutton."

She paused to take breath, and the inspector seized the opportunity.

"What's the good of all that?" he said reprovingly. "It isn't a matter of whether you were doing ten, or twenty, or a hundred miles an hour—as well you know."

"It was only nine and a half! Mr. Medhurst is prepared to swear that it was only nine and a half."

"That's neither here nor there. What you're charged with is theft, and what this gentleman is here for is to identify you."

Paul Craddock swung round sharply.

"This isn't Miss Lee."

"Of course it isn't," said Candida. "I kept telling them there was a mistake, and they wouldn't listen, so Ambrose went to find his solicitor—and who's Miss Lee anyhow?"

Paul Craddock came away from the station with something very like despair in his heart. Mally Lee had got away, and Candida had told him with a charming smile that she was engaged to Ambrose Medhurst. He left her explaining affably to the inspector how it came about that she had happened to be driving a friend's car instead of her own. It was a very ingenious explanation, and Candida seemed to be enjoying it very much.

Paul crossed the cold tessellated hall and entered the study. It was empty. A note addressed to himself lay on the writing-table. He picked it up, opened it, and read:

MY DEAR PAUL,

I'm taking a little trip abroad. It is one which I have been planning for some time. I feel much in need of a holiday, and as I shall be moving from one place to another, I do not wish any correspondence to be forwarded. I enclose a cheque to cover your salary for two months.

Yours,

G.P.

Craddock remained staring at the signature. In the face of this calamity his mind refused to work. If Sir George thought it time to be gone, then what about Paul Craddock? What about—Varney?

As he stood, dreadfully irresolute, a footman came in with the evening papers. He put them down on the edge of the writing-table and withdrew. Craddock picked up the one that lay uppermost, and a staring headline jumped at him from the page:

"ARREST OF MR. LAWRENCE MARRINGTON"

Late that evening, Mr. Ethan Messenger was bidding Miss Mally Lee a somewhat prolonged goodnight.

"Your cousin Janet said ten minutes—you know she did."

"My cousin Janet's a sensible woman. She didn't mean ten minutes—it was just her tactful way of putting it."

"She's a darling," said Mally. "I do love fat, comfortable cousins who call you 'My dear' and behave like heavenly angels of kindness when they might *quite* easily not have anything to do with you."

"Janet's a good sort. I say, she's awfully like Sir Piggy—isn't she?"

Mally gurgled.

"She's like an angel pig—the very, very nicest sort."

Ethan kissed her, and suddenly she stopped laughing and drew a long, quivering sigh.

"D-don't!"

"Why not, little funny thing?"

"I'm not f-funny—I'm sad."

"You're not to be sad. I won't have it. Oh, Mally, you're not to cry. What is it?"

"It's the *horridness*."

"What do you mean?"

"It comes over me. Ethan, they seemed just ordinary people when I went there, and I thought Sir George was nice until I saw that bust of him on the stairs. And then I felt perfectly awful—I don't know why, but I did. It must have been the horridness coming out."

"I expect it was."

"And there's poor little Barbara!" She choked on a sob.

"Mally darling, don't!"

"I c-can't help it."

"But, Mally, you wouldn't want that poor kid to grow up in the middle of a rotten business like that!"

"N-no. Mrs. Craddock's kind—she'll look after Barbara." She paused, and then said, *"Ethan."*

"What is it?"

"Ethan, is there any more news? You were speaking to your cousin Mansell. Did he tell you anything?"

"Yes, he did. They've arrested Sir George."

She called out sharply.

"Mally, you didn't want him to get away!"

"N-no. But I do hate it all. I thought I wouldn't mind what happened to Paul Craddock; but when I heard they'd got him, I wanted to cry, and I was s-sorry I called him a slug. Ethan, if you laugh at me—I'll—"

"What will you do?"

"I'll let your Aunt Serena *convert* me. She'd love to—I know she would."

"I'm not laughing," said Ethan hastily. He picked Mally up and hugged her. "Don't think any more about the horridness."

"I don't want to. I don't want to think about it. It's just that I c-can't bear to think of even a slug in prison."

"Think about the nice people. Think about Mansell, and Janet, and Piggy, and Aunt Angel, and Bunty, and Candida—and ME. Hang it all, Mally, you've got me to think about—haven't you? What more do you want?"

"Are you nice? Are you sure you're nice?"

"I'm *frightfully* nice. You ask my Aunt Angel. She'll tell you how nice I am."

"Ethan." She rubbed her cheek against his. *"Ethan."*

"What is it?"

"Will you always be nice to me?"

"Yes, I'll always be nice to you, Mally."

"You're quite sure? You're quite, *quite* sure?"

Ethan laughed—a strong, happy, confident laugh.

"Wait and see!" he said.

THE END

Lightning Source UK Ltd.
Milton Keynes UK
UKHW02f2007230718
326164UK00023B/949/P